Julia's Baby

Natasha Murray

Best Wishes
Natasha Murray
2022
♡

Chapter One

From the deck of a ferry bound for Rosslare, Seth Hearn and Julia Bridgewater watched the port of Fishguard fade into the dark night. The coastal line was now just a series of tiny lighted dots, sparkling brightly in the darkness. They held their gaze, and then quietly the lights slipped away into a sea mist, shielding them both from a troubled past. The gentle hum of the engines and the sea breeze promised them sanctuary. Ireland was only a few hours away.

Tired from the long drive from Southampton, Seth, with his arms around Jules, rested his chin on the top of her head as they watched the wake behind the ferry lengthen, a surreal, euphoric feeling swept over him. "Are you happy? Do you have any regrets about leaving Sussex?"

"No, I have none. We did the right thing. It's better to be on the run, rather than facing the wrath of the Hearns. I hope your sister got home ok and Patrick didn't give her a hard time."

"I do too. Patrick can be a bit of a bully sometimes but Charlene won't take any of his nonsense."

"Your sister now knows that your mother killed my Aunt Ann. Do you think Charlene will ask her about it?"

"Now, here's the thing. I don't think she will say anything. If she did, then Charlene will put herself and her family in danger. Mam... I can't really call her that anymore.

1

The woman who brought me up has a way of manipulating those around her. Nobody can prove that she did it. Like the detective Simon Black said, Ann's murder happened nearly twenty years ago and there is very little evidence left."

"If we had stayed in Sussex, then we could have gone to the police. We both heard her say that she hit Ann over the head and killed her."

"I don't think that would have made much of a difference. That evil woman would find a way to pay us back. She could use the fact that I drowned my Dad against us. Either way, I am a wanted man!"

"Seth! You mustn't think like that. You are innocent. I saw what happened. Your Dad was trying to kill you. He nearly drowned you; you were just defending yourself. I nearly lost you. Please don't blame yourself; it will only eat you up inside. Promise me, or I will be cross with you!"

"I promise. I will try, but what happened to us is haunting me at the moment. This is a fresh start for us both. You are shaking. Are you nervous or are you just a little cold?" he asked, holding her tighter. *My poor little dote.*

"The breeze has picked up a bit, and I am worn-out. Shall we go in and find a place to sleep? I didn't realise how long it takes to get to Ireland. It was a good idea to get the last ferry so we don't have to find and pay for accommodation in Rosslare. Are you tired?"

"Yes, I am almost asleep standing up. Come on, let's go and find a couple of sofas each to sleep on."

It was the end of the summer holidays and past midnight. The ferry was quiet. They found two soft seats in the lounge area and then settled down to sleep. There were a few other foot passengers in the dimly lit lounge, unable to afford a cabin. They were asleep or were sitting looking at their phones, oblivious to the two new arrivals.

Jules watched Seth make himself a pillow out of his hoodie and before he lay down he came over to her and kissed her. "I love you, you know," he whispered in her ear.

She smiled back at him. His big brown eyes looked sleepy. "I love you too. Sleep well," she whispered back as she lay down. He walked back to his sofa and lay on his side. With his head on his makeshift pillow, he looked over at her, deep in thought. She smiled, mesmerized by his eyes and longed to be in his arms and feel the warmth from his sweet-smelling body. His eyes closed. *My lovely Seth is so tired.*

Jules sat back up and looked around her, just to check that there was nobody watching them. She wondered if she would always be looking over her shoulder for a dark and menacing presence. Although she knew that his Dad was dead and could not harm them, it did not ease her troubled mind. *Just get a grip! You are on a ferry in the middle of the Irish Sea, where nobody can hurt you.*

Annoyed with herself for feeling so paranoid, she folded her mac into a pillow and pulled out of her suitcase a hoodie to use as a blanket. Quietly, she lay back down and arranged her pillow under her head until she was comfortable. She hoped that she would wake up before the ferry docked at Rosslare; she didn't want to oversleep.

Ideally, she would have liked to have set an alarm for four. It was such a nuisance not having a phone and she realised how dependent she had become on having one. Apart from not seeing what everyone was doing on Facebook and keeping up with friends, she didn't know what time it was or how to get to places. It was most annoying and difficult to function properly. *I* think we should get one, so we have access to the internet. Surely, you can set up a phone without having to give any personal details? I will see what Seth says in the morning.

***

Seth opened his eyes, not knowing where he was. Realising that he was on the ferry, he shut his eyes for a few more precious moments of slumber. Unable to sleep anymore, he sat up and stretched. He looked over at Jules and saw that she was sound asleep. The hoodie she had covered herself with had slipped down onto the cushion next to her. Her black eye was a strange colour and looked swollen. The skin around her eye was various shades of yellow, green and black. *We will have to get some makeup when we get to Rosslare. I hope people don't think I've been beating her. How could my Dad hit her like that and then try and rape her? What a sick bastard!*

He got up and gently covered her up. He then looked at all the other passengers asleep around them. Some of them had elected to sleep on the floor. There were plenty of sofas available, and he couldn't understand why. *Perhaps they have got bad backs.*

He walked over to a display screen to see how far they were across the Irish Sea. They only had another forty-five minutes to go before they got to Rosslare. *I need the toilet.* He looked back over to her and hoped that she wouldn't wake before he got back. *I don't like to leave her at the moment. Look what happened when I left her the last time! If I had a phone, then I could leave her a message.* He also wanted to see what buses they should get to travel to Waterfall. *We will have to get a phone, just for internet access.* He felt the stubble on his chin as he thought, *Perhaps we should stay in Cork, for a couple of nights. That way, we can leave our luggage in our room and then go and see May. I don't want to just turn up on her doorstep, homeless and jobless with all our luggage in tow. I wonder if there are any rooms at the hostel. When I last stayed there, it was really cheap. If I had a phone, then I could see where the cheapest place is to stay. We will have to get a phone. It's driving me mad, not having one. I'll talk to Jules about it when she wakes up.*

Fellow passengers were stirring as they became aware of their imminent arrival at Rosslare. He could hear the wind howling outside and felt a little sad that Jules would see Ireland for the first time in an August wind squall.

It was a shame to wake her; she looked so peaceful when she was asleep. She was lying on her side, her soft curls the colour of hay were framing her face. Her hands, as if in prayer, were placed under her cheek acting as a makeshift pillow. He crouched down next to her. "Jules, my sweet girl, it's time to wake up." He kissed her on her cheek. "Jules?"

"Morning… Oh, is it that time already? I was dreaming of you. Are we at Rosslare yet?"

"A good dream, I hope. We will be there in about fifteen minutes."

She sat up and felt with her fingertips the skin around her left eye. "The swelling has gone down a little, but it really hurts. I must look a fright."

He sat next to her. "You will always look beautiful to me. Did you bring any makeup with you? He really hurt you, didn't he?"

"Does it look bad? I'll have a look in my wash bag. I might have a concealer, but I'm not sure. I don't really use makeup, and what I have is probably dried up."

"We can get some in Waterford. I think that we will have to change buses there to get to Cork. Hey, I was going to say. I think we should stay in a cheap hotel in Cork for two nights. I haven't been able to ring May to tell her that we would like to stay with her. I want to talk to her first and would like her to ask us to stay, rather than us turning up with our cases and looking hopeless. What do you think?"

"Yes, that seems like a good idea. As I was dropping off last night, I was thinking about us getting a cheap smartphone." Jules bit her lip. "I know it is an expense but it would be so handy to have internet access and be able to contact people. Can you set a phone up without having to give out your personal details? Do they call a phone like that a burner?"

"You watch way too many films! Funnily enough, I was just thinking the very same thing. A burner is a phone you throw away. I am sure we will be able to work out a way to set a phone up without giving away our location or identities. The best deals are online but as that option is not possible, then the next best place to buy one will be a supermarket. It would be so good to have a phone. We could ring Charlene and your brother and let them know we are ok."

"Oh dear, I don't know his number. All my contact numbers are on my phone at the bottom of Silent Pool with all those bodies."

"Damn! I haven't got any contact numbers with me either. God knows where my phone is now. It is probably at the bottom of the pond with my Dad."

"We will think of a way. I hope your mad family aren't beating Peter senseless, trying to find out where we are. Oh no! You don't think they are, do you?"

"I am pretty certain nobody apart from Jake and Charlene know that we are alive. I don't like to think about Crow Farm. The Hearns will be out in the fields working the land as usual; Patrick doesn't like to lose money. Mam, Margaret... will be playing happy families again. Let's not think about her." He shook his head and smiled. "Are you hungry? I doubt whether there will be a bus until six. We can see what the terminal building has to offer us in the way of breakfast. Is that ok?"

"Yes, that sounds great. I so need a cup of tea. Let's hope it's not too expensive."

"We will manage. I am looking forward to taking you to Waterford. It is a beautiful Viking city. I think it is the oldest city in Ireland. You did history 'A' level, didn't you? We will have lunch there, and you can tell me all about the Vikings and why they founded Waterford."

"Goodness! I know nothing about Viking history. Although I have seen the film 'Viking Blood' so I could tell you about that movie. I think that Waterford is famous for its crystal. My mum had a few pieces in her collection."

He laughed. "I was only joking. It's ok, you don't have to give me a talk. We will just wander around Waterford and explore," he said as he looked towards the windows. "I think we are about to dock. Is my sweet girl ready to go on a little adventure?"

Chapter Two

Sulky grey clouds flew purposefully over Waterford, ready to do battle with any blue sky that dared to appear. Jules and Seth found it hard going, pulling their suitcases along the streets of the city. Seth had insisted on carrying her guitar and she had felt a little bit guilty for bringing it. They had visited a few landmarks and walked past the House of Waterford Crystal, but it had been such a bleak and windy day that they had surrendered and had taken refuge in a warm café in Maylor Street.

Jules leaned her guitar against the wall next to their table and patted it, glad that she had brought it with her. *I'd be lost without music.* Then she took off her coat and hung it on the back of her chair. She sat down and looked back at her guitar. *I am so glad you are with me. If we run out of money, then I can sing for our supper.* She grinned. *That's not a bad idea! I could busk in Cork to make us some money. I wonder if Seth is up for a bit of busking too.*

Not wanting to wear sunglasses in the café, Jules had bought some concealer and foundation in Boots. "I'm just going to the toilet to sort out my eye. I won't be a minute. Could you order me whatever you are having and some tap water, please?" she asked. He said that he would, and she headed off to the toilets with a small plastic bag containing the makeup. She couldn't help feeling like she was in a spy movie and was about to disguise her identity. *The Fugitive, perhaps.*

Jules had done her best to cover the bruise around her eye but it really was a shiner. She looked at herself in the mirror again and was pleased with her efforts. *Not a bad job. I look almost decent again.* Her hair, however, was out of control. She had forgotten to bring her anti-frizz serum. At times like this, she was tempted to shave all her hair off. She decided to tie it back in a ponytail again and hoped it would recover when she washed it later on.

Seth had ordered their lunch and while they waited, he set up the phone, which they had bought in Argos, along with a pay-as-you-go sim card. She smiled to herself as she watched him concentrating on this task. The instructions leaflet was left on the side unread. Her brother was the same and never read instructions either. *Why is that?*

Their lunch was served by a very talkative Irish lady with an infectious smile. Jules had difficulty understanding her Cork accent. She had told them that the potato bake Seth had chosen for them was famous in Cork. It smelt and looked good. The waitress, seeing Seth insert the sim card into the phone, gave them the café's Wi-Fi password.

The potato pie was surprisingly good. Jules could only manage half of it. *I could eat more, but I just don't want to get fat.* Seth had finished hers for her, but as always, he was concerned that she wasn't eating enough.

"Look, Jules, we are in business. That wasn't too hard to do. I didn't need to enter my email address or my name. The internet connection is strong and we have a brand-new number. It's good to be back in the real world again! We will need to charge it up soon, though."

"Well done; you clever thing. Do you want me to keep it in my bag?"

"Do you mind? My pockets aren't that deep. I'll just look up hostels first. Is it ok if we stay in a hostel in Cork? It's the cheapest option. If I travel and don't sleep under the stars, then I usually stay in one."

"I don't mind. You haven't slept rough, have you? Weren't you scared of getting eaten by wild animals?"

"No," he said, laughing. "I had a tent. That was just a figure of speech. Wild animals didn't bother me. It is the mosquitoes that like to feast on me, so I had a small one-man tent that kept the beasties away."

"Mosquitoes like me too. We must have sweet blood."

"If I was a mosquito, then I would come and find you. You are irresistible. Hey, I've found several hostels in Cork. We will have to find a shop to top up the minutes and then when we are on the bus to, I will give the hostels a ring to see if they have any rooms available."

"Do you have to sleep in dorms in a hostel?"

"Some have dorms, which is the cheapest option, but you can have a private room with an ensuite too. I'd prefer that, if it is ok. I'm loving having a phone, by the way! Now, let me see; when is the next bus to Cork?"

The number forty bus wound its way down through Killarney and Macroom on its way to Cork. Jules was sitting by the window trying her best to stay awake, eager to watch the leafy green countryside go by. She was surprised how rural Ireland was and she could understand why Seth loved the country so much. *He needs to live in open spaces and be part of the land.* She looked over at him and felt sad. *You must have hated being in prison.* She stared out of the window again, not wanting to miss anything, but the desire to sleep was too strong, and she drifted off, with her head on the window.

"I've found us a private room in Kinlay House. It doesn't have a bathroom. Jules?" *She's fast asleep again. I've never seen anyone sleep so much. I don't think she realises how much her diet is affecting her energy levels. I will have to see if I can help her change the way she eats without upsetting her. I know she is getting tired of me encouraging her to eat more all the time. I will have to tread carefully.*

It was late afternoon when Jules and Seth got off the bus at Cork Bus Station. They had decided to go straight to Kinlay House and then go out to eat. The wind had dropped and the sun shone on them as they walked. Seth had taken a screenshot of the route they needed to take as they couldn't use Google Maps as they had no data. It didn't take them long to get to the hostel and they had stopped for a while on one of the twenty bridges, to admire the river Lee.

From the window of their room in Kinlay House, Jules could see a barren park across the road. She looked harder and could see what looked to be large slabs of stone lying in the grass. *Are those graves?* She turned around and surveyed the small room. It was basic but clean and had a double bunk bed. She hadn't seen a double before. The room did also have an adjoining shower room which was an added bonus. *This will be our home for a few days. It will do.*

"Do you want the top or bottom bunk?" Seth asked, but he had a mischievous twinkle in his eye.

"So now that you have slept with me, you're going to banish me to another bed – unwanted and unloved!"

He looked shocked for a moment. "No, I didn't mean it like that. I can't sleep without you now."

11

"I know, I was just teasing. Is it ok if I shower before we go out again? I must look a fright."

"You look fine. Come here and kiss me before you go, to make up for being so cruel to me."

She walked over to him and put her hands on his cheeks and ran her fingers over his dark stubble on his chin. "You're going to have to be gentle, though. I don't want to get carpet burn!"

"So you don't appreciate a little designer stubble then? Do you want me to shave first?"

"No, I can't wait that long," she said, finding his lips with hers.

He kissed her passionately, drawing her close to him so she could feel that he wanted her. "Let's shower together and then I can show you how much I love you. Only if you are not too tired that is. Or are you hungry and want to eat first?"

"Seth, stop talking. I am hungry for you. You are driving me wild! Is it so wrong to want you all the time? I don't want to wear you out."

"It's a good job I am as fit as a fiddle then. I see that I am going to have my work cut out keeping you satisfied. Let's start with a shower, shall we?" he said, grinning. He embraced her, swept his hands under her buttocks and then lifted her up off the floor so that each leg was either side of his hips. She put her arms around his neck and kissed him hard, her body crying out for his. As he carried her through to the shower room, he whispered in her ear. "You don't know what you do to me."

***

It was starting to get dark outside. Jules lay on the bottom bunk in Seth's arms, her warm naked body against his. *I love her so much it hurts. I might have driven her a little bit crazy but it was worth it. Her look of surprise when I asked her to put the condom on me.* He kissed her neck. She smelt of vanilla. "Are you ok, my sweet girl? Are you asleep?"

"I was just dozing. Are you ok? Do you want to go out?"

"We should; I'm starving. Are you?"

"No not really. I had quite a large meal at lunchtime, but we should go and get you something."

I thought you would say that. This might work. We will see. "There's a shop not far from here. I'll get some eggs and cheese to make an omelette. There is a kitchen downstairs. I don't want to eat alone. Will you come with me and have a little too?"

"You sound sad! Of course I'll come with you. Do you want me to cook? I can make a mean cheese omelette."

"That will be grand. Let's get dressed and go out before the shop shuts."

They dressed and walked hand in hand along Bob and Joan's Walk. After a five minute walk, they reached the quiet high street with its eclectic mix of small run down shops. Jules was surprised how old-fashioned Cork was. They found a convenience store and bought what they needed and headed back to the hostel.

As they walked, Seth ran his hand along the side wall of an end of terrace house, so that he could feel the history of the building. *Each brick has a story.* "This part of Cork is quaint, isn't it? Some of the buildings are really old. I like to walk along by the river best. It is pretty along there. There is a lot to see in Cork. In the morning, before we go to visit May, I will take you to The English Market. You will like it. It reminds me of Borough Market in London. Have you ever been there?"

"I've never been to London, or on a train. Can you believe that?"

He grinned. "It's a good job you are going to marry a wanderlusting, wild gypsy. One day, I will take you to London and then, if you want to, we can travel the world together."

Jules and Seth were sitting in the courtyard at the back of the hostel, waiting for their turn to cook in the kitchen. They had found a picnic table to themselves and sat side by side, watching the other residents chatting and eating together. In the corner of the garden, an old man strummed on a guitar and he was singing quietly to himself. He had a faraway look in his eyes. "Do you think that man with the guitar owns the hostel," Seth asked as he opened a can of lager. He offered it to Jules. "It's still cold."

"Thanks," she said, putting the can on her hot cheek. "I think that he is a resident. I saw him letting himself into one of the rooms when we were looking for ours. It's warm out here tonight, his room might be too hot or he might not want to disturb anyone while he has a little practice."

"I think he is playing 'I walk The Line' by Johnny Cash. What do you think?"

"Is he? Who is Johnny Cash?"

"Seriously? Sometimes, I forget how young you are and how old I am getting."

A pretty Polish girl with blue hair appeared at the back door and waved to Jules.

"Oh, it's my turn to cook. I won't be long. I hope there are some plates left."

"Do you need my help?"

"No, it's ok. You save us the table. I'll take this with me," she said, picking up the cool can. "It's baking hot in there."

Seth took a sip of the lager and let the cool liquid slip down his throat. *Heaven.* He looked at everyone sharing their travelling stories and wondered if Jules would like to see more of the world. I would like her to, but... *I forget that I have jumped* parole. *A wanted man is no longer a free man. Will I ever be free again? Will I ever be able to travel out of Ireland?* He felt a little sad. Seth became aware of a young couple standing in front of him and snapped out of his musing. They were both wearing short sleeved checked shirts and jeans. *Are they cowboys?*

"Is this side of the table free?" they asked in unison and then both laughed at each other. "Are you Seth? Your girl said all the tables are busy, and we can sit with you," the young fair-haired man declared. He had an American accent.

I was right about them being American.

"Your girl told us to look out for a tall dark and handsome man with muscles," the woman said and laughed. "I am going to be so embarrassed if you are not Seth. We bring Cork's finest pizza with us," she added.

"Yes, I'm Seth. I don't know about tall, dark and handsome, though. Yes, please sit here and have a beer with Jules and me," he said, offering them the last few cans.

"That's mighty kind of you," the girl replied as she sat down and then she quickly tied back her blond curls into a band. "It's a warm evening but we are used to the heat. Are you a Cork man?" she asked. "You have an Irish accent, but it doesn't sound like you are from around here."

He smiled. *Do I have an Irish accent?* "I was born in Dingle, which is on the west coast. But I've lived in England for most of my life."

"We're off to England, to London in a few days. We are going up to Rosslare tomorrow," the man said as he climbed onto his seat.

"Are you on holiday?" Seth asked.

"As good as. We are YouTube travel vloggers. Have you heard of the Montana Wanderers?" he asked.

"No, sorry, I haven't. Are you from Montana then?"

"We sure are. Allow us to introduce ourselves. This is my wife Lucy, and I am Kenny Miller. Are you guys on holiday then?"

"No, Jules and I are planning to live near Cork. I teach people how to ride horses and I am hoping to get a job south of here, in Waterfall. Do you two ride? I have a feeling that you do. I don't know why."

"We were born and raised in the saddle. Montana is made for horses. Would you like some pizza?" Lucy asked as she opened the box.

"That is very nice of you, but Jules will be out in a minute with our dinner. You are quite welcome to share that too."

Kenny opened a can of lager. "That's mighty kind, but we're just fine with pizza and your beer."

Seth saw Jules emerge from the house, and she had in each hand a plate, some cutlery and her beer can. Her cheeks were flushed from being in the hot kitchen. She looked over at him and smiled as she walked across the garden.

"You found him then?" she said as she put the plates of food on the table.

"It's very kind of you to let us join you. We are finding everyone in Cork to be so generous and friendly. Would you like a slice of pizza?" Lucy asked her.

Jules sat down. "That's ok, thanks, I've got more than enough here. I didn't ask, are you two on holiday?"

"Kind of. We are YouTube travel vloggers. We make a living from advertising eco-friendly products on our channel. We film ourselves on our travels and show how anyone can enjoy the wonders of the world, and survive on very little money without destroying the environment. We have over thirty vlogs online and we have filmed some super places to visit in America.

We also film any pollution we find and try our best to clean it up. We got a whole community together once and cleaned up a section of the Grand Canyon. We have millions of followers, and we have been approached by companies asking us to promote their products. We only choose companies that care about the environment," Kenny explained as he took a slice of pizza.

"Two weeks ago, we travelled from New York by cargo ship to Dublin. We are travelling around the world and Cork is on our list of destinations. We have visited and kissed the Blarney stone and have explored Cork city. When we travelled across America to get to New York, we rode on horseback when we could. It took us a week on a cargo ship to get to Dublin. We would like to continue on horseback, but we have decided to use electric solar powered bikes we were given to test and see if they compare to riding a horse," Lucy said, laughing. "It is going to be super fun."

"I am green with envy," Seth said. "No pun intended. That sounds like a dream job. You have a difficult task on your hands; persuading the people of the world to change their ways and become environmentally friendly. Not many are willing to look beyond their noses. I admire what you two are doing."

"We hope that we can help people to see how easy it is to reduce their carbon footprint. The world is still a beautiful place to live in. And it is not too late to repair it." Kenny said.

"I spent nearly six years backpacking across Europe, the Far East and Australia. I have seen some beautiful places and I have also seen polluted waters, poverty and war zones. Man has a lot to answer for. It is a crying shame. I really do wish you well. It sounds like you are going to be away from your home for a while. Are you going to miss Montana?" Seth asked.

"We are happy for now but when we return home, we hope to start a family. I think that we will settle then. I don't think you can really take a baby backpacking with you," Kenny said, looking wistfully at Lucy.

"You will have to run a vlog about bringing children up in an ecological way," Jules suggested.

Lucy laughed. "You might have something there!"

Seth smiled at her. *You have the best ideas.* "Jules, this is a great omelette, by the way. So have you been recording yourselves in Cork?" he asked them.

"Yes, we went on a tour of Cork today and tonight we plan to visit pubs that have traditional music playing. Someone recommended that we go and visit The Elbow. They have some new bands there but we really wanted to hear some of the old songs. Can you recommend any bars with good folk bands playing?" Kenny asked.

"You are going to be spoilt for choice. Why don't you see what is going on in Sin E and The Oliver Plunkett?"

"Are you two heading out this evening?" Lucy asked.

Jules looked over at Seth, to make sure he wouldn't be disappointed when she said she wanted to stay in. He looked tired too. "We've had a busy few days travelling here and all I can think about is sleeping," she said.

"She's right. We are on our knees. We are going to have an early night. Tomorrow, we are going south of here to Waterfall to see if we can get work and accommodation there."

"I am sure you will. You both have the nicest of smiles," Lucy said, grinning at them.

"Later, I will look you up on YouTube and subscribe to your channel. We will both be interested to see where you go and what you find," Jules said, unable to stop smiling. "What is your channel called?"

"Look up Montana Wanderers. Or Lucy and Kenny go wild," Kenny replied, laughing.

Chapter Three

Unable to sleep any longer, Seth was standing by the window of their room and looked out onto the sunny street below. A small boy was kicking a ball to his mother in the park across the way. *Is it a park, or is it a graveyard?* He remembered playing football with his brothers and some of his sisters too, in the bottom field of Crow Farm where the land was level. *I can't have been more than ten.* He remembered his Dad standing on the side-lines, pretending to be their coach. He had taken that job far too seriously and there had been lots of fights over who was going to be on each team.

A distorted image of his Dad's evil grimacing face filled his mind when they had fought under the water in the silent pool. He remembered his father's hands squeezing him around his throat. There was no doubt that his very own Dad would have killed him, had he been weaker than him. *What father in their right mind would want to kill their own son? It was his own fault he drowned. I have to move on for Jules's sake. Like she says, it will eat me inside if I let it.*

He sighed with despair, but then a more pleasant thought filled his head. Today he would see his horse, Moss, and this made him smile. *I can't wait. We should go soon. I will show Jules Cork tomorrow. I am looking forward to seeing May too. Jules will like her. May is so kind and friendly. I wonder if Sinead will be working at the stables today? Should I tell Jules that I slept with her once? We were drunk, it was a mistake and it was a long time ago. I don't think that I should... It's going to be tricky to get to Waterfall West. I hope Jules doesn't mind a bit of a walk.*

He got up, picked up the phone and then sat on the edge of the bed. It was seven thirty-four and he wondered how long Jules would sleep in. He didn't like to wake her. She looked so lovely wrapped up in the duvet. *Right then, how do we get to Waterfall?*

Jules slept for another half an hour, and seeing her beautiful blue eyes when she woke filled his heart with joy. He leaned over her and kissed her gently on the lips. "Morning, my lovely. How did you sleep?" *She is so gorgeous!*

Jules stretched her arms out and then placed them around his neck and hugged him. "Oh Seth, that was the best sleep I've had in ages. I think that you were in my dreams. How about you? How did you sleep?"

"Not so great; I think I was awake every hour thinking about things. I've been up since five and I have had a workout, right next to you. I have showered too. You didn't even stir. Bombs could drop, and I don't think you would notice."

Jules laughed. "Dad used to say that I could sleep for England! Poor Dad, I hope he is ok. So, what's worrying you?"

"I just keep re-enacting Patrick's nightmare party and what happened to us. I am doing my best to get over it, but it is going to take a while. Don't you worry about me, though; I am tough as old boots. You seem to be faring better than me."

"I'm ok. I just think of happy things instead of brooding about the past. Knowing you are there for me helps. You know I am there for you too, don't you?"

"I do. I couldn't be without you. Now then, you are going to have to get dressed. I need to see Moss. That was another reason why I woke so early. It's been too long since I saw my horse. Excited isn't close to how I am feeling right now."

***

They took the bus to the quiet village of Waterfall. In some ways, the village reminded Jules of Findon, but the land was a lot flatter. For a moment she felt homesick for Sussex. Her new life in Ireland was, to her, just a surreal dream. *I hope I grow to love it here like Seth does.* Jules was feeling unsettled and as they walked up a quiet lane to Waterfall West, she found that she was constantly looking over her shoulder for the police. *I wonder if they are aware that he has skipped parole and fled the country? Stop worrying, Jules! Maybe I should worry in a week or so.* She was happy for him. He had come home to the country he loved and had been born in. Breaking his parole did not seem to be bothering him.

A leafy twisted lane and a ten minute walk took them to the home of Seth's old friend, May. She could see that he was happy as his eyes were lit up with excitement. *I hope that May will let us work and stay here. I hope that his horse is ok.*

A large faded sign stuck in the grass verge announced to all that they had arrived at 'Waterfall West Riding School and Livery Yard.' Seth hesitated for a moment and looked up the long shingle drive, and then at the old Manor House and the surrounding grounds. *The house, gardens and the verge used to look immaculate.* The once formal gardens had become a mass of weeds and brambles. *There is something wrong here.*

Hand in hand, they passed the old Manor House. Many of the windows had been covered over with ivy. He frowned. *This is really not good. May can't be living here anymore.*

The stable yard, however, was a hive of activity. Jules was pleased to see this, as she feared that they might have found them closed up too. A group of children were being helped onto ponies of various colours and sizes by stable hands wearing blue polo shirts with white logos. Once mounted, and the girth strap tightened, with a rider on top, the ponies wandered towards a sand school adjacent to the stable block. Some of the riders looked confident, but others had fear in their eyes.

As the last pony made its way to the school, Jules noticed a pretty girl with shiny black hair, tied back in two small bunches, maybe a little older than herself, walking out of the bookings office. She had a nose piercing and the bluest of eyes. Her face lit up when she saw Seth. He ran over to her and as he hugged her, he lifted her and swung her off of her feet.

"Sinead, it's so good to see you again. How have you been?" He put her down and stepped back, smiling broadly at her.

"Oh my goodness! I'm fine, Seth. Very busy, but fine. How long has it been? Three years? It's gone so fast. I can't believe that you are here. You're a bad boy! You should have kept in touch," she said in her broad northern accent. "May has been keeping me up to date, though."

"I know. I'm sorry. It's a long story. Sinead, this is Jules, my wife-to-be."

Jules smiled at Sinead. "Hi, it is nice to meet you," she said brightly, determined not to let her anxieties show. *Who are you? How well does Seth know you?*

"It's nice to meet you too. Wife-to-be? So when are you two going to get hitched? This is so exciting. I love a good wedding."

Jules was feeling uneasy, and a knot was tightening in her stomach. "We haven't set a date yet. Soon, I hope."

"Look, you two, I've got to teach this lesson but when I'm done, in an hour, then we will catch up."

"Ok, that's grand. We will come and watch you. Where's May?" he asked.

"Seth, there's lots to tell you. May had a stroke a couple of weeks ago. She is in a nursing home at the moment. Her brother, Tom, is coming over from Australia soon. Do you remember that git? There are going to be some interesting times ahead."

Jules looked at his face and could see that he was shaken.

He sighed. "I remember him. I'm sorry, that's such a shame about May. You get on and we will catch up later." *I didn't see that one coming!*

Sinead walked into the sand school and shut the gate. "Go and see Moss," she called. "He is in the summer field with the other cobs. You are going to be so shocked when you see him. He has been winning prizes!"

"Has he? Thanks, Sinead. We will see you in a bit."

Jules looked up at him and she could see a sadness in his eyes. "I'm sorry about May, perhaps we could go and see her later."

"Yes, I'd like that. We can't really stay here now, can we? Sinead said that she was busy, so we might be able to get work here. We will see. Come on, Jules, let's go and see my boy. I've waited long enough for this day."

As they walked to the summer field, Jules couldn't stop thinking about Sinead. She could tell that Seth and her were, or had been, close. *How close were they? I will have to be careful how I ask him about her. I don't want him to think that I am jealous. Am I jealous? No, it's something else. Just ask him, Jules! Dad gave mum such a hard time. Jealousy is a terrible thing. I am better than that.* "Sinead seems nice. Has she worked here long?"

"She's lovely. She is like a sister to me. Before we came to the stable yard, she had been backpacking like me. We met in Sydney and travelled around Australia together. When we were out there, we worked at a ranch to earn some money. That's where we met May. May was on a riding holiday with her brother, Tom. We used to take them out for rides and she must have liked what she saw as she asked if we would come over to Ireland and work at her stable yard. Tom was... How can I put this politely? An arrogant bastard. He tried it on with Sinead and then when he discovered that she preferred girls, he said some terrible things to her. I shouldn't have punched him, but he really was out of order. May said he deserved it but I am not proud of myself."

All of her anxieties and worries vanished, and she was pleased with herself for not causing a row. "That's awful. You do have a bit of a short fuse. You are going to have to learn to walk away."

"I know. I am working on it."

"It sounds like you were happy here. Why did you go back to Crow Farm?"

"Can you believe this? I missed my family and wanted to spend some time with them. I intended to come back here, but life didn't turn out that way. Now, where's my boy? Oh, goodness! Look under the oak tree. Do you see that great black horse, covering one of the mares? I don't think you should look. Here, let me hug you and hide your eyes for a moment until he is done. How embarrassing," he said, laughing.

Chapter Four

"MOSS...MOSS! COME HERE BOY." *Please let him remember me.* Much to Seth's relief, his beloved horse cantered across the grassy field towards him. Seth climbed through the post and rail fence to greet him. The delight in Moss's eyes at seeing his owner again was evident. Too excited to stand still, his horse danced about him, eager to hear his master's voice again and to be stroked. "Jules, he remembers me. Come on, boy, settle down and let me pet you. It's been too long, my old friend. Look at you now, all fine and dandy. Who would have thought that you would have turned out so well? Come on, Moss, calm down, boy." Hearing his soothing voice, Moss began to relax and finally stood still, allowing him to run his hands over his strong neck and shoulders. "He looks far too grand to be ridden. Look at the shine on his coat."

Jules was astounded. Moss was probably the most beautiful horse that she had ever seen. His large stocky body was muscular yet svelte. His coat was completely black and despite being turned out in a field, his fur shone in the light and it was almost as if he had been polished. He had the longest, silkiest black mane and tail that she had ever seen and the feathers below his hocks were full and fluffy. "Seth, he is incredible. I didn't imagine that he would look like this. I'm not surprised that he has been winning prizes. If only I could take a photo of him and put it on Instagram. You must be really proud of him."

"I am so proud. This is May's doing. She really knows how to bring out the best in a horse. I am so sad that she has had a stroke. I only spoke to her a month ago and she was fine then. I asked her if I could come back to work for her in June next year and she told me that I would always be welcome. She is so kind. She really didn't deserve to have a stroke."

"May should recover. People get over strokes. It doesn't sound like it was a bad one. Sinead said that she was in a nursing home. May is obviously well enough to leave the hospital."

"That's true, but they didn't let her come home. Let's hope she gets better. It's a shame her brother is visiting. Like I told you, he is a real pain in the arse. May used to be able to handle him, but she could only take him in small doses. I imagine that he is rubbing his hands together, hoping that she dies. May has no family, so he will get the lot when she goes."

"That's awful. Seth, I was going to ask you, before I put my foot in it. Do May and Sinead know that you went to prison?"

He shook his head. "I haven't told Sinead, she thinks I had to stay in Sussex because I had family problems; which wasn't a complete lie. I did tell May, though. I wasn't going to, but I couldn't help myself. She doesn't know about me going to prison instead of Jake, of course. She thinks I was sentenced for causing a major traffic incident. I don't think she bought it, though. It's not like me to be careless. She promised that she wouldn't say anything to Sinead. Talking about Sinead, shall I let my handsome boy go back to his women, and we go and watch her teach?"

"Ok, but I don't think he wants you to leave him. You can see that he is love-struck. He really is stunning."

After teaching a chaotic riding lesson, Sinead took them to the office and cleared some body protectors and bags from a couple of chairs so they could sit down. She looked tired, and her cheeks were red from exertion. She was sitting behind the booking desk, resting her feet on the corner and then switched on a small desk fan. "Is it me, or is it really hot out there?"

Seth got up and walked over to a mini kitchenette in the corner. "It was all that running about in the sand school you were doing. No wonder you are hot. You must be thirsty. Is it ok if I make us all some tea?"

"You don't have to ask, silly."

"What do you have these days? Black Redbush?"

"You remembered! I think there is some milk in the fridge for you both. I would sniff it first. So, Seth, how's your family doing. You said that you had some trouble with one of your brothers?"

Now what am I going to say? Fuck! "Well... a lot has been going on at End Farm and Crow Farm. Jules's father didn't want us to be together. Jake's girlfriend died and my brother had a bit of a breakdown but he is on the mend. Mam and Dad needed more help on the farm so I have been out in the fields, working the land. Dad passed away recently, and Mam has gone off her trolley. Patrick is running the farm now, and we don't really see eye to eye. That's why I am back here early."

"Goodness! You were right. You have been through it. I'm sorry to hear about your Dad."

Jules listened to his account of his past life and was impressed by his ability to gloss over the ghastly details without faltering or lying too much.

"So, Sinead, I told May that I would come and work for her next year and she was fine about it. Do you think I should visit her and see if it is ok to start now instead?"

"Seth, she will be made up! I am made up too. You won't need to ask her. You are like a son to her. Only the other day, she was talking about you and wishing you were here."

"That's good to hear. How is she doing? When did she have her stroke?"

"About ten days ago. She was sitting where I am sitting now and she was taking a call from someone wanting to book a lesson. When May put the phone down, she just sat there and was staring off into the distance. I actually saw the left side of her face drop before my eyes. I asked her if she was feeling ok but she couldn't speak properly and she wasn't making sense. I took her to hospital straight away and because we got there so quickly, they were able to give her that drug that reverses strokes.

It was touch and go for twenty-four hours, but she survived and now she can't walk without a frame and her speech is slurred. She was very tired for the first week, but when I saw her yesterday, she was making jokes and is sharp as a button. She is improving each day. This evening, I'm going to see her after work. Do you want to come along? The nursing home is in the next village."

"Yes, that will be grand. I will have to check when the last bus goes back to Cork."

"I'll drive you to Cork. It's only a twenty minute drive from here. So how are you finding Ireland, Jules? Have you been here before?"

"No, it's my first time. I like to travel, and I've always wanted to visit Ireland."

"Where did you two meet?"

"I met Jules in Sussex. She lived at Farm End, the next farm to ours," he replied.

"That was handy. How long have you two been going out together?"

Jules had to think for a moment and realised that they had only been together for a month. "Quite a while," she said, smiling at Seth.

"That is so cool. I can see that you two are meant for each other. I didn't think that he would ever meet the right girl. Well done for finding her before you got too old!"

"Cheek! I am still in my twenties. Although I do hit the big three zero on the thirtieth."

Jules inhaled with surprise. "No way! Seth, it's my birthday on the thirtieth of September too!"

"Well, I never!" he said, laughing. "What a party we are going to have! The thirtieth you say?"

Jules nodded "I can't believe it. Mum and Dad had the same birthdays too. How weird is that?"

He handed out the tea he had made. "So, will I be doing my old job, teaching and mucking out?"

"Yes, of course, you are a qualified instructor and you are still on the payroll. You don't have to muck out. We have lots of stable hands to do that. If it is ok with you, I will put you in charge of looking after all the cobs, and your Moss, of course. Oh, I need your help at the shows too. There's one this weekend, and Moss has been entered. I can't keep up with him when I run him around the ring. I fell over last time. What did you think of him? He's looking pretty dapper, isn't he?"

"It was so good to see him again. He has turned into a real fine horse. Who would have thought it? Jules, when I got him, he was underweight and a real scrawny thing. May laughed when I bought him for a song but now look at him. Jules has a cob back home in Sussex. When we are settled, we are going to bring him over here. Aren't we?"

"I'd like that, but he is no show horse. He is a kind old thing and is a nice ride, even though he is far too big for me."

"Are there any vacancies in the yard for Jules?"

"I'm sorry, we have all the stable hands we need at the moment. I have an idea, though. Jules, how do you feel about cleaning? I know it is not that glamorous but we are going to need a cleaner for the main house from next week."

"I'll do anything, and I don't mind cleaning. What did you have in mind?"

"So, you two saw the Manor House as you came in, didn't you? May has had it all converted into bed and breakfast accommodation. Next week, the front of the house is going to be tidied up and the gardens are going to be landscaped. The website will go live and a new sign will be put up on the road.

The renovations have been a headache and has stressed May out. I think that is why she had a stroke. She took too much on starting up this new venture but you know how she likes a challenge. It is a little late in the season to open for business but she is hoping to attract people that like riding. So it will be a bit of a riding holiday business. I think it will attract people all year round. I just hope May recovers and gets to see all her hard work pay off."

He sat down. "I was a bit shocked when I saw the state of the house. I guess that my old room has been converted. I was hoping that we could stay there."

"You wouldn't recognise your room now. I had to move out of my room too. I've been staying in an old mobile home near the summer field. Hey, I know. You could both stay with me. It has two bedrooms. What do you think?"

"You are an amazing girl! Yes, that will do us just fine. I've missed you so much. Is that ok with you, Jules?"

"I'd like to stay with you very much. If you are sure? You really have solved so many problems for us. We are so grateful," she replied.

"That's no problem. I have to warn you both. I've been so busy that the mobile is in a bit of a state. I know how you like order and to straighten things, Seth!" she said with a cheeky grin. "Hey, I know this is a lot to ask, but would you mind helping with the next lesson? I've got to teach Mr Farrow and his daughter at two. Last time I taught them together, they ended up arguing. I think it would be better if they were taught separately. We could split the sand school fifty-fifty. Would you, pretty please?"

"That is no problem at all. I can't wait to teach again."

Jules followed the two riders, Seth and Sinead down to the sand school. She had noticed that Mr Farrow and his daughter had been arguing when they came into the stable yard. She had overheard him say to her that he wouldn't spend any money on lessons if she wasn't going to try. He was speaking to her as if she was a child. His daughter was, in actual fact, a woman in her thirties. *I wonder why they keep coming here for lessons together.*

Seth talked to Mr Farrow and he agreed to let him teach him separately. Sinead led his daughter and her horse to the far end of the school. Jules leaned on the fence rail and watched the lessons with fascination. *Could I become an instructor, I wonder?* It was mesmerising watching him teach. She admired his confidence and knowledge. Mr Farrow was prone to answer back negatively. Jules soon decided that his daughter was a much better rider than he was but just lacked confidence. He never argued with him and just asked him to try something new each time. Eventually, Mr Farrow just did as he was asked and he started to do a little better.

After an hour, the two students left the sand school with their horses and a couple of stable hands came out of a barn to help put their horses away.

Sinead's face was flushed red from running around the sand school. She waited with Jules as Seth dismantled a jump. "It's good to see him happy again," she said, fanning her face with her hands. "This is going to be a new chapter for you both. You can leave your horrid past lives behind and start afresh. I really hope you like living in Waterfall. It was the making of me. Like I said, you two are really meant for each other. I've never seen Seth this much in love before."

Chapter Five

It was late in the evening when Sinead drove Jules and Seth to the nursing home in her new Mini. Sinead had insisted that Jules sit with her in the front, and Seth sit in the back. He spread himself over the two seats and he was feeling happy that Jules and Sinead were getting on so well and that he and Jules had both got themselves jobs and had found a place to live.

Jules thought that Sinead was probably the most confident driver that she had ever been with. She thought back to the drives she had been on with her brother, Peter, and realised how afraid she had been. *I really must learn to drive. Perhaps Sinead will teach me?*

The visit to see May had gone better than Jules had expected. May was not as she had imagined her to be. In her mind, she had an image of a frail, elderly woman with short white curly hair. May was in fact a tall, large-boned woman, with long dyed blond hair. She looked at least twenty years younger than her seventy years. They had found May was sitting in a wheelchair, reading in the nursing home's picturesque gardens. When she had seen Seth, her crooked face had lit up and she had put her good arm out to welcome him. Jules could see from his expression that he was shocked by her appearance. He had hidden it well, and had run over to her and had given her a big hug. May had not let go of his hand as she tried her best to talk to him. Jules could see how much she liked him.

Sinead had told May about her plan to employ them both and May had patted his knee and nodded. It had been quite hard going trying to decipher her words when she spoke. She had laughed at herself and rolled her eyes when everyone eventually worked out what she was saying. They had only stayed an hour, as a nurse had come into the garden to take her back to her room. May was looking a bit weary when they waved goodbye to her.

As they continued on to Cork, Seth watched Jules chatting away to Sinead and he smiled. It was good to see his beautiful girl so happy and loving life. He had been sad to see May in such a state, but after sitting with her, he realised how strong she really was. *It will only be a matter of time before she is back at the stables again.* Things were working out better than he had hoped. *I mustn't get too complacent, though. Tomorrow, I should be going for a meeting with my parole officer. When they realise I am missing, will they come all this way to find me? I hope not. Don't think about it.* "So, Sinead, are you up for a bite to eat with us in Cork? Our treat."

"Oh, yes. That's a good idea. Please come," Jules said as she looked back at him.

"I suppose I could. I can't stay out too late. I'm up early tomorrow. Ok, I will. Where shall we go then?"

"Do you know any good vegan restaurants?" he asked.

"We could go to Quay Co-op. I haven't been there, but I've heard that it is good."

"Jules, my poor meat-eating girl. Will you be able to dine with two vegetarians tonight?"

"Seth, you bad thing! You make me sound like a T-Rex! That sounds great. I am actually really hungry and could eat a horse!" she said, laughing. "I'm interested in seeing what's on the menu so I know what I can cook for you both when you come home tired and hungry from work."

"This is good news! I'm going to enjoy having you stay. It will be great to have a home cooked meal for a change. Do you like cooking, then?" Sinead asked.

"I don't mind it. After my Mum died, I had to cook for my Dad and brother. They are useless in the kitchen and seemed to like what I cooked."

"I'm sorry about your Mum. I can't cook either and I survive on very little, really. So what time are you two coming over tomorrow?"

"In the morning I am going to show Jules Cork, and then we will do some shopping. We are going to visit the English Market. They've got some great cheese there!"

Jules looked back at him and saw his cheeky grin and smiled. "Cheese tonight as well, I guess!"

"Maybe, probably. We will see. I quite like tofu if it is done the right way. Is late afternoon all right for you Sinead? Or do you need me to teach tomorrow?"

"I feel bad setting you to work straight away, but you couldn't take the four o'clock lesson, could you? Time-wise, I am really up against it. May wants the bed and breakfast open next week. I need to go online and sort out some advertising for her."

"Sure, no problem. It was fun teaching this afternoon. I'd forgotten how much I had missed doing it. What kind of class is it?"

"It will be the children from Munster House. Jules, these kids have special needs and you should see their faces light up when they are riding. I might need your help leading one of the ponies. Will that be ok?"

"I'd love to do that," she replied as they entered Cork.

***

Back at Kinlay House, Seth stretched himself out on the bed and smiled at Jules. "Come here and give your boyfriend a hug."

Jules crawled on the bed and lay next to him. He put his arm around her and she snuggled into him and laid her arm across his muscular chest. She couldn't help running her hand across his contours, marvelling at how firm his chest felt.

"Did you enjoy your meal? Did you miss not having meat?"

"I actually enjoyed my fake burger. It tasted really nice. I could get used to being a vegetarian."

"Will it be ok if we only buy vegetarian food from now on? Sinead will freak out if we put meat in her fridge. It is much healthier to eat this way. You can eat well without putting weight on. What do you say?"

"I am sure that I will survive. I like a challenge. I can always nibble on some jerky in secret if I am desperate."

He laughed. "I promise that I will take you out every month to satisfy any meat craving you may have. It was good to have a meal out with Sinead, wasn't it? A little bit expensive, though."

"Our savings are going down quickly, aren't they? Earlier, I was thinking about our money situation. When we work at Waterfall West, our wages will go into our bank accounts. That is not going to work. When we draw out our money, the police will know where we are. We are going to have to be paid in cash or just offer our services for free, in exchange for rent and bills."

"I hadn't thought of that. Most people pay for lessons or a room by card these days, so there won't be much cash available. I don't like to ask Sinead to go into Cork and draw cash out of the business account for us. Damn! That's thrown a spanner in the works. Our savings are not going to last for much longer and we need money for food. Don't worry, I'll think of something."

Jules smiled. "Don't be downhearted. I've got a plan to make us some cash and it involves this," she said as she slipped out of his arms. She crawled off the bed and walked over to her guitar and picked it up.

"You don't have to sell your guitar. I'll get a cash-in-hand job as well as working at the stables."

She looked out of the window to make sure that it was still dry outside. "Come outside with me. I want to run an idea past you. It's late and if I show you in here, then we might wake people up. Let's find a quiet spot. There's a bench in the graveyard across the road. This won't take long."

"You're scaring me a little. You threw a 'we' into the mix. Does this involve us singing together?"

"It might."

They found the bench and sat side by side. The street lamps in Bob and Joan's Walk gave them enough light to see each other in the eerie graveyard.

"You really couldn't have picked a quieter spot. It's a bit spooky here," he said as he watched Jules unpack her guitar.

"This is the perfect spot to play the guitar and sing."

"Ok." *She obviously feels confident enough to sing outside and be heard by people passing by. She's not going to get me to sing too, is she? She did say we.*

Jules put her guitar on her knee and started to tune it. She smiled at him mischievously. "So, I've been thinking. I've done this once before in Chichester and actually made some decent money by busking. Dad didn't allow me to go out a second time, so I don't know if I just got lucky that day. I surprised myself and I really love performing. It's still the tourist season here in Cork and if we hit the streets at lunchtime and busk, then we might be able to make some money. I'd rather we make us some money now, before our savings run out."

"You're saying 'we' again!"

"I did. I've heard you sing, and you have a great voice. If we sang popular crowd-pleasing songs, then I think we have a good chance of making money. I have the feeling, because your family all seem to like performing, then there is a chance that you do too. What do you think?"

"I don't know. It is one thing singing in front of your family, but it is another thing singing to the public. What if we get pelted with rotten tomatoes?"

Jules smiled. "We won't, not if we sing the right songs. I was thinking of singing some of the popular Irish folk songs, but not the ones that mention hard times and the IRA. Which is most of them, really. We will just sing the songs that lift the spirits, mixed with some modern-day songs that we can sing together." *He's gone quiet, I'm scaring him. I'll sing while he thinks about it.* "Ok, I would call on Ed Sheeran again and sing Galway Girl but I think that would be a good song for us both to sing. I've got a voice similar to Meghan Trainor, so I'll sing 'Friends' for you. Tell me what you think," Jules said as she started to play her guitar.

Seth watched his sweet girl strum on her guitar and sing. Her surprise announcement had startled him. He liked singing but he wasn't as confident as she was. It wasn't that he was shy, it was just that he found singing to be an emotional experience. He suspected that performing to the public would make him feel exposed. *This girl can really sing!* He was blown away by her confidence. She clearly loved singing in public and was enjoying herself. He couldn't help smiling at her. She had an amazing deep and husky voice that drew you in. *How does such a strong voice come out of someone so small?*

When her song ended, he was beaming at her. "You have just blown me away! I never knew that you could play or sing like that. You never said."

"Thank you. Do you think that I am good then? Do you want to sing with me as a duet?"

"You are amazing. I don't know about me singing. I'd sing to you, but singing to everyone else is another matter."

"Do you know any songs off by heart? I can usually pick up the chords for any song. I just know that we would do well. Can you think of any popular songs that we could sing together?" *He's smiling so that's a good sign. Oh, no! He's looking serious now.*

"I know most of the words to all of Coldplay's songs but if you are going for crowd pleasing, then apart from the Dubliners, you'd be looking at songs by popular Irish bands. I like Snow Patrol. They are an Irish band. I know 'Chasing Cars'. I hate to say it, but Westlife would go down well too. I told you that I went to my sister, Maureen's wedding a few years back. The night I was coming down with the flu and Jake had the big accident… that night when… Anyway, she's a big fan of that band so some of us got together and did a few Westlife songs for her. 'Unbreakable' was one of them and it would be a good one for us to sing," he suggested. *What am I getting myself into here?*

Good, he is smiling again. "That sounds great. Do you want to have a go? Will you sing Unbreakable to me? I think that I should be able to play along and join in with the chorus."

"I do remember it. Ok. I'm feeling nervous now," he said, looking up and down the path to make sure nobody else could hear him. Satisfied that the coast was clear, he closed his eyes and started to sing.

Unable to play, Jules listened to him sing with her mouth open, astounded by his voice. *He sounds more Irish when he sings. He sounds a bit like Shawn Mendes and Shane Filan. Seth is way better than his brother, Patrick. I didn't expect this. He doesn't need to be accompanied. We can sing acapella if we need to.*

As Seth got to the chorus, she joined in and chills went up and down her spine. *Our voices complement each other's. Busking is going to be amazing with you!*

He finished singing and he knew that he was crying as he could feel tears streaming down his face.

"You're crying. Don't cry, Seth. You were incredible!"

"I knew that was going to happen. I am a mess when I sing. I don't know why. We will have to sing happy songs, otherwise this won't work," he said, brushing his tears away with his hands.

"So you are up for a little busking with me?"

"It won't hurt to try but if anyone throws a rotten tomato at me, then it will be all over and I will find myself a cash-in-hand job in the fields."

"I think that you are going to be surprised. We are going to be awesome together!"

JULIA'S BABY

Chapter Six

It was early and Kinlay House was starting to wake up. This was Jules and Seth's last morning at the hostel. From her bed, she could hear the sounds of people in the rooms around them. Some of the guests were packing or were just getting ready for the day ahead.

Jules had surprised herself and had woken up first. Not wanting to go back to sleep, she had plugged her headphones into the phone and had searched for songs that they could sing together. *I can't wait to sing with Seth. He is so hot when he sings.* She had compiled a playlist of twelve songs that she thought would go down well on the streets of Cork. Jules had listened to the Dubliners and had done her best to remember the chords and the words of some of their songs. *Today we will busk together and start our new life at Waterfall West. I can't wait!*

The night had been warm, and she had slept lightly. Seth had been restless, and she suspected that he had been awake for most of the night. It was good to see him resting and looking so peaceful. She left the phone and earphones on the side and turned over so that she was facing him. He had taken his top off in the night and his strong shoulder and arm were exposed. She sighed and couldn't take her eyes off him. *You are just so good-looking. You make me feel weak and again my body yearns for you. Is this normal? It is better if you sleep like this for a while.*

Please don't let the past destroy you. I couldn't bear it if you ended up like my Dad. Poor Dad. I wonder if he has been allowed to leave Meadowfield Hospital yet? She felt very guilty for leaving her brother to deal with him alone.

Seth opened his eyes and saw her lovingly watching him. He smiled, and putting his arms around her, he pulled her to him and kissed her. "Morning, my little Nancy Mulligan. How are you doing? No nerves then?"

"Nerves? Oh, for our busking adventure later. No, I'm looking forward to it. I am so excited. That is probably why I am awake before you. Who is Nancy Mulligan, by the way?"

"I'm surprised you don't know. Your second love, Ed Sheeran, sang that. I know the words to that one. Back home, that song was popular with my sisters. I'll sing it today, if you like."

"Oh, yes. I remember now. I can play that one. I'd like that. I have just been lying here, admiring you while you slept. I love you so much."

"I'm glad to hear it. Do you want me to show you how much I love you?" he said with a naughty twinkle in his dark brown eyes.

"You must be tired. I don't think that you slept much last night, did you? You should save all your energy for our busking session later?"

"No, I didn't sleep well but that is not going to stop me making love to you. I am ready for you."

She smiled. "I think that you should rest and let me pleasure you. It only seems fair. Earlier, while I was looking for songs to sing together, I came across twenty ways to please your man in the bedroom."

"Just twenty?"

"I doubt that you will be able to survive all twenty. Lie on your back, Seth, and let me put my hot plan into action."

He turned over, feeling a little surprised by her boldness and waited for her to kiss him. She was smiling at him in a seductive way, and he realised that he was about to be tortured.

"Close your eyes," she whispered. She leaned over him and gently kissed his forehead, then each eyelid. She turned his head to the side, kissed his ear, bit gently on his earlobe and then licked deep inside it.

He inhaled sharply as a shockwave of pleasure ran down his body. *What is she doing to me?*

Slowly, she kissed and nibbled her way down his neck and muscular chest, licking and kissing his nipples. His body quivered with pleasure. She continued her journey downward, enjoying seeing how each kiss or bite affected him.

*"*Oh my!*" Where is she going now?* He could feel her teeth tugging at the skin and hairs below his navel and he gasped as his body shook again. "I can't take much more of this!" He opened his eyes. "I am going to have to take you now. I can't hold on for much longer. There are condoms in my wash bag. Please, Jules, stop! You are driving me mad!"

She paused and smiled at him. "Close your eyes again. We won't need a condom for what I've got in mind. I like driving you wild and see you lose control. I've just got twelve more zones to find before we get to twenty. I'll get to you in time," she said as she ran her fingers along the inside of his thighs towards his groin.

"Dear God! You crazy girl!"

***

Jules and Seth were sitting by the river Lee and were soaking up the last of the summer sun. Cork had turned out to be a really interesting city to visit. After a late breakfast, they left their luggage in the reception of Kinlay House and arranged to collect it after the grand tour of the city. Hand in hand, they had wandered along the streets and lanes, through Fitzgerald Park, visited cathedrals and rang the Shandon Bells in St. Anne's Church. Later, they planned to visit the English Market to buy some local cheese.

Seth had discovered that their phone had a decent camera and he had taken a few photos. She flicked through them, admiring his ability to take such interesting shots of Cork's bridges and the buildings that lined the river Lee. "You really do take some excellent photos. You've got a good eye for it. If we don't make any money busking, then we could get some of the photos you've taken, blow them up, frame them, and sell them at a market. We could make a fortune."

"Now there's an idea. I just love your positive outlook on life. I don't think that I am going to go too far wrong with you by my side. Jules, I am really hungry. Are you? I think it's time to feed my sweet little bird. How does a McDonalds sound? I promise that I will turn a blind eye if you need to satisfy your carnivore cravings."

"I'm starving too. I might have to. I don't know what's wrong with me. I've never felt this hungry before."

"It's the healing Cork air. And... I think that you may have over exerted yourself this morning. It must have been exhausting torturing me like that. That was a first for me."

Jules smiled. "I don't think you suffered that much. Although at one point, I thought that you were going to have a heart attack! Perhaps later, I can find the last six erogenous zones

I missed. However, you will need to earn that reward by singing with me on the corner of Princes Street."

"You drive a hard bargain, my wife to be. I will do my best to please you. But I fear my heart may give out before we get to Princes Street."

Jules laughed. "Seth, seriously, you only need to sing if you want to. We will do half an hour and see how it goes. We've got nothing to lose."

After lunch, they had gone back to Kinlay House and had collected their cases and the guitar. It was a few minutes past one by the time they got to Princes Street. Seth spotted another busker further up the road, but he was far enough away from them not to hear him. The sun was out, and the street was full of shoppers, tourists and office workers.

Jules took her guitar out from its case and lay it open in front of her. She found some change and threw it into the case to make it look like they had already made some money. Her heart was beating hard in her chest. *Just last minute nerves. I will feel better when we've sung the first song.* She slipped her guitar strap over her shoulder and tuned the guitar. Jules looked across at him to make sure he hadn't passed out with anxiety and she was relieved to see that he was smiling and looked relaxed. *He's got this.*

"Shall we start with 'The Whiskey in the Jar'? It's about Cork, I think. I learnt the chords and words yesterday. I was singing it in my head before we went to sleep last night. We could do 'Chasing Cars' and 'Nancy Mulligan' after, if you like."

"Jules, this is your baby. You just have fun and I'll do my best to follow you."

"Ok, thanks. Here goes. Ready?" She started to strum her guitar and looked up and down Princes Street at the people passing by and noticed a group of Japanese tourists were heading towards them. *I wonder if they will stop?* She looked back at him and smiled. *Good, he is ok and looks like he wants to sing.*

"As I was goin' over
The Cork and Kerry Mountains
I saw Captain Farrell
And his money, he was countin'
I first produced my pistol
And then produced my rapier
I said, "Stand and deliver or the devil he may take ya"

I took all of his money
And it was a pretty penny
I took all of his money,
Yeah, and I brought it home to Molly
She swore that she loved me,
No, never would she leave me
But the devil take that woman,
Yeah, for you know she tricked me easy

Musha rain dum a doo, dum a da
Whack for my daddy, oh
Whack for my daddy, oh
There's whiskey in the jar, oh

Being drunk and weary
I went to Molly's chamber

Takin' Molly with me
But I never knew the danger
For about six or maybe seven,
Yeah, in walked Captain Farrell
I jumped up, fired my pistols
And I shot him with both…

***

The bus was full, but Jules and Seth had managed to find a seat together at the back of the bus and had squeezed their cases into the small luggage rack. The guitar she slotted next to her by the window. Seth put a large shopping bag between his feet and sat back in his seat. Exhausted from their busy day, they waited patiently for the bus to leave the station.

Seth was beaming at her. "I am so proud of us. In forty-five minutes, we made thirty pounds and now we have enough food for the week. You were right. There is money to be made from busking."

An elderly woman a couple of seats down from them turned towards them. "I couldn't help overhearing. Was it the two of you I saw on Princes Street?"

"Yes," he replied, leaning forward to talk to her. "Did you see us singing then?"

"I did, and you brought a tear to my eye. You both sing like angels. I wish the best of luck to you both. It's good to see youngsters like yourselves getting off their arses and doing something for the people of Cork."

"Thanks. I'm glad you enjoyed it."

"You're welcome," she replied, turning back in her seat and then she started to talk to another elderly woman who was sitting opposite to her.

"That was nice of her," whispered Jules. "I really enjoyed singing with you today. Do you think we could busk once a week, until it gets too cold to be out?"

"Why not. That would be grand. I didn't think that I would like performing, but it really gives you a buzz and it makes people smile too. When we get to the stables, I am going to tell Moss all about our day. I'm itching to take him out for a ride. I am sure Sinead will be able to lend you a horse to ride. What do you say to a gentle evening hack through the fields?"

***

While Seth saddled up Moss and a mare named Sasha, Jules hung up their clothes in a musty wardrobe in their bedroom. The evening sun shone down on the roof and the heat inside the mobile home was almost unbearable.

When Jules had entered their new home, she hadn't been that impressed. It was like stepping back into the 1970s. She had done her best to look pleased but she couldn't help noticing the smell of mould. The horrid orange curtains hanging limply in the windows disturbed her too. Jules felt like she was in a time capsule but she was also grateful that she had a home.

Sinead was in the lounge area doing her best to tidy up. Jules finished what she was doing and then changed into some riding trousers. They stuck to her legs as she pulled them on. She looked at herself in the wardrobe door mirror and tutted. The makeup over her eye was starting to slide off her face in the heat and her bruise was showing. She wiped off the old makeup and then added some more, hoping that Sinead hadn't noticed the state she was in.

"Jules, Seth is coming over with Sasha and Moss," Sinead called. "You will like riding her. She is a darling. Moss hasn't been ridden for a while now. He's going to be full of beans. He only likes Seth to ride him, but I think he is going to have trouble."

Jules came out of the bedroom. Sinead had arranged all the clutter into neat piles and was lying on the sofa, exhausted. She looked around and smiled. Sinead laughed. "I did my best. I know! It can't stay like this. I'll put it away when you two are out. That's if I can move again. It's so hot this evening."

"I'll help you when we get back. I am going to make a vegetarian curry. Are you ok with spice?"

"I love a curry. They say, when it is hot, a curry will cool you down from the inside. You really are spoiling me. I am so glad you two are staying here. I don't like living by myself."

Feeling a little bit nervous about riding a horse she didn't know, Jules put on the hat Sinead had given her and emerged from the mobile home and then eyed Sasha up suspiciously.

Seth looked over at her and knew that she was worried. "It's ok, she's a sound horse. Come and say hello to her first."

"You can read me like a book," she said, trying her best to look confident. She petted Sasha's nose and then neck. The mare didn't object to being stroked and she thought that it was a good sign. "She seems ok."

Sinead came outside and her cheeks were scarlet. "Thank goodness it's cooler out here!"

"Sinead, will you hold Moss while I help Jules up?"

"It's ok, Sinead. I should be alright. Sasha is so much smaller than Connor. I can easily get onto her back."

"I'll hold the saddle this side," Seth said. "She tends to blow herself out when you do up the girth."

Jules, holding the reins, put her foot in the stirrup and climbed up into the saddle. "It would have slipped if he hadn't been holding the other side."

"There I told you. Let me tighten it for you."

"Thanks. She is lovely."

Seeing that Jules was ready to go, he mounted Moss and he grinned at her. "It is so good to be on him again. I think he is smiling too."

"You look like a knight on him."

Moss started to dance about, eager to get moving. "Come on then, let's get going. Will you ride next to me? It will calm him down."

As they walked past the mobile home, he called out to Sinead, thanking her for taking such good care of Moss. Jules smiled. *Seth is just the sweetest thing.*

They had walked and trotted through fields, woodland and down tracks. She didn't realise how vast Waterfall West Estate was and she was surprised that Seth still remembered where to go. The landscape around them seemed to go on for as far as the eye could see. "How many acres is Waterfall West?"

"About a hundred acres, I think. I haven't seen it all." he replied as he tried his best to keep Moss on the track.

"That's huge. How do you remember where to go?"

He laughed. "I've brought people out on hacks hundreds of times and Moss usually remembers the way home. How are you finding Sasha?"

"She's lovely. She's willing but calm. Just how I like a horse. Moss is lovely too, but he is a bit of a handful. You are going to be exhausted when you get back. He is such a fidget."

"He just needs a gallop. Are you up for a run or do you want to wait for me and I will take him around the field and come back to you?"

"You go, Seth. He is going crazy. I'll wait here for you."

"Ok, I'll see you in a minute."

Jules watched them take off and Sasha's ears pricked up as she wondered if she should go too. "It's ok, you sweet girl. We are just going to watch. Look at them go. We couldn't keep up with them even if we tried, could we?"

Chapter Seven

The night was hot, sticky and humid. Jules and Seth had found it difficult to sleep. The small window of their tiny bedroom was wide open, but it made little difference and the temperature continued to rise in the airless room.

"Jules, are you awake?" Seth whispered. He got no reply. *Good, she's asleep at last. I can't sleep. I am too hot and restless. I need water and fresh air. I'll sit outside for a bit.* Being as quiet as he could, he slipped out of bed and checked the time on the phone; it was three, twenty-three. *It's nearly morning.* Exasperated, he shook his head, walked through to the kitchen and got himself a glass of water. The water was cold and refreshing which surprised him as he fully expected it to be hot. He sighed and wished he could go back to bed and sleep, but he knew that would not be possible.

Their time spent in Cork had been wonderful, and he couldn't remember a better few days. *Why then is my mind in turmoil? We are safe here and there is no need to keep replaying the past. If only I could sleep through the night. If I could, then I know I will be able to get over the last few weeks.*

Seth opened the front door and sat on the step outside. It was a dark night, and he was unable to see farther than the edge of the summer field. He listened out for Moss and the other cobs but couldn't hear them. He could, however, see millions of bright stars above. *Thank you for being there. I don't feel quite so alone now. If only I could stop my crazy mind from over thinking.* His anxiety levels were now off the Richter scale and he was struggling to cope. This wasn't the first time he had felt this way. When he had gone into prison, memories of Jake hitting and killing the old man and the car turning over had kept him awake for weeks. *I managed to get over that madness before. I am sure I can again.* He put his head into his hands.

"Seth, are you ok?" Sinead asked. "I heard someone open the door. I was just making sure that we weren't being broken into."

He sat back up feeling a little embarrassed. "Sorry, I was too hot to sleep. It's September now. It shouldn't be this hot. I didn't wake you, did I?"

"No, not at all. I haven't managed to sleep yet. I was thinking of having a shower to cool down. You look so tired and haunted. There's something up, isn't there? Are you happy? Is everything alright with you and Jules?" she asked, sitting down next to him on the step.

"We are grand. No, it's not that. I just keep having nightmares about something that happened back home. I've had night terrors since we left Sussex and I am not sleeping well or at all some nights. The nightmares are doing my head in. I am just so, so tired. I've had them before, and they will pass. I would give anything for a good night's sleep. I sound like a crazy person, don't I?"

"No, you don't. You should see someone. I don't know if you can deal with this all by yourself."

"I saw someone a long time ago, but they just wanted to give me Sertraline. I'd rather cure myself naturally. You know what I am like. In the past, I used to listen to music to calm my troubled brain, and I read a lot too. Music and reading books probably saved my life."

"So what kind of dreams have you been having?"

"We had some serious family problems before we came out here. Jules's Dad tried to hang himself and we had to cut him down. As for my family, it turns out that I am not Mam's at all and she would prefer it if I was dead."

"You've both had a tough time. This is your home now. You can forget the past and have a fresh start here. You just need something to relax you."

"I know where this is going," he said smiling. "You're going to get your whacky baccy out, aren't you?"

"It relaxes me. A friend of mine had PTSD and cannabis helped her to sleep. Do you want to try? You used to have a little smoke when we were in Australia. I remember a very chilled out Seth back then."

"Just a little, it might help. Ok, thanks."

Sinead jumped up and went back into the mobile home. She reappeared with a lit cigarette, took a puff and then passed it to him. He sighed and then he inhaled the sweet fumes, taking them deep into his lungs. As he exhaled, he smiled, "It's been a while since we did this."

"We were young then and free to go where the fancy took us. I like working here, but I do miss travelling with you. We had some good times, didn't we? Seth... you're crying?" she said as she put her arm around him. "Please tell me what's wrong."

Jules appeared behind them. "What's going on? What the hell? Are you smoking a joint?" She was fuming and glared at Sinead. Seth shook his head, stood up and then walked off into the darkness.

"He was crying. I only put my arm around him because he was upset. You don't think that anything is going on, do you?"

Jules took a deep breath in, trying her best to calm herself down. "No, I didn't think that at all. I was just shocked to see him smoking. I didn't know he smoked. It wasn't just a cigarette, was it?" She remembered Jake smoking weed in the Hearn's barn – it had a very distinctive smell.

"When we travelled together, we shared the odd joint but that was it. He's been having nightmares, and he's not sleeping. I thought a joint might relax him. He said that you have had a few family problems, but there's something else you are not telling me, isn't there?"

"There is a lot going on. His mother is a psychopath, his dad tried to rape me and we have fled to Ireland to save our lives!"

"Shit! He didn't tell me that."

"He said he was coping. Where do you think he has gone to?" she asked.

"He needs you, Jules. I think that you are all he has to live for at the moment. He will be with Moss. Take a torch; there's one on the hook by the door. I've never seen him cry before. I don't think the joint helped him much. I'm sorry if I made things worse for him."

"It's ok, you were only trying to help. I guess it is better to cry than to keep everything bottled up."

Jules found Seth by the summer field, leaning against the fence. She saw him put the joint out and she wasn't sure what to say to him. It was too dark to read his face properly. "How are you doing?" she asked gently. "I'm sorry if I startled you. I didn't know that you smoked weed."

"Don't be sorry; you've nothing to be sorry for."

She was relieved that he wasn't mad at her and she started to cry. *Why am I crying? It is Seth that needs my help.*

"You're not crying, are you? You are. Please don't cry. Come here and let me hold you. I don't want you to think badly of me. I have smoked the odd joint in the past but nothing serious. Please don't cry, or you will set me off again."

Secured in his arms, Jules breathed in the heavenly smell of his warm body and rubbed her tears away with her hand. "I think the world of you. I don't like to see you hurting. You should have told me that you are suffering."

"You've seen me cry a lot recently. I'm sorry for that. Sinead thought a smoke would relax me. My mind is being bombarded with images of my Dad and me fighting, you nearly being raped, Mam disowning me and her leaving us to drown in the silent pool. If I could just sleep, then I would be ok. As soon as my head touches the pillow, I feel like I am going crazy."

"Seth, if smoking a joint is going to calm you down so that you can rest, then I can see nothing wrong in it. I don't want you to end up like my Dad. So come back and finish that joint. We have to try something to help you sleep. But if it doesn't work, then you have to promise me that you will get help."

"I will, but I am tough and I know that I can get over this by myself. I think Sinead was right. The joint is kicking in. I am starting to feel more chilled. Or it could just be because I am with you. I love you."

"I love you too. Come back to the caravan. Sinead is worried about us. We need to tell her everything. And I mean everything! Talking about what happened to us will make all the difference to you. I might have a quick drag too. I don't want you drifting off to a happy place without me."

"What! You wouldn't? Would you?"
"No, probably not, but it does smell nice."

Chapter Eight

White clouds scurried across the blue sky. The shadows they cast challenged each other to race across the fields. Jules was sitting on the step outside of their mobile home and she zipped up her hoodie. She looked up at the sky, hoping to feel the warmth of the sun again, but the sun was covered over for the moment.

Although the mobile home was tiny, it was an ideal place to stay. Despite her initial shock at seeing the old-fashioned interior, she had felt at home there straight away. That morning, determined to get rid of the smell of mould, she had cleaned their home from head to toe, and she hoped that Sinead would be pleased. Two bags of rubbish were at her feet, ready to take to the bins at the Manor House.

This is the most idyllic place to sit. This can be my new happy spot. From where she was sat, all she could see around her were fields, trees and horses grazing. Moss was peacefully grazing in the middle of the herd. The only thing that spoiled the view was the roof and chimneys of May's old Manor House, poking out behind the tree line in the distance. Sinead had shown them around Waterfall West House, and despite it being finished to a high standard, there was still something odd and perhaps eerie about all the dark rooms. Just thinking about the house made the hair on the back of her neck stand up. *I've got to clean there soon! When the ivy is removed from the windows on Monday, then I'm sure it will feel much better inside. I hope so.*

They had taken Moss out the past two evenings and she had ridden Sasha. The grey mare was easy to handle, but she did miss Connor's plodding gait. The Irish countryside was stunning and she could see how much Seth enjoyed their trips out together. Riding seemed to calm him. He said that he was still having bad dreams but the joint he smoked before they went to sleep was making a big difference and relaxed him too. He had been able to sleep for most of the night and he was looking less tired.

They had told Sinead their sorry tale and the reason why they were on the run. She had listened to them with her mouth open. She was shocked and said that she had always imagined Seth's parents to be sweet and caring like he was. For some reason, he had found it difficult to tell her about him going to prison. Sinead had sworn when she heard that he had gone to prison instead of Jake. Jules knew that he was embarrassed about it. She couldn't understand why.

Saturday was one of the stable's busiest days and both Sinead and Seth had lessons to teach or hacks to take out throughout the day. There was a lot more to running a riding school than met the eye. Jules couldn't imagine how Sinead had managed all by herself when May had gone into hospital.

Today was also the local harvest fair in a nearby village, with rides and a ploughing competition. If May had been around, then she would have found someone to teach for the day and they would have taken some of the cobs to the show. Sinead said that May had planned to show the horses there as a favour. All the big prize winning shows were over with for the summer, so it was really just an excuse to show off her coloured cobs, and Moss, of course.

Sinead had contacted the event manager, and she had explained to him that May was too ill to attend. Since Seth had started teaching, the bookings for lessons had doubled and they were all too busy to go to the fair anyway. Sinead had laughed and said that the increase was due to them having a new hot instructor on their books. He had been mortified and had asked Jules if she thought that it was true. She had raised her eyebrows at him, agreeing with Sinead, and he had looked surprised. *My lovely hot Seth!*

Jules got the phone out of her pocket and found a site with vegetarian recipes and then flicked through them looking for something to cook. Her attempts to cook healthy meals for everyone was not going well. She was feeling a bit disappointed with herself. Sinead had told her not to worry and that she was grateful for a hot meal every evening but Jules really wanted to excel at this task. She was also feeling like she was a bit of a spare part and was eager to earn her keep somehow. *It's Saturday today, I should be busy in Cork, busking and making some money. Seth is too busy to come. I will be fine on my own. I should do this. I'll get the bus into town. I will see what he thinks first.*

One of the horses in the field neighed and she realised that it was Moss. He started to canter across the field. Jules looked up from the phone and saw that Seth had appeared. She grinned. *This really is like a scene from Black Beauty. I should film it.* She pressed the camera icon, video and then record and caught Moss flying across the field with his mane flowing behind him. Finally, Moss was standing by the fence and stamped his hoof, waiting for Seth to give him some attention.

She watched him hug and pat his strong neck. This would be a priceless moment. She was glad that she had caught it all on camera. *This is true love.*

After a few minutes, he walked over to her.

"How's my gorgeous girl then?" he asked, pulling her up from the step and kissing her.

"She's a lot better since you came along. I didn't think that I would see you until after work."

"My lesson was just cancelled, so I have an hour spare to have lunch with you. I was missing you too. It hurts me when we are apart. What delights are you going to rustle up in the kitchen for me then?"

"Oh, dear! All I can think of is cheese on toast for us. I'm not very inventive in the kitchen, am I? I think Sinead nearly choked on what I gave her last night."

He laughed. "It really wasn't that bad. You don't have to worry about cooking up anything fancy. I am happy as long as there are plenty of vegetables and cheese involved. I don't mind soya mince or tofu too. I bet you could do lots of things with those. Sinead isn't used to eating decent food. From what I can remember, her diet has always been chocolate, crisps and coke."

"Seth, we really need to buy some more food. I've been thinking. Rather than me just sitting here doing nothing except being a domestic goddess; perhaps I could get the bus into Cork and do a little busking. I could then buy a few groceries in the supermarket on the way home. What do you think?"

He was taken aback for a moment. He hadn't realised just how independent she was. *I must let her do exactly as she wants and allow my sweet little bird to fly. I will worry, though.*

She studied his face. "You've gone quiet. You don't like the idea do you?"

"No, it's not that. I do like the idea. It's just that I would worry about you on the streets of Cork on your own. There are some scallywags out there who would rob their own grandmothers. I don't want you to get robbed or worse. After all we've been through, I can't help feeling protective towards you. On the other hand, I want you to experience life and do what your heart is telling you to do. I will throw myself into teaching and try and stop myself from worrying if you choose to go."

"I will be fine. I will watch out for the scallywags, earn us a little money and bring home the bac... the cheese. I won't make as much money as we did the other day as I will be missing the dulcet tones of my hot husband-to-be."

"I really don't understand what you or Sinead are going on about. Do you think I am attractive to the ladies then?"

"Seth, you are like an Adonis. You must know how good looking and hot you are? I am proud to be your girlfriend. I'm feeling warm now," she said, taking off her hoodie.

"I think that you flatter me. You are pretty hot yourself. You are not wearing a bra under that sundress, are you? I might have to show you how hot you are!"

"Now I really am feeling hot and my heart is racing."

"It doesn't take much to get you going, does it? Jules, I've just had a thought. Let's go dancing tonight. We have tomorrow off so why don't we go to Cork this evening and hunt down all the bars with live music? We can dance into the small hours of the morning. We could both go busking together tomorrow afternoon. What do you say?"

"Great! That sounds exciting. I hope you remembered your dancing shoes."

"I think they were the first thing I put into the case when we left. Now then, my hot wife-to-be. Do you want me before or after lunch?"

He saw a smile spread over her pretty little face. *I love it when she wears that sundress, she looks so sexy in it.*

"Wait here for a moment; I want to show you something."

She disappeared into the mobile home and he waited patiently for her. She reappeared with a blanket over her arm and in her hand she was holding the phone and a small packet. *Is that a condom!*

"We are going to need this," she said, slipping the packet into his breeches' pocket. "Come with me," she said, taking his hand.

He was puzzled. "Are you going to have your wicked way with me in the barn? I wouldn't if I were you. All the stable hands will be in there having their lunch."

"No, I don't do barns. Trust me," she said, pulling him towards the corner of the summer field. "Yesterday, I took a walk up the side of the field and I noticed a gap in the yew tree hedging that we could squeeze through. Let me show you." She led him along to the side of the field and they came to a small gap in the foliage. "You will be amazed when you go through here," she said as she parted the branches.

Seth followed her and they found themselves on the edge of a huge meadow. He looked around him and all he could see for miles were multi-coloured wild flowers, entwined in waist high, yellow grass. "It's beautiful. I've never been here before. Who knew this field was just behind our mobile," he said.

Jules started to walk into the field and he watched her slip through the grass until all he could see of her was the top half of her bronzed body. Her honey coloured curls shone in the sunshine. *She is so beautiful.*

Jules spread the blanket out and then looked over her shoulder at him and smiled seductively. "Will you come and lie with me? Nobody will see us," she called as she lay down and disappeared from view.

He looked around him to make sure that they were alone. He was a little shocked and his heart was beating in his chest. *Am I excited about this or am I nervous?* He walked over to her and then sat down next to her. "I don't know if I can do this," he said as he looked around him again. All he could see was flowers and long grass.

She was lying on her back looking lovingly up at him. "This is just a little fantasy I've had since I found this field. Just lie next to me for a while and if you can't handle the risk factor then we can go back to the mobile."

He lay down next to her and hand in hand they lay looking up at the blue sky and white clouds floating by. She breathed in the sweet smell of the meadow and sighed a happy sigh. "This is such a lovely spot. I was missing the Findon hills but now I've found a new happy place to share with you; I am the happiest girl alive. It's lovely here, don't you agree?"

"Just beautiful. It feels like there is nobody in the world here but us. I am glad that you brought me here. You make me the happiest man alive."

"Would you be able to give me a kiss then?"

He smiled. "How can I resist?" he said as he rolled over to her. She put her hands around his neck and found his lips. He kissed her passionately, almost taking her breath away. Kissing him back, she ran her fingers through his hair. She was throbbing hard and wanted him desperately. She reached down and undid his trousers. He was aroused and ready for her. She stopped kissing him and smiled at him, wanting to reveal her secret. "Seth," she whispered breathlessly. "I'm not wearing anything under my dress."

He smiled, and she could see the longing in his beautiful eyes. "You naughty thing!"

She felt his hand run up the inside of her thighs and then between her legs. Gently, his fingers caressed her and she moaned with pleasure.

"Turn over, Jules, you are driving me crazy. Will you get on your hands and knees for me?"

Chapter Nine

After a dinner of homemade pizza, pleased with her domestic goddess effort to produce an edible meal, Jules sifted through her suitcase looking for something decent to wear. *Do trainers go with a sundress? No, I had better not. If only I had brought my pumps.* Seth had decided to wear his black jeans with trainers instead of his reel shoes. He had pulled out a short-sleeved white shirt from his suitcase and he had looked pleadingly at her to iron it for him.

Sinead had an iron but no ironing board and Jules had managed to do a decent job on the crumpled shirt and she had left it on the bed for him. Most of the clothes they had brought with them needed a wash. *I will just have to wear jeans and this clean white t-shirt. I have nothing else. I wonder where Sinead washes her clothes. I'll ask her.*

Jules checked her makeup in the mirror and she was pleased to see that the bruising around her eye was starting to fade. Her hair was her next challenge and she brushed it through, adding plenty of anti-frizz lotion. *Please don't puff up and make me look like a poodle. I shouldn't have brushed it!*

Seth was half-dressed and was wearing his black jeans. He was shaving over the sink in the cramped shower room. *I'm looking forward to going out on the town with Jules.* This was the first time he had actually taken her out on a proper date. *I*

69

wonder if she will mind if I have a couple of beers. He heard a knock on the door.

"Seth, is it ok to come in? There's something I want to ask you."

"Sure, Sinead, the door is open. I'm just shaving."

She popped her head around the door and laughed. "There's not much room in here for someone your size. I don't remember you being so broad. You're looking really fit these days."

"Don't you mean hot? You're not going to swoon are you? It has been known."

"No, not over you. Now if an attractive girl should come along, then maybe."

"Are there any attractive girls in Waterfall then?"

"No, just single buxom women looking for a farmer to marry."

"So where would a fine northern lass, like yourself, go to find herself a girl round here?"

"There is a club and a few bars in Cork. I usually hook up with someone there and end up wasted. I'm getting a bit old for all that now. Can you believe that I am going to be thirty-six soon? I'm too old to fool around anymore. I'll have to check out the dating sites when I get a spare moment and find myself a decent woman. Tonight, I have to do some washing. What a bore."

"So come out with us for a bit of harmless fun. I might yet get you to dance a jig with me."

"You know I can't dance but if you and Jules don't mind an old spinster tagging along, then it would be good to go out for a change."

Jules having changed and wanting to use the bathroom, overheard Seth inviting Sinead out. "Yes, please come out with us."

"Ok then. Why not? I'll get ready. Oh, Seth. I was going to ask if you or Jules would be able to come with me on Monday to collect May's brother from the airport. I don't like to ask, but I really don't want to go by myself."

"How did you end up with that job?" he asked. "You should have told him to get a taxi. I can't really go as Tom is not going to be pleased to see me, is he? He's such a knob end!"

"I know, but I can handle him now. May asked me to do it. I couldn't say no to her. He's going to stay in the Manor House. I'm not sure how long he will be staying. Not long, I hope."

Jules looked at Seth and could see the serious look on his face. *He really doesn't like him.* "I'll come with you," she offered.

***

Cork on a Saturday night was nothing like Jules had imagined. *It's so busy.* The city was heaving with euphoric crowds of people weaving their way to bars and clubs, eager to dance and drink. Merry tunes from folk bands playing in the pubs filled their ears as they passed by; enticing them to enter and promising them a good time. Sinead, a little overwhelmed by it all, found them a quiet bar to sit in and talk. She insisted on buying them a round of drinks. Seth had argued at first but had given in to her pleas and had let her treat them.

When they had finished their drinks, Seth, wanting to dance, had found them a lively pub with a dance floor that had a large folk band playing. The pub was busy, but they had managed to find a table in the corner. Seth went off to get them some drinks, and feeling hot, Jules took off her hoodie and pulled out a chair to sit on. A large black and white cat was asleep on it. *How can you sleep in such a noisy place like this?*

She turned to Sinead, who was stripping off too and then she was surprised to see that the top half of her body was completely covered in tattoos of animals, colourful flowers and intricate patterns. She couldn't help staring. *So many tattoos and oh, my! A Celtic Knot too.* This particular tattoo was at the top of her right arm. Silently, she inhaled as a warning bell went off in her head. *That tattoo is exactly the same as Seth's!*

She managed to persuade the cat to move on and then she sat down to watch the band and people of all ages, dancing the familiar square dances that Seth had taught her. Her attention returned to Sinead's tattoos and her eyes settled on the Dara Knot again.

"Are you shocked by the amount of tattoos I have?"

"A little," Jules replied. *I'm not going to cry, am I?* "They are beautiful... Where did you have them done?"

"Every time I visit a country, I have a tattoo inked to remind me of the places I've been to. I only choose the best artists. Before I went travelling, I worked in Inky as a tattoo artist. I have all the inks at home. Would you like a tattoo? I will create one for you, if you like."

"I would like that. I'd like a Dara Knot. You have one on your arm like Seth's."

"Yes, I do. I did Seth's tattoos."

"Oh, did you? You are very talented. I..."

"Are you upset, Jules? I am picking up on something here. What's wrong?"

"I'm sorry. You are really close to Seth. I think that I am just a little jealous that you have such a tight bond with him. I wish I had known him as long as you have. Ignore me; I am being stupid."

"No, you're not stupid. I understand. You haven't been going out with Seth for long, have you?"

"No, not that long but in some ways we both feel like we have known each other all our lives. I wish I had met him a long time ago. Which doesn't make sense, as I would have been a child then."

"So, you do know that you have nothing to worry about. I love him to bits, but sexually, he is a complete turn off. I'd rather sleep with you than Seth. Are you into threesomes?"

Jules gasped with surprise. "No way, Sinead! You're lovely but…" she said, laughing. *She was joking, wasn't she?* "When you are able to, then I would like you to do a tattoo for me. I'd like you to draw one at the top of my back," she said as she got the phone out of her bag. "I have seen a picture of a Celtic oak tree I like. In the leaves, could you do a fancy S and J within a heart? Could you do that for me?" Jules asked, showing Sinead the picture she had seen.

"I'd love to."

Seth appeared with a tray of beers and put it on the table. He was grinning. "Well, here's a thing! Jules, you're not going to believe this! Mick the landlord saw us busking the other day and he wants us to sing some of our songs tonight. The band on the stage usually has a singer but he is off sick. If we sing with them, then he thinks that we will draw in the crowds. I didn't realise it but this is The Elbow that Kenny and Lucy told us about. Mick likes to showcase new talent. What do you say, Nancy Mulligan? Will you come and sing with me?"

Sinead laughed. "Seth, you sly old dog. I didn't know you could sing. You two didn't tell me that you have been busking. Is the landlord going to pay you?"

"I've only recently had the courage to sing to the public, thanks to Jules. Wait until you hear her voice. You'll be blown away. We're being paid in drinks tonight and the landlord thinks he might have more paid work for us. What do you say? I'm up for it, if you are."

Jules looked at the large folk band with wide eyes. "I've never sung with a band before or in front of a crowd this large. I'm not sure. I haven't brought my guitar. It will be strange to stand on stage without it. What will I do with my hands?"

He smiled. "You'll think of something. The band only plays all the old Irish songs. We could start with Whisky in the Jar. We nailed that one the other day. If you don't know some of the songs, then just join in with the chorus."

Jules nodded. "Ok, this might be fun. Do you mind being stuck here by yourself for a while, Sinead?" she asked.

"No, you too go and do your thing. I am dying to see you two perform."

Chapter Ten

It was a bright but cold morning as Jules and Sinead left Waterfall West, on their way to collect Tom Stone from Cork airport. As they drove down the drive, Jules noticed that the landscapers were hard at work in the gardens of the Manor House. Two of the workers were up ladders, stripping the ivy away from the walls. She wished that she could stay and watch as she could already see that the ugly house was starting to wake up and shine.

Some of the leaves on the trees in the lane were turning orange, and she knew that autumn was well on its way. *Is it nearly autumn at Farm End? I wonder what's happening at the farm and how my brother and Dad are doing. I hope Peter is coping with the crazy Hearns. I feel bad for leaving him and Charlene to deal with everything.*

"A penny for them?"

"Oh, Sinead! Sorry, yes. I was deep in thought. I was just thinking about my Dad and brother. I miss them, and I hope Peter is coping. Do you have family up north?"

"No, not really. I was brought up in the care system, and I don't like to think about those days. Are you able to contact your family?"

"I can't think of a way to talk to them without giving away our location."

"You could ring them using my phone."

"Thanks, but I still think the police would be able to track us. We both lost our phones before we came over here and we don't have access to our contact list. It's mad that I don't know anyone's number off by heart. I could write a note and post it. If I send a letter then there will be a local post office stamp printed on the envelope. I would be mortified if Seth got caught because of me."

"You need to find someone who is travelling to England or any other country to post it from their hometown. I still can't believe that he went to prison for his brother. That is totally insane."

"I know, but you know Seth; he would do anything for anyone he loved. Do you think Tom will post a letter for me when he gets back to Australia? It would be hard to explain why I wanted to do that."

"He is probably the last man on earth that I would ask. Jules, I've never met anyone like him. He comes across as charming, but beneath that façade is an evil snake. I am so grateful that you are here with me. I don't think I could have collected him otherwise."

"Seth's Dad was like that too. He was totally nuts but charming and helpful. Until… he tried to..."

"Don't think about him, he was another evil bastard. Just keep away from Tom. I've got a feeling that he is going to like you a lot. He just thinks he is God's gift to all young women."

"How old is he then?"

"I would guess that he is in his late fifties, but he thinks he is in his twenties. He owns a large pharmaceutical company in Australia and likes the finer things in life. He detests staying at Waterfall as it is too down market for him. I know that he is going to complain about the room I put him in. It was the smallest one," she said, laughing. "He'll just have to put up with it. We have guests staying in the other rooms soon. Can you believe that? I only started advertising a few days ago and already the Manor House is full for the rest of September and the first two weeks of October."

"Goodness! That was quick work. May will be pleased. Seth wants to go and see her later. We were thinking of riding over there."

"You'll have to go on the roads. I think Moss is too highly strung to go out. I'll drive you both. I wanted to see May anyway."

"I feel bad relying on you to take us everywhere. I must learn to drive. Seth hasn't got a license now."

"I'll teach you."

"I'd love to learn, but wouldn't I have to get a provisional license?"

"We won't worry about that. I could give you a few lessons on the estate as it is private land and then I am sure we can find a private car park somewhere."

"You're the best. I'd love you to teach me. I am so glad we came here. I just need to start work and then I will feel more useful."

"You are going to wish you hadn't said that. Soon, you are going to be run off your feet. If it's ok with you, I need you to start work at the Manor House from Sunday. Will you be ok putting the breakfast things out each morning? The rooms are ready but there will be rooms to clean, laundry to do and beds to be made up. I feel bad that I can't pay you a wage. I am sure that I can give you and Seth some money from petty cash. However, you two seem to be doing pretty well busking. How did busking go yesterday? I forgot to ask."

"Really well. I just love singing with Seth. He is gaining in confidence all the time and seems to love being out there performing. The tourist season is nearly over so I don't know how busy Cork will be in the coming weeks."

"You need to busk at the Cork Folk Festival at the beginning of October. Thousands come to Cork so there will be plenty of money to be made then."

"That should help. We could go busking every evening during the festival. We are also hoping that we will get some work from the pub owner that let us sing on Saturday. I think Seth said his name is Mick. He said he will pay us in cash, so I think we should get by without starving this winter."

"Talking of starving, we need to get some supplies in," Sinead said. "After work, we will drive over to Tesco and stock up. In May's business plan, there is a list of what she wants to give the guests for breakfast. I hate shopping."

"I got a few things for us yesterday. If you set up an online account with Tesco on your laptop using a debit card, then I can shop online for us and get it delivered. We could give you cash for our share. That's how I used to do the shopping when I was at Farm End."

"I would never have thought of that. Yes, we will set an account up for the business when we get back from the airport. By the way, I have to say it again, I thought you two were amazing on Saturday. You both sound so good together when you sing. If you weren't on the run, then you could make it big. You got everyone up dancing and even I was tempted to have a go. I liked watching you and Seth dance too. You two are pretty hot together; it made me horny," she said, laughing.

"Sinead! You're terrible!"

There was a lot of traffic at Cork airport which made them late. They found Tom waiting for them outside the airport. It was easy to spot him as he was a tall man with long blond shoulder-length hair. His skin was bronzed, and he was wearing a white linen suit. Sinead eyed the back seat of her car despairingly. "I'm really sorry Jules, I'd forgotten how tall he is. Do you mind going in the back of the car?" she asked as she drew up next to him.

"No, I don't mind. Poor you, having to sit next to him."

They both got out of the car and then Tom came over to them. "Morning girls. It's Sinead, isn't it? I hardly recognised you. Didn't you have red hair the last time I saw you?"

"I did. Are you wearing a wig, Tom?"

Jules could see his face twitch with annoyance but he didn't lash out. "No, it is all natural. It's amazing how spending time on a yacht in the Med can regenerate you," he said, climbing into the passenger seat. He had left his huge suitcase on the pavement for them to deal with. She was surprised that he had such a posh English accent. *Was I expecting him to be like Crocodile Dundee?*

"Pompous arse!" Sinead whispered to her as they tried to get the suitcase in the boot. The suitcase wouldn't fit, so between them they managed to get it onto the back seat and then Jules squeezed herself into the car next to it.

Tom looked across at her and raised his eyebrows. "Are you Sinead's girlfriend then? I don't think I have had the pleasure."

"No! I'm Julia. I'm Seth Hearn's fiancée."

"Oh, heavens! May didn't say that he'd be around. Mind you, I haven't spoken to her recently. How is she doing Sinead?

79

The nursing home was vague, and I could barely understand the woman that spoke to me."

"She's doing a lot better. Each day I see an improvement," replied Sinead as she started up the car. "You'll see when you visit. Are you going to rent a car while you are here? It's a long walk to the nursing home from Waterfall West. I can't take you. We are really busy at the stables at the moment."

"I suppose I will have to. Does May still have her gippo ponies then?"

Jules could see Sinead's eyes narrow in the rear view mirror, and she knew that it was only a matter of time before she exploded. "They are gypsy vanner horses or coloured cobs. Ireland is famous for them. They are incredible and win prizes at shows. Do you still ride?"

"Is that so? I have a couple of horses back home but I don't have much time to ride them these days."

When they reached the Manor House, Jules was amazed to see how different the house looked. The ivy had gone, and the windows had been polished. A new sign had been erected at the entrance, declaring to all that Waterfall West's bed and breakfast and riding school was ready to do business. Jules was impressed with how much better the house looked. "I barely recognise the place," she said as they veered off the drive and drove up to the parking area at the side of the house. The landscapers were still working in the gardens and looked up for a moment and then continued with their work.

They got out of the car, and Tom waited for Sinead and Jules to remove his suitcase from the back seat. "Such a waste of time opening a bed and breakfast in the middle of nowhere. My sister has no sense at all," he declared.

Jules could see that Sinead was furious. "I am sure that he is trying to wind you up. Keep your cool and don't let him," she whispered.

Sinead gave Tom the keys, told him the room number and got back in the car. Tom's mouth was open with surprise.

Jules got back into the car. *I don't believe him. You actually expected Sinead to take your luggage into the house and take it to your room. You really are an arse!*

When they reached the stable yard, Jules noticed a group of women mounting horses ready to go out on a hack. Seth was in the sand school giving an elderly lady a private riding lesson. He looked over to Jules, and he waved at her. She smiled back. *I'll go and watch him in a minute.*

Sinead looked at her watch. "We only just made it back in time. These ladies are going to be disappointed that it's going to be me taking them out on a hack today," she whispered. "Look at them all ogling at our hot Seth."

It was true, most of the women were staring at him. "We are going to have to charge them extra for looking," Jules whispered as she headed off to watch him teach. *You can look all you want, but that is all!*

***

Jules was sitting in the lounge area of the mobile home with Sinead's laptop on an old brown table. They had set up two accounts with Tesco. They had already ordered provisions for the Manor House. Sinead was looking in the fridge and was trying to work out what shopping they needed for themselves.

Seth was stretched out on the sofa, tired from a hard day's work. He had got up early and had gone out to the barn and had worked out the best he could. He had probably worked a little too hard as his muscles were sore. He felt drowsy and knew that he would sleep well that night without having to smoke anything. He could feel his eyes closing.

"Are you sleeping?" Jules asked.

"No, I was just resting my eyes. Have you ordered yet? Do I have time to have a shower before we go and see May?" Seth asked as he stretched. "It will wake me up."

"Yes, if you are quick," Sinead said as she looked in the overhead cupboard. He stood up and then walked to the window. Tom was standing by the summer field looking at all the cobs. He was sure that he was looking at Moss in particular.

"What is he doing out here? Why is he looking at the horses like that?"

"Who's looking at them?" Jules asked.

"Tom! He's dressed ready to ride. I hope he's not looking to ride Moss. Oh no, he's coming this way."

"Seth, stay calm. I'll deal with him," Sinead said as she went outside to meet him. She returned with a cross look on her face. "He did want to ride Moss, and I told him that he belongs to you and that he will only let you ride him. I'm going to saddle up Kiran for him. I won't be a minute and then we can go over to the nursing home. You go and have your shower."

Seth and Jules watched them go towards the stables. "Tom is such a knob head. What decent man his age has a ponytail? I'll be glad when he goes back to Australia. Did he say how long he was going to be here?" he asked.

"No, but if we keep away from him, then he will get bored and go home," Jules said, completing their shopping order.

Seth looked out the window again to make sure that he had gone. "I'm not really sure why he is here. He doesn't care about May. I just know that there is more to him being here than meets the eye. He is going to need watching."

Chapter Eleven

Jules ran newly washed and dried sheets through a steam press in the laundry of the Manor House. As she worked, she listened and sang to music on the radio. When a song came up that she thought that they could sing, she found it on YouTube and then saved it to show Seth later. Moments earlier, she had scribbled down Let Her Go by Passenger. *I wonder if Seth knows that one. I hope it doesn't make him cry.*

It had been a busy couple of weeks for her at the bed and breakfast and she had enjoyed the hard work. *It's good to be earning my keep.* She had got the room turnaround time down to half an hour and Sinead had been pleased with her and thankful that she didn't need her help as she had her hands full coping with the extra riding lessons generated by the visitors.

The guests had left some lovely comments about the cleanliness of the rooms and had said that the staff were friendly and helpful. An American couple who had stayed for a week had left her a tip of twenty pounds with a thank you note. She wanted to share the money with Sinead, but she wouldn't let her.

The only downside of working at Waterfall West was having to deal with Tom. He was creeping her out. Wherever she went in the house, he just happened to bump into her. All he wanted to do was chat, and he was always very polite and complimentary but he really got on her nerves. She did her very best to keep out of his way and she made sure he was out of the building before she cleaned his room. Jules shivered as she thought about the moment she had knocked over his bin, allowing an oozing mass of used condoms to spill out across the floor. Jules had almost thrown up when she had cleaned up the mess. Since then, she had used disposable gloves when she cleaned his room and she tried not to look when she emptied the bin.

Jules looked up at the sky through the skylight window above. The sun was out, and she could feel the heat of the sun on her shoulders. She thought about her new tattoo. Two days ago, Sinead had inked a Dara oak tree tattoo with S&J in a heart entwined in the branches at the top of her back. The tattoo had been hot to touch for a while as it healed. She had seen it by using mirrors and thought that it was beautiful. *This is for Seth really. I hope he likes it.*

Jules and Seth had planned, if the weather was good, to busk on the streets of Cork in the evening. They also had a gig at The Elbow. Mick had rung them to ask if they would perform for two hours. He was going to pay them two hundred pounds cash and they would have the use of the microphones again but not the band.

Each evening since the call, they had gone through a few new songs together and they now had a playlist of twenty songs to perform. Being part of the Cork music scene was giving them both a buzz. It was fascinating seeing how the public reacted when they sang a popular up beat song rather than the more traditional Irish tunes. Never Be Alone was a particular crowd favourite. The people that visited The Elbow were open to listening to all kinds of music.

It was going to be a good day as May was coming home. Her speech was a lot better, and she was now able to walk well with a stick. Yesterday, everyone except Tom had cleared up the annex, ready for her return. Jules liked her very much and thought that she was a courageous lady. May had a bubbly personality and she wasn't going to let a little thing like a stroke get in the way of her ability to enjoy life to the full. She had volunteered to cook for May, but Tom, much to everyone's surprise, had said that he would take care of her. He had only visited her once in the nursing home and this hadn't gone unnoticed.

Oh goodness, I've just remembered, it's going to be our birthdays tomorrow. Seth was not looking forward to being thirty but he was looking forward to celebrating and sharing a birthday with Jules. She still couldn't get her head around them both being born on the thirtieth of September. They were both Librans and she had found out on Google, that Libran partners form the most agreeable, romantic and well-balanced relationships. Things were going really well between them and she had never been so happy.

She had wanted to get Seth something for his birthday but he said that he didn't need anything and made her promise not to. She had said the same, but she had seen him smile and knew he was planning something. The tattoo on her back was a declaration of her love for him. That was her gift to him.

She heard footsteps and she turned to see the door open. *Is that Tom?* Her heart was thudding in her chest. Seth appeared. *Thank God it's Seth and not creepy Tom.*

"How's my sweet little maid doing?" he asked as he came up behind her and embraced her. "You smell of clean washing and fresh air." He moved her hair back and kissed her neck.

I hope he hasn't seen my tattoo. No, he hasn't, my t-shirt is covering it.

"Is it bad of me to want you all the time?" he asked. "Just let me breathe you in for a moment and then I will let you work. Are you ok?"

"You're sending goosebumps down me, Master Hearn. As much as your poor little maid wants to please her master, she has piles of ironing to get through this morning. Six visitors will be checking out today and the rooms will all need cleaning and fresh linen. Can you hold out until later? I thought you were teaching all morning."

"You drive a hard bargain. Your Master could get into role-playing," he said with a cheeky grin. "My eleven o'clock lesson was cancelled at the last minute. The kid I was going to teach threw up in the car on the way here. So here I am, ready to give you a hand or make you a cup of tea."

"I could do with both. It really has been hard going today. I know what would help me a lot. Our washing has just finished. You couldn't put it in the dryer, could you? You will need to put the dryer on low, for thirty minutes, otherwise things will shrink and I can't have my Master going out in short jeans."

"Ok, no problem," he said, opening the washing machine door. "Has Goldilocks been to see you today?"

"Shush, Seth. He might hear you. No, not yet. But if you say that it has just gone eleven, then he will be on his way to get May in his fancy hire car. Don't worry about me. I can handle him. I think he is just a bit lonely."

"I don't like him near you. Do your best to keep your distance from him."

"That's easier said than done. He spends a lot of his time in the house. I keep our conversations down to the minimum, though."

"I know. Just let me know if he is annoying you."

She nodded. "I will." She knew that things would end badly if she said anything. "I hope May likes how we have rearranged everything in the annex. I've noticed that she is a bit of a hoarder and people like that don't like their piles of things touched."

"She will understand. We did a grand job. It had to be done; otherwise she would have been tripping over everything. She is going to be so happy when she sees the front of the house and gardens back to how they used to be. I don't know why she let them get so overgrown. So, where can I make tea then?" he asked.

"The nearest place is the dining room. There is a tea and coffee station there with instant hot water. May has thought of everything for her guests. I reckon that this business is going to make a bomb. Sinead said that she has taken bookings for the whole of October and November. There have been a few bookings for Christmas too."

"You've all worked so hard and this place deserves to do well. I'll be back in a minute. Do you want sugar?"

"No, not today, thanks. I am putting on weight with all this healthy eating."

"You are looking grand. I should know, I've inspected every gorgeous inch. Maybe you are a little, but it's all in the right places. I know I shouldn't have said that but you are looking so much better these days."

God, he thinks I'm getting fat!

***

The Elbow was really busy, and Jules and Seth made their way to the bar and sat there watching another band play. They had half an hour before they were due to go on. A banner with the name Sonar Cell was hanging from the front of the stage. The band was made up of four lads. They played on guitars, a keyboard, and the lead singer played an electric violin when he wasn't singing. Their music was current, and the songs they were playing were their own. They were excellent musicians and they had many fans all crowded around the stage.

Seth could see that Jules was looking worried. "They are first-rate, aren't they? In our own way, we're just as good," he said. "I think that we should sing our favourite songs and leave the old traditional songs out. It might be an idea to write our own songs one day."

"This time, it is just you and me and my guitar on stage. I don't want to be booed off. Can I sing 'Linger' by the Cranberries? I like that one and I think the crowd here tonight will too. What do you think?"

"Of course. Why don't we follow that with 'Wake Me Up' by Avicii? That's always a popular song and you play that so well on the guitar. We've got something special going on, you and me. You can see it in the faces of the people when we perform. We might get tomatoes thrown at us in the more traditional pubs if we sing these modern songs. Do you want another drink? Do you need a shot to calm your nerves?"

"No! Thanks, I'll be fine. Just a diet coke, please. If I had a shot now, then I would be on the floor."

As Jules and Seth walked on to the stage, they were introduced as S&J and she was surprised that Mick had given

89

them a name. *It's ok, I guess. Has Mick seen my tattoo? Is that why he has named our duet S&J?*

The Sonar Cell fans were slowly being replaced by others, eager to hear them sing. Jules smiled as she recognised some familiar faces in the crowd and she realised that they were starting to get fans of their own. Not wanting to keep them waiting, she looked across at Seth and she whispered to him to sing Wake Me Up first as this song showed off his voice beautifully. Earlier, a crowd had gathered around them when they had sung that song by the river and had made them ten pounds. As they started to perform, some of the crowd clapped them. It was a heart-warming moment.

Halfway through their gig, Jules took a sip of her coke and then started to play Galway Girl which was a popular dance number in The Elbow. As they sang, someone caught her eye at the back of the dancing area. She recognised the white linen suit and his blond hair immediately. It was Tom, but he was not alone. He had his arm around a young teenage girl who was wearing very little and she couldn't help but stare at them. *How odd. I don't think it's registered with him that Seth and I are singing.* She kept watching Tom and waited for the penny to drop. *This moment is going to be priceless.*

And there it was! A look of absolute horror spread across his pallid face. Tom's mouth opened in shock as his eyes caught hers. His arm quickly dropped from the girl's shoulder and she saw him pull her along as he headed towards the exit.

Just priceless!

Chapter Twelve

"Seth, did you see Tom with that girl?" Jules asked as they got into the back of a taxi. They had waited in the taxi office for nearly an hour before a car became available. She hadn't wanted to ask him before then, as it had been too noisy in the office. Everyone had been chatting to each other as they waited for their taxis to arrive.

"Yes, I saw him. He left pretty quickly when he saw us singing. I wonder if May knows that he likes to prey on children. That girl was young, really young. She was covered in makeup, but I don't think she could have been more than fifteen."

"He needs locking up," she said with disgust. "I think that girl could have been younger than that. I think he brings them back to his room. His bin is always full of used condoms," she whispered.

"A lot of bad things happen in Cork, drugs, prostitution, muggings. It's not like it used to be," announced the taxi driver. He was a large man with a mass of grey hair, and he was wearing a thick jumper. The evening was pleasantly warm and she thought that he must be sweating profusely beneath it.

"That's a shame. We like living in Waterfall. Nobody bothers you there. That's where we want to go, by the way. To Waterfall West Manor House," Seth said to him. He picked up her hand, squeezed it and then smiled mischievously at her.

He is up to something. I just know he is.

"I like Dingle myself. It is where I would prefer to be," the driver said as he drove off. "I've had to move to Cork to get work. There's nothing going on work wise in Dingle but it is a wonderful place to live, nonetheless."

Jules was finding it hard to understand him as he had a strong Dingle accent and spoke very quickly. Seth didn't seem to be having a problem following what he said.

"I was born in Dingle too," he said.

"Were you now! I am sure to know your family then? What is your family name?"

"It's Hearn. Maybe you know my Aunt Bridie and my granny, Joan Hearn? Most of the Hearns moved to England in the nineties, though."

"I know that name and remember Jethro Hearn only too well. He was one for the ladies; if I remember rightly."

"That's my Dad. Was my Dad. He died a few months ago."

"I'm sorry to hear that. We can't choose our parents, can we? Hearn, yes, I know that name, to be sure."

The taxi driver pulled up outside the Manor House. Jules was relieved to get out of the car as the driver had talked non-stop the entire way. Seth paid him and they stood out of his way as he turned the car around to go back to Cork. They watched the red lights of the car disappear up the lane. When the car had gone, it was so dark that they were unable to see more than a meter around them. They could see a light in one of the windows of the Manor House. Jules got the phone out of her bag and turned on the torch.

"That taxi driver was friendly. I had no idea what he was saying half the time. Your family don't speak like he did."

"He was probably born in a remote part of Dingle. Granny and grandpa were travellers and settled in Dingle. I think Granny may have a Dublin accent. Some of us have a bit of a mix. Do you think I have an accent?"

"A little. You sound very Irish when you sing. It's cute."

"Ah here, will you leave it out!"

She giggled. "You were putting it on then, weren't you?"

"A little, to be sure."

They walked hand in hand up the drive, the crunch of the gravel beneath their feet more noticeable in the darkness.

"What time is it?" he asked. He was feeling nervous and hoped that Sinead had done what he had asked her to do. *Why am I worrying so much? I know Jules loves me.*

"It's nearly twelve and time for bed."

"Do you mind staying up a little longer? I know you have an early start tomorrow. If you give me five minutes more, then I will help you do the breakfast at the Manor House in the morning. There's something I want to show you."

"You are sounding very mysterious. Is it something to do with our birthdays?"

"It might be. Come with me and I'll show you."

He took her past the stable yard and towards the summer field. As they approached their mobile home, she noticed that the path was lit by a series of candles in jars. "Oh look, I can see candles ahead. Why are they...?"

"We are nearly there. Hold on a second," he said as Moss appeared by the fence. The horse snorted at him and ran along the edge of the field, impatient to be made a fuss of. "I've just got to give my boy a hug." He put his arms around his strong neck and Moss instantly calmed down. He patted him and hugged him again. "There you go, Moss. You are holding me up. I'll take you out tomorrow. Tonight it is all about my girl."

She watched them and then looked at the trail of lights leading up to the mobile home. *What is he up to?*

They reached a circle of lights and Seth invited Jules to join him at the centre.

"Seth?"

"I want to sing to you and I know it sounds really soft but I want to sing a song for you from my heart. Do you mind? Even if you see tears; don't stop me."

"I'd love you to sing to me. Are you going to sing Happy Birthday? It must be midnight now."

"No, yes; you'll see. Hold my hands, that's an important part. Ok, if I sound a bit hoarse then forgive me. We sang a lot tonight, didn't we?"

Jules grinned. "Don't worry, I'll understand." *He's almost crying and he hasn't started yet.*

"Good. I hope I can remember the words. I only wrote this song a couple of days ago. I'm nervous now."

"Oh, my! Your own song! Don't be nervous."

My heart is your heart
Take pity on a poor farm boy
I'll show you the way
If you promise you'll stay
We'll walk through the fields
And make love in the grass
Only time will tell
But I'm under your spell
I'm under your spell
Under your spell

JULIA'S BABY

I want to wake up with you
You know that I do
Let me hold you tight
We've got this, right?
I want to wake up with you
And breathe you in, breathe you in
Wake up with you and breathe you in
Breathe you in

I'll hold your hand
If you've got nothing planned
We'll walk through the snow
And then you will know
If I see you smile
Then I know it's worthwhile
I can't help but love you
Will you love me too?
Will you love me too?
Love me too?

I want to wake up with you
You know that I do
Let me hold you tight
We've got this right?
I want to wake up with you
And breathe you in, breathe you in
Wake up with you and breathe you in
Breathe you in

I will know that you care.
When I feel your heart beat
You're staring at me
What do you see?
I feel your hand on my chest
Have I passed the test?
Your lips are on mine
We're going to be just fine
Just fine, just fine
Just fine

I want to wake up with you.
You know that I do.
Let me hold you tight.
We've got this, right?
I want to wake up with you.
And breathe you in, breathe you in.
Wake up with you and breathe you in.
Breathe you in

Jules hugged him and then wiped his tears away with her fingers. "That was lovely. You are a dear thing." She was crying now. "When did you set up all these candles? It is such a lovely thing to do."

"Don't cry. I love you so much. I didn't want to make you cry. Sinead helped me. She's staying at May's tonight."

"Is she? Why?"

"I wanted us two to be alone. I wanted to ask you something."

"What do you want to ask?" She inhaled sharply as she realised what he was about to say.

He smiled. "Jules, my gorgeous girl. You know that I want you to be my wife. Well, I haven't asked you properly yet, have I? I love you with all my heart. My heart is yours. I want to walk through the fields with you for the rest of my life. Will you handfast and tie the knot with me? Will you marry me and be my wife?"

"Yes, Seth. I want that more than anything."

"I want you to marry me on the nineteenth of April, when there is a full pink moon," he announced, and she could see his eyes were full of tears again. He grinned and let go of her hands. From a pocket he produced two gold rings. "Will you wear this Claddagh ring on your left ring finger? I'll wear one too. Each ring has a small crown symbolising loyalty. The heart is for love and the hands each side are hands of friendship. While we are engaged, the tip of the heart points away from our hearts. On our wedding day, when we are married, by handfasting, on the top of a hill somewhere, then we turn the rings around, so that the tip of the heart points to our hearts. Will you wear a ring with me?"

"Of course I will. I love you so much."

"You've made a thirty-year-old man very happy. I couldn't have asked for a better birthday present." He took up her left hand and slipped the ring on her fourth finger and then kissed her hand. "Happy birthday, my sweet girl."

"Happy birthday, Seth," she said, holding her hand out to admire the delicately carved ring in the candle light. "It fits perfectly. Can I put your ring on you? It only seems right," she said, holding her hand out for his ring.

"Sure." He gave the ring to her, and she took his hand and held up the ring to make sure she had it facing the right way and then placed it on his finger.

"I have Sinead to thank for choosing the right size ring for you. Sinead ordered them online for us. I am feeling a little guilty. I spent our earnings today on them. Are you mad with me?"

"No, it was a wonderful idea. We can easily make the money back. Sinead is a star. She did a little something for me too. You'll need the torch on the phone to see it properly," she said, handing him the phone.

"It is better if I take my t-shirt off, so you can see it." She slipped off her top and shivered a little as the night air grazed her skin. Seth was looking confused. She kissed him gently on the lips and then turned around. "Lift up my hair, and tell me what you see," she asked.

"A very tempting bra clip!"

"No, not that! Lift up my hair so you can see my back."

"You are shivering."

She felt his fingers run across her back as he swept her long curly hair over her shoulder. She shivered again with pleasure.

"Oh, my! It's beautiful. It's a Dara Knot but it looks more like a tree. Sinead has done you proud. It's amazing."

"Do you see our initials in a heart in the leaves?"

"I do. You have the name of our band on your back, Jules! I'm only teasing. It is touching. You have made us immortal. You are a brave thing. It must have hurt when you had it done. How long have you had it for?" *How did I not notice?*

"Just a couple of days. It's not sore now, but it still tingles in places. You'll have to take a photo of it when we get in, so I can see it properly. I wanted a tattoo similar to yours, to show that we are strong, like oaks and my love for you will last forever. I do love you so and I can't wait to be your wife."

"I am a very lucky man." He turned off the torch and put the phone in his back pocket. She turned to face him, and began to put her t-shirt on. He was smiling broadly, and she knew that he was up to something. As she pulled her head through her top, she felt his strong arm around her body and the other behind her knees. He scooped her up into the air and she squealed with surprise.

"You have now officially been grabbed! I am going to carry you off to our bed and have my wicked way with you!"

She laughed. "Seth, you bad gypsy boy! I am going to have to teach you some manners."

Chapter Thirteen

Seth had done all he could to help Jules get breakfast ready for the guests at the Manor House. He was standing by the dining room window and looked out onto the immaculate front garden. Where there had been a tangled mass of weeds, ivy and wild garlic, there was now a new front path lined with rose bushes. New turf had been laid and formed two lawns on either side of the path. The landscapers came regularly to tidy the garden. He liked working outdoors and he wondered if he would make a good gardener. *It might be worth considering if the money dries up from busking.*

He looked over at his beautiful Jules. She was singing along to the radio as she arranged the croissants, juice, jams and cereals on a table at the side of the room. He tried to work out if he had heard the tune before but he didn't recognise it. They were both feeling tired as they hadn't slept much. He smiled as he remembered proposing to her; it had gone better than he had hoped. He looked down at his ring. Although it felt new and unfamiliar on his finger, it also made him feel complete and not so alone in the world.

"Seth, would you mind going to the kitchen and getting me a few more knives? I've just got to change the cloth on table seven and put some serviettes out. The guests will be down soon, and I like to disappear before they arrive; otherwise they will keep me chatting."

"Of course, I'll get them. No problem at all."

He wandered down the corridor inspecting the workmanship of the decoration as he passed. He saw Tom walking towards him. He was dressed in his riding kit and had his hair drawn back in a ponytail. *What an eejit!*

"Is the dining room open for breakfast yet? Oh, it's you! Is Julia around?"

"Morning, Tom. The dining room will be open in five minutes."

Tom hesitated for a moment and then frowned.

Seth passed him by and smiled; doing his best not to be rude. *What an arse. So Jules has told him her name is Julia. Only friends and family call her Jules.*

She turned around expecting to see Seth and then saw Tom standing there, staring at her.

"Julia, I'm sorry about last night."

"I don't understand. Why are you sorry?"

"She meant nothing to me."

Jules was a bit shocked. *Does he think I care about him? Oh, God!* "I don't care who you see, Tom. Why would I? I got engaged to Seth last night."

He frowned at her. "Happy birthday, by the way."

Seth came into the room and glared at Tom. He gave Jules the knives and she put them in a pot on the side table.

"Seth, we're done here. I saw Sinead earlier and she told me that May wants us to have breakfast with her." They left the dining room without saying anything to Tom.

"Was everything ok in there? I asked him to wait five minutes. He didn't, did he?"

"He just wanted an early breakfast," she lied. *He won't be able to deal with what Tom just said to me. I've got to try harder not to engage with that creep.*

May was sitting in the conservatory and was doing a crossword. Papers and magazines were thrown around her.

"Happy birthday, you two. I hope last night went well. I think it did, as you are both grinning like Cheshire cats." Her speech was a little slurred but her words were clear.

"Jules is going to make me the happiest man that ever lived. We are going to be married on April the nineteenth, up on a hill nearby. How are you doing, May? You're looking grand."

"It's a good day for me too. I think I have just turned a corner. I've read every paper, and I have done half a crossword. And it's not even nine o'clock! Now then, how about if we have scrambled eggs and salmon for breakfast with a little champagne? Special occasions like ours should be celebrated. You never know when it's going to be your last day. Jules, my lovely, could you make breakfast for us? I would, but it would take a while and I know what Seth is like in the kitchen."

"You wound me, May! But it's true, I have let Jules spoil me and now I am dependent on her to stop me from starving. I'll open the bottle. I'd like to do my bit," he said, laughing.

"I'll cook, it won't take a minute. Seth, do you eat fish?"

"I'll have a little. I don't think I've had smoked salmon before."

As Jules went off to the kitchen, she could hear May and Seth chatting and laughing together. *It's good to hear them laugh.*

The fridge didn't have a lot inside it. *I wonder what Tom has been cooking for May? There is nothing but milk and eggs.* She had a quick look in the freezer and noticed that it was full of ready meals. *That's good, she has food. I'll bring her something homemade now and again. It's not good to eat ready meals all the time.*

She found a bowl and six eggs. She beat four of the eggs together with a little milk. The salmon packet had been opened and as she pulled back the cover a strong fishy smell hit her nostrils causing her to retch. She flipped the lid back to mask the smell and noticed that it was in date, which surprised her. *I won't have any of that. It's way too fishy for me.*

They ate breakfast together and Jules could see that May was having difficulty chewing her toast. Jules found it strange to be drinking champagne so early in the day. It was refreshing but it was making her head spin and she was feeling drowsy. *I know it's our birthdays, but I wonder if Seth will mind us going back to the caravan to sleep. Just to sleep.* She thought about them making love through the night, and she could feel her body start to ache for him again. *Seriously? Control yourself!*

"Sinead told me that you two sing together at The Elbow in Cork and that you are fantastic."

He smiled. "I wouldn't say that exactly, but we do our best and people applaud so I guess we are holding our own. We enjoy singing, don't we, Jules?"

"It's great fun and we're getting paid to sing too. Seth is an amazing singer. We could sing for you later if you like. I'll bring my guitar over. We could get an Indian take-away delivered here. Sinead should be free. Look at me inviting everyone to your house! Would that be ok? Do they deliver take-away in Ireland?"

"Yes, they do deliver to Waterfall. That sounds like a lot of fun," laughed May. "I'd love to hear you both sing.

Seth, there is another reason I asked you over this morning. There is something I need to share with you and Sinead. I talked to Sinead this morning. I have a gift for you both. When I finally meet my maker, which I hope won't be for a very long time, I want you and Sinead to have the stables, the horses and the land. I want my riding school to continue and the cobs to win prizes at the shows. I know that my penny pincher of a brother would sell the lot, and then what would happen to my beautiful cobs? I'll leave him with the house of course, and he can do what he likes with that."

"Oh my, no May. That is too much. I couldn't..."

"Nonsense, you and Sinead have earned it. Although I am not understanding why you are not taking a wage at the moment. Sinead says that there is a problem with both your bank accounts. We will have to work something out. It isn't right that you don't get paid. I know, I will give you the stable's bank card and you can draw your wages out in cash. Yes, that will work.

Anyway, Grayson Solicitors in Cork hold the will in their office. Tom will kick off but it is all there in black and white. We will leave him in the dark until you need to visit the solicitor. I have no children, so let me do something worthwhile with my money. You all mean so much to me. I consider you, Sinead and Jules as my own and you must let me treat you as such."

He exhaled. "I'm blown away. I don't know what to say. What did Sinead say?"

May laughed. "Much the same as you."

After they had seen May, they went back to the Manor House to tidy up the dining room. Seth loaded the dishwasher while Jules put away the cereals and jams.

"You are quiet. Are you thinking about what May said to you? Are you in shock?"

"I don't think shock is the right word. I'm dumbfounded and lost for words. Things like that do not happen to someone like me. She didn't have to do that. If she wants to give away her property, then she should have given it all to Sinead. I haven't worked as hard as she has here and she has been working at the stables longer than I have. It doesn't seem right. I feel like I am having a working holiday and Sinead is running around like a headless chicken, running the place."

"So, maybe, you should make up for lost time and do more to promote and grow the business and then earn your share that way."

He smiled. "You are the best. You make everything sound so simple and straightforward. I have to admit that I am looking forward to seeing Goldilocks's face when he finds out that we are included in the will."

"He will probably contest the will, but we mustn't worry about that until we have to. I am done here and I need to sleep for a bit. Do you mind if I have a rest before we go out for a ride?"

"I really was a bad boy last night! You're exhausted. We can go out this afternoon, and I will let you rest. I will have a look at the stable's accounts to see if there is room for improvement. I've also want to work out. I'll ask Sinead if she wants to join us for an Indian tonight."

"Aren't you tired?"

"I was earlier but now I think May's news has energised me. I'm dying to hear what Sinead thinks about May's gift."

When they got to the stables, Sinead was teaching in the sand school. They waved and carried on walking. Sinead saw them and ran over to the fence and called out to them to come over to her.

"Seth, Tom has taken Moss out for a ride. I didn't see him take his tack. I just saw them in the field over there," she said, pointing to the fields beyond.

Seth was horrified and angry. *Stay calm.* "Is it ok if I saddle up Soldier for him?"

"Yes, he's not being used until four. Seth, don't do anything rash!" Sinead said, biting her lip.

"No, don't worry. With a bit of luck Moss will throw him, and I'll find him lying on the floor with a broken neck," he said and then stormed off up towards the stable block.

Jules followed behind him quietly; she could see that he was fuming and needed time to calm down.

Seth collected Soldier's saddle and bridle from the tack room and took these to his stable. Jules went to the office to get Seth a hat as she suspected that he would ride out without one. She waited a few minutes for him to appear again. She could feel her stomach knotting up with anxiety. Finally, he came out into the yard and led Soldier towards the mounting block. *He looks calm now.* She went over to him and handed him the hat and could tell that he hadn't even thought about wearing one.

He smiled weakly. "I'm not thinking straight," he said as he put on the riding hat. "Go and rest. I promise I won't hit him. I am cross, though. What was he thinking?"

"He is probably trying to wind you up. Don't rise to it."

"I won't," he said as he mounted Soldier. "I might give him a piece of my mind, though. I don't want you to hear me. He won't be riding Moss again, that's for sure! I'll see you in a bit."

She watched him go. *I hope he keeps his cool. But I doubt that he will.*

JULIA'S BABY

Chapter Fourteen

Breathless, Jules stopped running, and with hands on her hips, she took in deep breaths of air to try and recover. It had seemed like a good idea to go running with Seth, but now she was not so sure. The gap between them was getting larger. *I have been running like a snail. I knew that I was unfit, but I hadn't realised how bad I was.*

As well as working out, Seth sometimes went for a run on a Sunday morning and he always left Jules in bed to sleep. She usually slept in until lunchtime and had begun to feel guilty about it.

The night before, she had decided to add exercise to her new healthy lifestyle. He had been pleased but sceptical about her plan. *He thought that I was going to find it difficult to get out of bed. It was hard but I managed it. Oh dear, he's had to stop for me. Come on, Jules, you can do this.* She started to run again, determined to show him that she had what it took to become an athlete.

She needs more protein to build up muscle. I'm proud of her, though. "How are you doing? I'll run with you and then we can chat."

"Thanks, I am sorry if I am holding you up. It's hard to talk and run at the same time."

"You need to breathe through both your mouth and your nose and that should steady your breathing."

"Ok, I'll try. How far are we going today?"

"I usually manage 10k in an hour, but we will just do a quarter of that today. You need to build up to that slowly. We have about five more minutes of slow running and then when we get to the Manor House we will walk up the drive to the mobile home to warm down."

"I can do that. I think my breathing is improving. Have you always run? Were you good at sports at school?"

"I didn't really go to secondary school much. I didn't like being cooped up in a classroom with eejits."

"I didn't know that. Did you get in trouble for not going?"

"Plenty! Dad gave me the belt a fair few times, but it didn't change anything."

"So how did you learn to read and write?"

"I learnt to read when I was at primary school and I have always read books. Travelling taught me a lot about the world and I have learnt a lot from the internet. I can add up and subtract in my head quite easily. So all in all, I don't feel that I have missed out on anything."

"I would have never of guessed. Seth, can we stop for a moment? My side is hurting."

"We can walk now if you like. We are nearly at the start of the drive."

"No, if we are nearly there, then I want to reach the finishing line."

"Ok, just hold where it hurts and try and get a rhythm going with your breathing. When you breathe out, release the pressure on the stitch."

"How do you know all this?"

"From a running guide on the internet," he said, laughing.

Jules managed to run to the drive, but she couldn't get rid of the stitch. She did, however, feel like she had achieved something. Although she was tired she walked up the drive, holding his hand feeling like she had just completed a marathon.

As they walked towards the Manor House, she could see someone at one of the windows and realised that it was Tom. She wished that she hadn't looked his way as he was staring at them. "Don't look now," she whispered. "But Tom is watching us from his bedroom window. He really gives me the creeps."

Seth looked up at the window and frowned. "He's staring right at us. Why is he standing there gawping at us like that?"

"Ignore him. He is just trying to intimidate us."

"He is still feeling sore that I left him without a horse to ride on. He thinks that he is safe behind glass. I'd like to see him try and look at us like that out here!"

"That was a bit mean. You shouldn't have left him stranded in the fields with no horse to ride home on."

"I know I shouldn't have done that, but he really was getting on my nerves and he needed putting in his place."

Jules resisted looking at him a second time and they continued on their way up to the stable yard.

As they got to the mobile home, it started to rain and they just made it inside before it poured down.

"That was lucky, we could have got soaked. Are you still up for busking at the Cork Folk Festival? Jules asked.

"I don't see why not. It is just a shower and I am sure it won't stop people going into Cork. I can't believe how well we did yesterday. I didn't realise how popular the folk festival is. We made nearly two hundred pounds," he said as he started to strip off, ready to go into the shower. "If the sun comes out then we should busk by the river. I've got a good feeling about this afternoon."

***

The bus had been busy with villagers heading into Cork. Jules and Seth had got to know the bus driver well and he always wished them luck as they got off the bus. The sun had come out, although there were a few dark clouds in the sky threatening rain. They had picked a spot on the river bank, near to the famous St. Patrick's Bridge. Before they started to play, Seth had taken a few photos of the bridge and the river. He showed Jules one that he was particularly proud of. The path by the river was busy with visitors and with local families taking a Sunday stroll.

"So are you ready to sing, my sweet girl? It's probably best to stick to the traditional songs with a few of Ed Sheeran's thrown in as well. What do you think?"

"Ok, but can I do Let It Go for the kids first?"

"Sure, I don't know that one. Is it a bit like the Wheels on the bus?"

Jules laughed. "No, Seth! It's from Frozen. Surely you have heard that one before?"

"No, I can't say that I have."

"Really? You'll know it when I sing it. Elsa had a long white plait and a pale blue gown."

"No, you've got me there."

"Please will you hold my guitar while I sing? Watch the children stop. I think that they still like this one."

Mystified, he took her guitar and watched her sing. *She looks so happy when she sings. No, I don't recognise the song.* He was amazed to see children stop and listen and drop coins into the guitar case.

When she had finished, she grinned at him. "You recognise it now, don't you?"

"No, I have never heard it in my life. You did a grand job, though. We are going to have to hire you out to kids' parties."

The afternoon passed by quickly and they had done well. They had decided to do one more song before they called it a day. Jules was looking forward to having a coffee and a cake in their favourite cafe and she hoped that they still had lemon drizzle cake left. They were halfway through Song for Ireland when she noticed that Seth was staring at someone standing on the bridge above. *Oh, God! It's Tom. Just get going. He is going to lose it if you stay watching us.* She then realised that he had stopped singing, and he was looking annoyed.

She kept singing and hoped that Tom would realise that his presence was not welcome. *Surely he must see Seth glaring at him?* Tom held up a camera with a long lens attached. He held the camera up to his eye and directed it at her, adjusting it so that he could see her clearly. Not at Seth, but just at her. *Oh, no! You arse!* She wanted to stop singing, but there was a crowd around them and she didn't want to disappoint them. Tom continued to watch her through the camera.

Seth was fuming "That's it! He's gone far enough!" He walked off, pushing his way through the crowd as a red mist enveloped him. *If he knows what is good for him then he will take himself off and never come back.* He found his way onto the bridge, and he stormed over to Tom. "You stop that now!" he yelled and shoved him in the chest. Tom hadn't seen him coming as he was too engrossed in watching Jules. He let go of his camera. It hit the top of the bridge, toppled off the edge and hit the river Lee with a splash. *He looks frightened.* Seth was ready to thump him but managed to resist the urge. *He is not worth it. Jules won't want to marry a thug.*

"You imbecile! That camera is worth over ten thousand pounds!"

"You shouldn't have been leching through it then! You keep your beady little eye off Jules. Don't talk to her and don't go near her. Do you hear me? You will be sorry if you do."

"I have no idea what you are talking about. Can't a man take photos of the river?"

"Just keep away from her," he said as he walked away. *I should have let him have it.*

Jules had continued to sing and had watched the scene above play out in slow motion. She had seen Seth push Tom and she had seen the camera fall into the water. Her heart had been beating so hard in her chest that it had made her ears ring. When she saw Seth walk away from Tom she had been so relieved. Tom had given her one last look before he went on his way. She shivered as her eyes met his.

The crowd clapped her and she thanked them as she packed away the guitar. Seth walked over to her and she could see that he was still angry. She wasn't sure what she should say. "Are you ok?"

"I am, now that I am back with you. Just give me a moment. I don't like losing my temper."

Chapter Fifteen

Seth shivered, zipped up his hoodie and rubbed his hands together to warm them up; the temperature in the mobile home was just above freezing point. It was the middle of November and there was a thick frost on the ground. *Frost already! I'd forgotten how cold the winters can get in Waterfall.*

The mobile home had heating, but it had gone off in the night. While the kettle boiled, he had a look at the heating controls. The control panel was blank, and pressing the start button did nothing. *Has a switch tripped somewhere? The kettle is working, though.* He had no idea where the fuse board was. *I'll ask Sinead when she gets up in a minute.* He got two cups out to make his tea and a cup of black coffee for her. Jules was sound asleep. When he had got out of bed, he had covered her over with his half of the duvet to warm her up.

Despite the cold weather, they were going to be busy all day at the riding school with group lessons and hacks. It was nearly light, so he looked over to see if he could see Moss in the summer field. He hoped the rug he had put on him hadn't slipped off. He could see him in the distance with the other cobs and was relieved to see him there with his coat still in place. He still hadn't got over Tom taking him out for a ride and fully expected him to take his horse out again without asking. He remembered riding Soldier up to him and seeing Tom's sly face and then the look of disgust at having to talk to him. *He thinks that I am a dirty traveller.* He had seen that look before on other people's faces.

He poured hot water into the cups and thought back to that day. He had demanded that Tom get down from his horse before he was thrown. Moss was not happy to have him on his back and was playing up. Tom had said that he didn't realise that he was doing wrong as he thought that the horse was owned by May. Seth had told him that he had paid for his horse. He had managed to persuade Tom to dismount to ride Soldier instead. Tom said that Moss hadn't been broken in properly and was dangerous. Without losing his temper, he had taken Moss's reins and had turned Soldier around and cantered off with both horses, leaving Tom behind to walk back. Seth smiled. The look on Tom's face had been a picture. *I shouldn't have done that but he really deserved it.*

After the incident on St Patrick's Bridge, Tom had kept away from him, and he hoped that he had kept away from Jules too.

Although Seth had paid for Moss, his horse's passport was registered with May, making him technically hers. *I will talk to her later about getting that changed. Would registering Moss in my name give my location away? Are the police still looking for me? I don't like being a wanted man.* Trying his best not to think about it, he got some bread out of the fridge and put a couple of slices in the toaster. He held his cup of hot tea in both hands to warm them up. The bedroom door opened and Sinead appeared with her duvet wrapped around her. Her face was almost blue with cold.

"Fuck, it's freezing!"

"There's a coffee here for you. The heating went off in the night. Where's the fuse box?"

"Fuck knows!"

He smiled. *It's best to talk to her after she has had a coffee.*

"There's a manual in the shoe cupboard," she said as she picked up her cup and headed towards the lounge. "Thanks for the coffee."

He flicked through the booklet and then located the fuse box in a cupboard by the door. One of the switches was down, so he flicked it back up and then reset the heating control panel which was live again. The boiler sprang to life. *We must have overloaded the circuit last night. I've no idea why as we were all asleep. We will see how it runs today.* He was glad it was working as he didn't want to start work and leave Jules to freeze. He could hear her in the bathroom and was surprised to see her up so early. She came through to the kitchen and smiled weakly at him. Her face was flushed, and she just had her nightshirt on. She didn't look well. "Are you ok, my sweet little dote? Are you hot?"

"I'm boiling and so thirsty. It's so hot in here! The duvet is too thick."

Her voice sounded husky and dry.

"Come here and let me feel your head." He put his cold hand on her forehead.

"Oh, that feels lovely. Your hand is so cool. I need both your hands on my cheeks. Seth placed them on her cheeks and kissed her forehead, and she sighed.

"You've got a fever. Do you feel ok?"

"I feel fine? My throat feels a bit sore, and I do feel really hot. I'll take a paracetamol and have some water. I've got to do breakfast at the Manor House soon."

"You've got a couple of hours before you have to do that. Take something and then go back to bed and rest and see if you can rally. I don't think you should go in. You don't look good."

"It's my job. It won't take me long. There's only two guests to deal with, and Tom, of course. I'm hoping May will be around and then..." Just saying Tom's name made her shudder. The past couple of months had been a nightmare. She knew that she had to tell Seth about him but after seeing him shove Tom on the bridge, she feared he would do worse if he knew how much he had been bothering her. *I can't handle this situation anymore.* Yesterday had been the last straw. He had been waiting for her in the kitchen and had declared his love for her. Despite her telling him to sod off, he hadn't listened to her and had tried to kiss her. *It's all too much.* Her stomach was aching with anxiety and she burst into tears.

"Oh, no! What is it? Is it Tom?"

She nodded. "He won't leave me alone. I told him to sod off but he won't listen. Can you talk to him later, and I won't care if you thump him but don't kill him. He is making my life Hell. He will be waiting for me in the kitchen again. I know it."

He wrapped his arms around her and hugged her. "Don't cry. I won't kill him. You should have said. Two breakfasts to make. I can do them before my first lesson and I'll sort him out. He won't bother you again."

"Thank you, Seth." The tears continued to flow and she couldn't stop them. It had been such a relief to unload her miserable secret.

"Just tell him to back off. Why is he still here? May can look after herself now."

"Don't fret. I'll take care of him. You go back to bed, and I'll bring you some tea and toast. Take some paracetamol."

Sinead came through to the kitchen for more coffee and then looked at Jules. "Is everything ok?"

"Do we have anything for a fever?"

"Yes, there's a box of tablets in the bathroom cabinet. Are you crying, Jules? Did I hear you mention Tom's name?"

"I'm going to have a word with him. He's been bothering her."

"I thought he might. He used to follow me around all the time. He can barely look at me now. I think you call that grooming. Can I come and watch you beat him to a pulp?"

"I hope it won't come to that. I'm allowed to maim but not kill. I won't do either. I've got enough blood on my hands."

Seth walked over to the Manor House and was not looking forward to seeing Tom. It pained him to see Jules so upset and he knew he would have trouble controlling his temper. He shivered and hoped the Manor House would be warm inside. *We will have to go into Cork and get some winter clothes soon.* A plan was forming in his head as he walked. As he got to the back door, he turned on the audio record button on the phone and hid it in his mac pocket. He found May and Tom in the kitchen together. He glared at Tom, and he glowered back at him with defiant eyes. *He knows I'm on to him.*

"Is everything alright, Seth? You look cross," asked May.

"I'm fine, but Jules is ill. She has a fever. I came to do the morning service."

"Don't worry, I'll cover her. I don't think she has had a day off for months. No wonder she is ill. I feel bad. I can help at the bed and breakfast more now that I am fully mobile again. You still look worried. Does she need to see a doctor?"

"No, not a doctor. She just needs Tom to leave her alone. She's really upset."

"I don't know what you're talking about!" he snapped. "If anything, it is her that is obsessed with me. I can't help it if women find me attractive."

"You should be ashamed of yourself!" May said, cutting in. "You are too old to be messing around with young girls. Don't think I haven't noticed you bringing them back here. You're old enough to be their grandfather, for heaven's sake!"

"They are just friends. Am I not allowed to have friends?"

"No, Tom! This can't go on anymore. Some of your so-called friends are still in school. You need to go home. I don't need your help here anymore."

Tom sneered. "You're not much better yourself, throwing yourself at this gypsy. It's disgusting!"

"You bastard! Get out and pack your bags. You are not welcome here. If you don't, then I will call the police and I am sure they will be interested to know that you are a paedophile!"

Seth was astonished, he hadn't had to say anything. May had told her brother, in no uncertain terms, to clear out. They both watched him leave the kitchen and then looked at each other.

"I'm sorry you had to hear that. I'm sorry Jules has had to deal with him. He is toxic and needs locking up. I am ashamed of him."

***

Jules lay in bed and watched the snow falling. Large white flakes fluttered past the window. It was just starting to get dark, and she guessed that it was late in the afternoon. *Have I been asleep all this time?* She felt warm but not as hot as she had been. Her throat was still sore. She sipped some cool water to soothe it. *Where's the phone? What time is it? Oh, it's three thirty in the afternoon.* Seth had stuck a note to the screen and it read.

I love you so much. PLAY ME!

His handwriting was neat, but the letters were very large. *He writes with confidence.* Jules sat up and pressed play, expecting to hear Seth's voice. As she listened, she realised that he had recorded his meeting with Tom that morning. May was there too. *Oh my, May is letting rip!* When she had listened to the whole recording she smiled. *May has asked Tom to leave. Thank God! Peace at last!*

She got out of bed and shivered. She was feeling cold and wanted to get back in. I can't, I have to go to the toilet. Jules put on her hoodie and went to the bathroom. *Should I bother getting dressed? Seth and Sinead will be back soon, and they will be hungry. I'll cook and then we can all watch a movie. Oh it's Saturday, oh no, we should be singing at The Elbow tonight. I forgot about that. I can't; not tonight. I hope Seth won't be disappointed.*

When Jules came out of the bathroom, Tom was waiting for her in the kitchen. He was brushing the snow from his black overcoat.

"GET OUT!" she spat.

"Julia, darling! That's not nice. I only came to see how you were."

"Get out, you shouldn't be here."

"You're not well. One day you will welcome me with open arms. You need to get dressed. We've got to catch the last flight to Sydney. I know you love me. Let's not make this any more difficult than it already is. Get dressed; there's a good girl."

"Just piss off, Tom. Didn't May and Seth tell you to leave me alone and fuck off back to Australia?" She had caught him off guard, and he frowned.

"I suppose your piss poor boyfriend told you that. Why stick with him when you can have everything and live the high life with me?"

"I don't love you, and I never will. I will call the police if you don't leave. I'm sure they will be interested in meeting your little friends."

"We both know that you don't want the police involved. I've done a bit of research. Did you know Sebastian Hearn is an escaped convict? It is in the Worthing Herald. Smell the roses, Julia. He is just using you. If you don't get dressed then I will have to do it myself. He held up a small gun loaded with a tranquiliser dart. Jules gasped, and fearing for her life desperately looked around her for an escape route. She turned to run back into the bathroom with the plan to lock the door behind her.

"No, don't you dare." He pulled the trigger, and she felt the dart hit her back and she screamed out with pain. As she slid down to the floor, she imagined the dart stuck in her tattoo between the S and the J. For a moment, she felt Tom's hand on her arm and then nothing.

There were snowflakes falling on her face. White flakes as large as saucers with rose buds printed on them. Jules laughed at the spectacle and then felt a wave of anxiety wash over her. *Where am I?* She wanted to scream but she had no voice. She was being carried by something horrible. A large black octopus was carrying her. Hundreds of arms were wrapped around her and she couldn't move. She couldn't breathe properly. She wanted to shout at the beast, but it didn't have ears and no words were leaving her mouth. *Where am I going?*

Seth looked up at the sky and realised that the snow was getting heavy and he would have to cancel the four o'clock lesson. *I wish we had an inside school.* His private lesson had finished ten minutes early as the weather was too bad to continue. A cold and miserable stable hand was busy unsaddling the pony, ready to take him back to his stable. *She should have a coat on.* "Gemma, I'll take Mini back to his stable. You head home, you must be frozen. The snow is laying, and I don't want you getting stranded here."

"Thanks, Seth, me Mam is waiting for me in the car park."

As Seth walked Mini across the yard he looked for Sinead. She had taken a group out for a hack and he hoped that she was ok and would head home early.

Although the snow was a bit of a nuisance, he couldn't help but like it. He remembered playing in knee deep snow with his brothers and sisters back at Crow Farm.

When he had put Mini away, he walked into the office and listened to the answering machine. He was pleased to hear that both four o'clock lessons had already cancelled. *That means Sinead can finish early too. I'll wait for her to return and then I'll go and see how Jules is doing. I hope she's feeling better. I wonder if she's listened to the recording I made earlier. There's no way we are going to make it into Cork this evening. I'll have to let Mick know.* He could hear hooves on the cobblestones in the yard and went outside to help Sinead put away the horses. One of her riding group, a young girl, was leading her horse and looked worried. He was puzzled. "Where's Sinead?"

"She's in the Manor House car park. She says that you need to come right away. She's having a row with a man with blond hair."

Seth's heart started to pound in his chest and alarm bells were ringing in his head. "Thanks, can you hold on to her horse for a minute? One of the stable hands will help you," he said as he started to run to the car park. The snow stung his eyes as he ran.

As he approached the house, through the snow, he could see Sinead struggling with Tom as she barred him from getting into his car. She was yelling at him as he tried to pull her away.

"Seth, thank God you are here. I think he is trying to steal something. Have a look in the boot. I came up the drive with the others and saw him put something large into it. It wasn't luggage and he was looking over his shoulder in case anyone was watching him."

"You deranged dyke! I'm going home. It's just luggage."

"Then you won't mind me having a look then?" Seth said as he tried to open the boot. It was locked. "Open the boot, Tom!"

"Piss off! Keep your slimy convict nose out of my business!"

Seth marched over to him and shoved him in the chest. "Give me the keys, or I'll just have to help myself." He glared at his sly face and knew he was hiding something. *Fuck, he knows I've been in prison.*

"Are you going to thump an old asthmatic man?"

"Just give me the keys!"

"I'll get them. Let me give you a kiss goodbye," Sinead said. Horrified, he backed away. She was too quick for him, and she kicked him in his groin. Tom doubled over in pain and swore. He was unable to stop her from searching his pockets. Triumphant, she found the keys to the car and a small empty bottle. She handed the keys to him and then read the label. "It had ketamine in it," she said, frowning.

Seth opened the boot and shook his head, unable to process her words. "You bastard!" Jules was lying in the boot with the duvet wrapped around her. She was awake but her pupils were dilated and she hadn't recognised him. "Did you give her ketamine?" he yelled.

"Just a little. I was taking her to the hospital. You obviously couldn't be bothered yourself. She wouldn't come with me, so I gave her a little something to relax her."

"Then why is she in the boot? You're a fucking liar. Just fuck off out of here!" He threw the keys at him so that they struck him hard in the chest. He scooped Jules up into his arms and glared at Tom. Sinead shut the boot.

"She wasn't my type anyway. You're welcome to the slut. They're all the same. Now I've had her, she bores me." He laughed out loud and then his eyes narrowed as he looked at Seth. "Just one thing," he said, as he climbed into the car. "That dangerous horse of yours likes ketamine too. I gave him a good dose. I'm sure that it was enough," he snarled.

Seth and Sinead didn't wait to see him go and went as quickly as they could to the summer field. The snow was ankle deep and made walking difficult.

"What does ketamine do to a horse, Sinead?"

"I don't know. I think it's used as an anaesthetic."

As they approached the field, he could see Moss laying on his side. His rug was covered in snow. There was nowhere to lay Jules down, so Seth continued on home and left her on the sofa, on her side. "I'm sorry. I won't be long, you're safe now." *I've let you down.*

When they reached the field, the snow was falling thick and fast. He climbed through the post and rail fence and joined Sinead. Silently, they were standing side by side staring at Moss's motionless body.

"I'm sorry, Seth, I think we're too late," Sinead said quietly.

He dropped down onto his knees and swept the snow off of Moss's face and neck. "No, no," he sobbed, resting his forehead on his cheek. Moss's eye was wide open and lifeless. "Please don't be dead," he whispered. He ran his hand over his neck, feeling his soft fur. "He can't be dead, please no. He's still warm for God's sake." The huge horse quivered, hearing his master's voice. Seth looked up at Sinead and rubbed his neck and ears. He put his hand over his soft muzzle and could feel hot air coming out of his nostrils. "Sinead, he's still with us! He's breathing. We need to get more blankets to keep him warm until the ketamine wears off. Don't let that bastard win. Keep breathing my beautiful boy," he whispered.

Chapter Sixteen

Sunlight filtered in through the dusty windows of the old barn, warming Jules up as she whitewashed the walls. The weather had been terrible and Jules had never seen snow like it. The roads around Waterfall had been blocked and they had been unable to get into Cork to sing at The Elbow. Jules missed singing with Seth and longed for the long summer nights to return.

The radio was on full blast playing Christmas songs and she sang along as she painted. In just over a month, they had managed to turn an abandoned barn into something that almost resembled a home. It had been May's idea for them to renovate it and she had called it an early inheritance present.

May had been mortified when she heard what her brother had done to Jules. She had cried with Seth when he told her about Moss. Seth had spent the whole night with him, talking to him and encouraging his horse to wake. The temperature had dropped below zero but by some miracle they had both survived the night. May had said that she could never make up for what Tom had done to them both. She had written Tom out of the will completely and thought that they should call the police. They had talked her out of doing that.

The past four weeks had been hard for Jules and Seth. The shock of nearly losing her and Moss had taken its toll. Jules could see a sadness in Seth's eyes, and she was doing her best to cheer him up. She looked forward to seeing him smile again.

Seth wasn't sleeping well either, and his night terrors had returned. He had spent a lot of time working out in the barn or listening to music if he couldn't sleep. Sometimes he decorated through the night. *He needs to smoke weed again to relax him. Why doesn't he? I think he's run out of it. It helped him before. I'll get Sinead to get us some more. If I go out and buy it then I'll probably end up being kidnapped by a drugs baron. Why do I keep attracting trolls? Do I have victim tattooed across my forehead?*

Jules hoped that their first Christmas together, their move into the barn and their wedding in April, would give Seth back his appetite for life. Their relationship, however, was stronger than it had ever been. They never hid how they were feeling and talked about anything that was worrying them. He had said that he felt guilty for letting a monster get to her and he was having trouble leaving her by herself in the house; fearing that she might be attacked again. She had assured him that she was fine. "I don't remember any of it. You mustn't worry about me," she had said. "I must have had more than my fair share of bad luck and now I can lead a peaceful life." He had called her his sweet ray of sunshine.

Jules had no recollection of Tom's attempted abduction. Sinead had told her everything that had happened that wintery afternoon, or nearly everything. She was sure there was something more to tell but she didn't want to ask, in case it was something awful. *Perhaps, it's better not to know.*

It was Monday and Seth was teaching. Sinead always had this day off, and he was left to run the school by himself. Only the most dedicated of riders took lessons over the winter and today he had a couple of private lessons to teach. With the weather set to improve next week, he knew that the phone calls would be flooding in and he and Sinead would be run off their feet again.

Seth dragged some trotting poles across the school and spaced them evenly along the ground. His student was a three-year-old girl who liked to talk a lot about her dog. She was riding a small white Shetland pony named Pringle. He had asked them to keep walking around the edge of the school, but the pony had decided to have a rest and had come into the middle to doze. The little girl's mother was watching the lesson and laughed when Seth looked surprised to see her daughter and pony had strayed off the track. "So did you lose your way?"

"No, he's naughty," the girl said, laughing.

Pringle was probably the laziest pony he had ever come across. Having laid out the poles, he took up the lead rein and asked the girl to use her legs and reins to ask Pringle to move back onto the track. Despite her best efforts, the pony refused to budge. Seth had to lean on him to get him to move and then reluctantly Pringle started to walk.

The lesson had ended, so he helped the little girl down from the pony's back, and then at the office her mother booked her in for a lesson the following week. Looking in the book, in the office he noticed that he had a new student to teach. In brackets, next to her name was the word 'nervous.' *I'll get Sasha saddled up for her. In forty-five minutes, I will be free to go and work on the barn with my lovely girl.* He liked decorating, it was relaxing and he liked being with Jules; she distracted him from thinking too much about the past.

Jules stopped painting; she needed a break and a cup of tea. She had brought a flask with her and some custard creams.

I'll just have two. I've got to cut down or Seth will be walking Godzilla up the aisle!

She looked at the bare walls. They would need a lot of artwork to fill them. *I've got an idea. I will get Seth to take some photographs of the local area, and we can get them blown up and frame them.* She was sure that being outdoors taking photographs would reconnect him with the earth and help heal his mind. *I'll ask him today. We will have to buy a decent camera. We can afford to.* Their wages had been accruing in May's business account, and they had been drawing out cash from it when they needed to. She missed busking with him and longed to be out on the streets again, singing their hearts out. There was no better feeling in the world. *If the weather is ok this weekend, then we will go and busk again. That will help him. Music heals the soul.*

After Seth put Sasha back in her stable to rest, he walked over to the barn with a heavy heart; not even the December sunshine was cheering him up today. One of his most annoying recurrent thoughts was eating him inside. His mind flashed back to the moment when he had found the used condom on the floor next to their bed. Before he had spent the night with Moss, waiting for the ketamine to wear off, he had gone back to the mobile home to check on Jules. He had carried her through to the bedroom. She had been asleep and seemed to be recovering. When he had laid her on the bed, he had almost stepped on the unfamiliar condom. Seeing this confirmed the brutal truth that Tom had actually abused her and he had felt sick. He sighed. *At least he used protection and didn't give her anything. It's still rape, though. I don't like keeping secrets from her, but I can't tell her this, can I? I don't want her to feel any more pain.*

Seth had told Sinead about what he had found, and she thought that it was better to pretend that it hadn't happened as Jules had no memory of that evening. Memory loss, apparently, was a side effect of taking ketamine. Seth wondered how many other girls Tom had drugged and date-raped. *Jules will get sick of me if I don't get my act together. Surely, I should be over nearly losing her and Moss? It's been a month. I've got to get over this. Weed helped last time. I wonder if Jules will mind if I smoke a joint now and then. I'll ask her. She will know what I should do.*

As he reached the front of the cobblestone barn, he noticed that daffodils were starting to grow outside. *I don't remember seeing daffodils in December. We must have warmer weather on its way.* He smiled as his spirits began to lift. *This is going to be our first proper home together. Where is she? I can't wait to see her sweet little face.*

When he walked into the barn, he found Jules sitting on a large box with her legs crossed. She was wearing paint splattered work dungarees and an old t-shirt. Her hair was tied up in a headscarf and a few of her curls sprang out from it, unwilling to be captured. *She looks so hot in overalls.* She was holding a large cup of tea and there was a packet of custard creams opened in front of her. He looked at the walls and realised that she had painted one of the sides of the barn. "Hello, beautiful. You've been busy. What a difference! You're doing a grand job."

Her eyes lit up and she smiled. "I'm on fire, and it's all thanks to good music and the power of a custard cream. Do you want some tea? There's some in the flask."

He walked over and kissed her and then pinched the custard cream she had just taken out of the packet. "If I'm going to keep up with you, then I will need one of these. Did you bring lunch or shall I go back to the mobile and make us some?"

"Oh, I hadn't thought that far ahead." She looked at the phone. "It's nearly midday. Shall we go over to the mobile together and then after lunch, I'd like to go shopping, if that's ok?"

"If you want to. There is loads to do in here, though."

"I know, but Sinead is off today and she has offered to drive us to Ikea. She is going Christmas shopping there. I thought that we could order everything we need for the barn, pay for it in cash and then get it delivered here."

"Oh my, this is going to be a mega trip but we have to do this at some point. Ok, but we need to eat first, I'm starving."

"I've added something else to the list."

"What's that then?"

"Photo frames. I don't want to buy Ikea's pictures to hang on the walls. I want you to go out and take us some photos of the landscape. Like the ones you took around Crow Farm. Would you do that for us? We could get a good second-hand camera for you. Please, Seth."

Her eyes were sparkling with enthusiasm. "I don't know if I still have an eye for it. You'll have to come with me and hold my hand. I'm a bit rusty."

Jules grinned. "I will. You take amazing photos. I think I've found a suitable digital camera on EBay for you and if you think it is ok, we could pick it up on the way to Ikea. We could give them a call and see if it's still available."

"You naughty thing! You knew that I wouldn't be able to resist. Yes, ok, we will give them a call." *She's working her magic on me. Before I know it, we will be out busking again.*

The camera was still available so Sinead, using her EBay account, had managed to contact the seller and had been given rough directions to his house. As they drew up, they noticed that there was a moving lorry outside and furniture was being uploaded into it. It was almost full. Seth and Jules got out of the car as a large man wearing shorts came out of the house, holding a camera in a black case.

"My friend contacted you about the camera you are selling. Sinead is in the car and she is buying it for me. Is it ok if I have a look?" he asked. "I see that you are moving. It's lucky we caught you. You look like you're nearly done."

"I'm off to Dublin in half an hour. It's been a busy morning," he said, handing the camera to him.

Seth unzipped the case and inspected it carefully. As he checked it over, a large white cat with a fluffy tail walked up the path and started rubbing itself on Jules's leg. She bent down to stroke it and the cat started to purr.

"You don't know anyone that wants a two-year-old cat, do you? My neighbour thinks he is about that age. His previous owner left him in this house and I have been looking after him ever since. I'm not really a cat person. I've asked around, but nobody wants him. He just needs biscuits and water. He is very friendly."

Jules hadn't owned a cat before and wasn't sure how to look after one. "What is he called? He's lovely."

"He's called Barney. Well, I named him that. I don't know what his name was before. I think he likes you. Do you have room for a cat?"

The camera was in good order, and Seth was happy with the price and said that he would take it. He gave the man the money and then noticed that Jules had picked up the cat and was smiling at him.

"He's called Barney; like my old pony. He likes me. He is like a baby in my arms. There will be room for him at the Old Barn, won't there? Please, Seth."

"I don't see why not," he said, grinning. "Anything for my gorgeous girl!"

Chapter Seventeen

Even though I am sick of the white stuff, I really hope that it snows today. Why do we all want it to snow on Christmas Day? I guess it is because all the best Christmas films have snow in them. Jules was sitting on the lid of the toilet and watched Seth take a shower in the tiny cubicle. Through the steamed up glass, she could see his muscular body which was always pleasing to see. *I miss showering with him. The shower in the Old Barn is big enough for two.* A shock of electricity ran through her body as she thought about them being in there together.

"You are very good, working out on Christmas Day. It's been too snowy for us to go out running. I do actually miss going out on a run with you. I nearly ran all the way last time."

"You are doing really well. This snow can't last forever. I think you should come down to the Old Barn and workout with me. I'll be kind and break you in gently," he said as he turned the shower off and stepped out onto the bath mat. Jules passed him a towel, and he started to dry himself off.

"I don't know. I like running. I don't think I am cut out for boot camp."

He laughed. "I wouldn't kill you. I promise. I love you too much. The weather is going to improve next week. We should be able to run soon."

"When you brought me to Ireland, you never told me that Cork was really the Arctic in disguise."

"Ah now, here's the thing. Cork normally has a mild climate like the South of England. May thinks we are having this snow because of global warming. The pollution in the atmosphere is causing the planet to warm up, giving us extreme weather conditions to deal with. One day, snow will be a thing of the past. Eventually, Cork will become a desert, and we will all have to find a new planet to live on."

"Do you think things are going to get that bad? I hope not. It won't be in our lifetime."

"Perhaps we can do something to change things before it's too late. I'd like to do something like Kenny and Lucy are doing. We could become the Waterfall Wanderers and vlog on YouTube about how we are helping to save the world. What do you think?" he asked as he put the towel around his waist and walked over to the sink and looked at himself in the mirror.

"We could vlog about our lives here and how we are turning our barn into an eco-friendly dwelling."

"Maybe. I forgot to shave. I don't look too bad, do I?"

"Designer stubble looks good on you. You'll be getting all May's female guests in a tizzy."

"Tizzy? I've not heard that word before," he said, chuckling.

"So, are you up for watching another film?" she asked. "We could watch Love Actually. We've got a couple of hours before we go down to May's for lunch. The Manor House is full, so there will be at least twenty guests to serve Christmas dinner to. I am amazed that so many people want to be away from home at Christmas. I hope I don't spill anything. I've never been a waitress before. Have you?"

"No, not a waitress. I am not pretty enough! I've worked in a pub before and had to take food to the tables. Sinead is going to be the one that throws everything everywhere. We worked in a bar in Melbourne, and she was carrying a tray of drinks to a table and tripped over nothing. The whole lot went flying and she drenched this guy from head to toe. Thankfully, he saw the funny side of it. She was mortified."

"Poor Sinead. She is clumsy, though. She's always tripping over Barney. Oh, I forgot to tell you. May wants me to play Christmas carols on my guitar after everyone has eaten and is having coffee. I'm glad I don't have to sing as I only know the words to carols in German. I don't think that will go down well. Don't let me forget my guitar when we walk down later.

I like Christmas. I can't wait to see what May thinks of the framed photos of her cobs. That was such a clever idea to do that. I wish that you would let me buy you something. You bought me a jacket. You don't like people giving you gifts, do you?"

"I'm sorry. I don't know why that is. I guess it is because there were too many of us at Crow Farm and we didn't get gifts at Christmas or birthdays as there wasn't the money for them back then. It didn't mean that we didn't have a good time. There was always a party with lots of food, and we danced, ate and were merry. When the grandchildren came along, Dad used to dress up as Santa and take presents to them. He really spoiled them. Recently, he bought cars for all his daughters but nothing for his sons. He was a strange man. How about you, what was Christmas like for you?"

"It was fine when Peter and I were small - when Mum was alive. When your Dad is in the army, you become part of a huge army family and go to each other's houses on Christmas Day. I have an old school friend called Anika – she is German. I used to spend Christmas Eve with her family as they really celebrate Christmas then. She was a real laugh. Her mother tried to give me carp to eat but I managed to feed it to their dog under the table," she laughed. "When I came back to England, we used to keep in touch by messenger. I do miss talking to her. I wonder what she is doing now. She wanted to become an au pair."

"Oh dear, you've had to leave all your friends behind. I am sure we can find a way for you to contact Anika again. Sinead is on Facebook. She might be able to find her and you could talk through Messenger on her account."

"Oh, do you think so? That would be great. It's only on days like these that I miss family and friends. You must miss Charlene and some of your brothers and sisters. After Mum died, Christmas wasn't quite the same at Farm End. Dad would hide himself away after lunch and Peter and I would watch films together and eat too many chocolates. Actually, those days weren't so bad. Talking of chocolate, I might have a little something tucked away for you and for me. I found some mini chocolate cheesecakes in Cork and thought we could have those this afternoon. I don't think one would hurt before lunch. What do you think?"

"Chocolate cheesecake, you say? You know how to please a man. Come here and let me thank you in person. It is not often that we are left on our own."

Jules grinned. "I need chocolate first. Come into the bedroom and help me find it," she said, standing up to go. Seth came over to her and drew her to him. He smelt of lemons and soap. She kissed him and took his hand. "Chocolate first," she said, leading him to the bedroom.

***

The walk to the Manor House was treacherous. It hadn't snowed for a couple of days, but the snow that remained had turned to ice. As it was Christmas and the stables were closed for the week, all the horses and ponies had been turned out into the lower fields. Moss and the other cobs remained in the summer field as the ground there was well drained because of the incline. The lower fields were a different story, and were wet and muddy. Some of the horses had taken refuge in the hay barn, and they huddled together, waiting for spring to arrive.

As Jules and Seth walked through the slippery stable yard, which was exceptionally icy, they walked slowly trying to find patches of ice-free ground. Some of the yard was covered in black ice and called them over to dance with death. Jules looked around her at the empty stables and noticed how silent it was. "It's funny not seeing any of the horses here. It's so quiet that you could hear a pin drop." Her foot slipped to the side and she wished she had worn her wellies. The bag of presents she was holding clunked on the cobbles. Seth grabbed her arm and nearly went over himself.

"Careful, you need to look where you are going. I don't want you to break your leg. Wait here a minute and don't move. I am going to throw some salt around, so we don't do just that when we walk home later." He gave her the guitar he had been carrying and then went to the store room to get some road salt.

Seth returned holding a bag on his shoulder and then opened it and threw handfuls of the salt around him. He smiled at Jules as he worked, she was watching the horses in the lower fields. The new snow jacket he had bought her with the fur around the hood looked cute on her. He liked buying her things. Her face had been a picture when he had given her the green coat. She had looked annoyed at first as they had said they wouldn't buy each other gifts. Her frown had been replaced by a broad smile as she tried it on. This time he had chosen the size of the coat himself, and he had been pleased how well it had fitted her. With the hood up, her blue eyes shone even brighter.

Seth put the empty bag in one hand and then picked up the guitar. "Come on then, let's go and help May. Hold on to me. My shoes have better grips than yours."

"Ok, I hope I don't slip again. We've only got twenty minutes before the guests start sitting down for lunch. I hope May and Sinead are coping. I feel a bit guilty for not helping them. Sinead doesn't like cooking."

"Believe me, you don't want to be in the kitchen when she is in there. Too many cooks and all that. Just because she doesn't like cooking, it doesn't mean that she can't cook. She will be stressed, though." He could see smoke coming from the Manor House chimneys. "Do you see the smoke, Jules? May has lit all the fires in the house. It is going to be roasting in there. I hope she hasn't got the heating on too."

"I like sitting around an open fire. I wonder if Barney would like to lie in front of a roaring fire. Cats like warm places, don't they? Would he be too afraid to sleep by the flames?"

"You do ask the strangest of questions. I would imagine that our boy would walk across hot coals if you were there beside him. Like me, he doesn't like being away from you."

"I am lucky to have two men in my life that dote on me. I am going to bring a little bit of turkey and gravy back later for my baby. At Farm End, George and Pip always had a Christmas dinner. I'll feed him outside so you and Sinead don't have to witness him feasting on meat. Seth, I might have a little turkey for lunch if that is ok?"

"You daft thing! You don't have to ask. I don't mind watching you eat meat. I always had my meals with my meat eating brothers and sisters. It didn't bother me."

They found May and Sinead in the kitchen. Sinead was relieved to see them. "Oh, I am so glad that you are here early. The turkey is huge and we need someone strong to get it out of the oven and carve it up."

"Hello, you two. Merry Christmas," May said, hugging them both. They wished her a Merry Christmas too. "I don't know how we got the turkey in the oven. It is ready. You can smell that it is. I better stick my probe into it to make sure it is cooked through. Seth, be a dear and get it out, please. I've made a space for it here on these mats. We need to let it rest for a moment," she said, patting the mats.

"Do you have oven gloves? I am sure I can get it out for you. I will do my best," he said, taking his coat off. Jules took it from him and took hers off too. The kitchen was hot and steamy.

"Here they are," May said, taking the gloves off the top of the microwave and giving them to him. "Sinead, how are the vegetables doing?"

"They are practically done. I hope they are not over cooked. They look a bit odd."

"They'll be fine. Jules, would you mind getting the plates out of the warmer in five minutes? I can hear people in the dining room already. I hope they all like turkey. Oh, yes! In the microwave, there is a nut roast for you two. Jane will be sitting next to you, Sinead, and she is going to have a portion. I cooked that earlier. It will just need a couple of minutes in the microwave, to heat it up."

He looked in the oven and couldn't believe how large the turkey was. "Goodness, this is a bit of a beast!" He held his breath as he slid the turkey out, not wanting to smell it. The heat of the oven hit his face. *I hope May's not going to ask me to carve it up.*

Jules looked at the turkey with surprise. She had never seen one so big. May took the temperature and said that it was above the required minimum and she looked pleased. "It's been in there for hours. I really don't want to poison anyone. We will let it rest for a bit."

Jules noticed that Seth was looking worried, and she knew that he was finding it difficult to be near the bird. *Somebody has to carve this thing up. I don't think May is strong enough. I'll have to have a go.* "I don't mind carving it up," she announced. "Do you have a carving knife, May?"

"I've got an electric one. You would be here to next Christmas if you did it by hand," May said, laughing.

Seth carried out the first set of Christmas dinners to the hungry guests. The fireplace had been decorated with garlands and candles. A fire roared below. May had arranged the tables in a row and had covered them with red tablecloths. She had decorated the centre of the long table with holly, crackers and jars with the candles inside. *They are the same candles we used when I proposed to Jules.* He smiled at the guests, and they stopped chatting when they realised that their lunch was about to be served. *Do I serve them from the left or the right? I'll start at the end of the table. Left I think?*

As he got to the last table by the window, he noticed that it was snowing again. *I must tell Jules that it is snowing. She wished for snow today. I wonder if it will lay on all that salt I threw on the stable yard?* He placed the plates he was holding in front of an elderly couple. "Please start, before it gets cold."

Sinead was serving the next guests, and she had a determined look on her face. When she set the plates down, she smiled in triumph. "There, made it. Come on, Seth, May is plating up like a crazy woman and she is running out of space. The dinner is looking good although the nut roast smells strange. We will just have to cover it with gravy. I brought our special gravy granules down with me this morning."

When all the plates of food had been given out, Seth and Jules joined May and Sinead at the head of the table to eat their lunch with the guests.

May stood up. "I just wanted to thank you all for spending Christmas Day with us. It has been an absolute pleasure cooking for you all and I hope that you will join us next year. Merry Christmas, everyone," she said, raising her wine glass. Everyone lifted their glass and wished her a happy Christmas too.

As May and Sinead carried out various desserts to the dining room, to leave on the side so that everyone could help themselves, Jules and Seth loaded the dishwasher. "That went well," Jules said. "Everyone seemed to enjoy that. I did. The turkey wasn't too dry. There is so much left. The guests will be having turkey for weeks to come. What was the nut roast like?"

"It was nutty. Kind of gritty. I much prefer what you cook for me."

"You are sweet. Ok, let's turn this machine on and find the cafetières for the coffee. Oh, no! It's not starting. I'll try again. No, it's not working."

He looked over at the microwave and cooker. "I think the power supply has been cut." He tried the light switch, but the light didn't work either. "The fuse board is in the hall cupboard, I think. I'll have a look and see if any switches have tripped."

While he went to check, Jules looked at the cooker and hoped that the gas hob was working. *I will boil water in a saucepan and make the coffee that way. I guess I will have to use a match to light the ring. May must have lit the fires with a match. I wonder where she keeps them.*

May and Seth returned together and looked worried. "The fuse board is fine," May said. "Last year, a snow laden tree went down on a cable and we didn't have power until the next day. Oh dear, the guests will have to stay by the fires and keep warm. Their rooms will be too cold to stay in tonight. I'm not sure what to do."

"I am sure that the power will be back on soon," Seth said, trying his best to sound cheerful. He didn't like to see May so worried. "Jules and I will entertain everyone. Are you up for a little singing, my beautiful wife-to-be?"

"Ok, why not. What songs shall we sing? Carols? I can play them but as I said I can only sing them in German. I should be able to sing them in English too. My brain is just having a moment!" she said, laughing.

"I don't know the words that well either but if you play carols, then I am sure there will be a few singers in the audience that will sing for us. We don't have to just play Christmas songs, we could sing some popular songs too and see what happens."

"Seth, I know that this is a bit cheesy but I really like 'Let It Snow'. If we sing it by the fire then I am sure everyone will want to join us. This is going to be fun. We need to make everyone tea and coffee first. I was thinking. We could heat up a huge saucepan of water on the gas ring. We just need to light it."

"You are a clever girl. I would never have thought of that," May said. "I mustn't get myself stressed. I am so glad that you three are here to help me and keep me sane."

An hour had passed since the power had cut and as everyone finished their coffees, Jules and Seth went into the lounge to arrange the chairs. They made a semi-circle of sofas and any comfortable chairs they could find around the fire. They had brought some of the jars with candles in with them as it was starting to get dark. They were sitting on dining room chairs to the right of the fireplace and waited for the guests to transfer from the dining room and join them.

Seth looked out of the window and could see the snow coming down thick and fast. "It is going to be really cold at home now. The boiler has probably stopped like it has here. Do you think we should sleep here tonight? Sinead is going to stay with May. I hope Moss and the other cobs will be ok. I should have brought them into the barn with the others."

"Moss will be fine, he is built for weather like this. We need to go and feed Barney. The power might come back. If it doesn't, then we can go and feed our boy and come back here. We will have to think of a way to warm up the guests' rooms. It might be best if they sit by the fire all night. Seth, I can hear people coming. May must be asking them to come through to us. Let's start singing Let it Snow," she suggested as she started to strum her guitar. "I know the words. Do you? I hadn't thought to ask."

"I do," he replied and he grinned at her. His big brown eyes looked so much brighter in the candle light.

When they had finished singing, Seth looked at everyone and smiled. Some of the guests were still wearing party hats, and some had brought glasses of Prosecco with them. He was concerned that they might be feeling worried at the prospect of being snowed in for Christmas without electricity. The majority of the guests were elderly, and some were beginning to doze as the heat of the fire hit them. Those that were awake were either looking at them or at the flames in a dream-like state. Seth stood up and picked up a couple of logs and lay them on the fire. One of the logs spat as the flames hit it. It made him jump.

"There is nothing better than an open fire on a day like this," remarked a man with an American accent. Jules felt like she was in the film The Day After Tomorrow. By sitting by the fire, they would all escape freezing to death.

Seth turned around to see who had spoken. He saw a man with wavy grey hair and a broad smile looking his way. "We have plenty of logs, so we should all survive the night. If we run out, then May has a whole library of books to burn."

Jules smiled. *Seth is thinking about that film too!*
He looked up and saw May and Sinead appear, holding armfuls of blankets. "If anyone is cold, then May and Sinead have plenty of blankets for you all," he said to everyone.

"So, that was a song about a snowy day. Does anyone have any Christmas memories they can share with us? I am sure we have some great singers here, so if you think of a song then I am sure that my talented fiancée, Jules, will be able to accompany you. I'm Seth Hearn by the way. I am a riding instructor here at Waterfall West. Jules and I are also known as S&J and we will sing a few songs for you too."

"I'm John Maguire," said the man with the American accent. "My grandfather, James Maguire married a Dublin girl, Carra Hearn. James was born in Waterfall, and they lived here until 1847. They survived the Great Potato Famine. Do you know the name Carra Hearn?"

"The Hearns are a huge family and cousins have married cousins. I don't recognise the name Carra. I think my family came from Dublin originally but they travelled a lot and then settled in Dingle. Most of them are in England now," he said. "We could be related. Is that why you are here? Have you come looking for lost relatives, John?"

"In a way. I'll tell you all our story, if you like."

"Yes, please do, John. It's a Christmas story too," his wife said as she took a sip of wine. Mrs Maguire was wearing a Christmas jumper with a large snowman on the front. Her hair was as white as snow.

"This is my story," John announced. "My great grandfather, John Maguire, he was born here and was one of eight children. His parents rented land from Waterfall West and grew root crops. It was difficult to eke a living out of the land and my great grandparents died before their time. They went without to feed their children and eventually starved to death. His son, my grandfather, James Maguire took on the tenancy and worked the land. He had no children and made a little money selling vegetables at the local market. He got by and provided the Manor House with produce. James fell in love with the housekeeper who worked here. He married Saoirse in 1844. There is an entry in the local church register. I doubt whether the marriage was approved of as James was just a peasant and Saoirse was a station above him. They were, however, good Catholics and were much respected in the village."

Jules noticed Seth give her a surprised look. *He is comparing us to them. You daft thing. You are not a peasant!*

"Then came the Great Famine in 1845," John continued. "As you probably know, after much rain over several days, a potato blight fungus destroyed all the potato crops overnight.

Most of the farming families around here depended on the potatoes to survive. After two years, over a million people had died of starvation or typhus. James lost everything and couldn't pay the rent. James and Saoirse decided to immigrate to America and start a new life. The Lord of the manor paid for their passage and they took their chances and travelled in a ship to New York. Not many people survived in these ships as conditions were brutal. Bodies were thrown overboard every day. They called them the coffin ships."

"Goodness!" Seth said. "That's quite a story. I didn't realise that the potato famine affected Waterfall. How did your grandparents do when they got to New York? Did they make it to America?"

"They did just swell, although it can't have been easy at first. They went on to have eight children themselves, and my father was their first born. He is one of the reasons we are here. He says that he dreams of Waterfall West as his father told him such vivid stories about the place. Especially about my grandfather's Christmases here. My Dad hasn't got long, and I wanted to take some photos and find out more about the house for him. May has been really helpful and has given us a few old photos. We wanted to take pictures of the house and the fields at Christmas. We couldn't have asked for more. The house is going to look amazing in the morning all covered in snow. The photos are going to be keepers for sure."

John looked sad for a moment.

"That was a lovely story," Jules said. "Your Dad is going to be so pleased. Seth, will you sing 'The Fields Of Athenry'? That song is about the potato famine."

"I don't know, Michael stole food and ended up in Botany Bay. We will all be crying. Me included."

"Oh, please do. John's father sings that sometimes. Although he hasn't got a voice as good as yours. John, you must record this for your Dad. Please sing it for us," Mrs Maguire pleaded.

"Ok, but we need to sing something cheerful afterwards. Can you play this one, Jules?"

"Yes, ready…" she said as she started to strum her guitar…

> *But a lonely prison wall,*
> *I heard a young girl calling*
> *Michael they have taken you away,*
> *For you stole Trevelyan's corn*
> *So the young might see the morn,*
> *Now a prison ship lies waiting in the bay*
>
> *Low lie, The Fields Of Athenry*
> *Where once we watched the small free birds fly*
> *Our love was on the wing*
> *We had dreams and songs to sing,*
> *It's so lonely round the Fields of Athenry*
>
> *By a lonely prison wall*
> *I heard a young man calling*
> *'Nothing matters Mary, when you're free'*
> *Against the famine and the crown,*
> *I rebelled, they brought me down*
> *Now it's lonely round the Fields of Athenry*
>
> *Low lie, The Fields Of Athenry*
> *Where once we watched the small free birds fly*

Our love was on the wing
We had dreams and songs to sing,
It's so lonely round the Fields of Athenry

By a lonely harbour wall
She watched the last star falling
As the prison ship sailed out against the sky
Sure she'll live in hope and pray
For her love in Botany Bay
It's so lonely round the Fields Of Athenry

Low lie, The Fields Of Athenry
Where once we watched the small free birds fly
Our love was on the wing
We had dreams and songs to sing,
It's so lonely round the Fields of Athenry

"Oh, Seth, you sang that beautifully," Mrs Maguire declared, clapping for him.

***

The power cut ended at one minute past midnight and when the light in the lounge went on, everyone had cheered. This was followed by a quiet moment as the guests looked sadly at each other as they realised that they would be leaving the warm fire and their new friends behind in exchange for an icy room and a cold bed.

Before they left the Manor House, Seth made sure that the boiler was working. May stood by him, and holding her glasses in front of her nose, changed the settings on the panel so that the heating stayed on all night.

"There, the rooms will soon be warm," she said. "That was an amazing evening, you and Jules bring the best out of people. Some of the stories and songs we heard were remarkable. I will never forget this Christmas Day. I am so proud of you both. It's late. You two need to get to bed. It has stopped snowing but the snow is deep. You will be ok getting back, won't you? I have some pull-out beds if you want to stay. I'd be happier if you stayed."

"We will be fine, May. Barney needs feeding and Jules won't rest until she sees him."

"Seth," Jules called as she spotted him in the laundry room with May. "I've got your coat. My baby will be climbing the walls. Let's give Barney his Christmas dinner."

Chapter Eighteen

It was a dark and cold wintery January night and only the foolish dared to step out into the foul weather. Jules and Seth, wearing thick coats, hats and gloves, had waited by the bus stop in Waterfall for over half an hour. The icy wind had cut through them, and they had bone chill by the time they got on the bus.

As they climbed aboard, Seth carried in the guitar and the bus driver, seeing it, chuckled. "You've picked a rare old night to go out and sing. I've heard that there's more snow on the way. You don't want to get stranded. It's lucky I saw you in time, or I would have sailed on to Cork."

Seth took off a glove and got some change out of his pocket. "It is a cold one for sure, and I doubt that we will be able to busk tonight. We will find ourselves a good pub with a roaring fire, music and somewhere to dance. We will soon warm up."

"Do you want a return?"

"No, just two singles, please."

"You two enjoy yourselves. You are only young once."

They were sitting at the back of the empty bus and could feel warm air blowing around their feet.

"That feels so good," Seth said as he rubbed his hands together.

Jules was so cold that she could barely move her jaw and she waited patiently for the warm air to thaw her out. "It is lovely and warm in here. That wind was evil. Do you think we made the right decision to go out tonight? It's Saturday and I thought that the bus would be full. Perhaps they've heard about the snow coming too and have stayed at home."

"I checked the forecast and snow is due, but I don't think it is going to hit Cork until the early hours of the morning. I've missed us singing together at the weekends. I know I said to the bus driver that we weren't going to busk but if the streets are busy, then we could give it a go. We will need to find a sheltered doorway of a shop to keep us out of the wind. If it does snow later and the taxi can't take us home, then we could always stay overnight. Hey, why don't we stay at a hotel tonight anyway?"

"That's a good idea. I'll let Sinead know and get her to feed Barney in the morning. It would be good to have time alone with you. We hardly get a moment together these days. I can't wait to move into the Old Barn with you and Barney, so we have our own space. I love Sinead, but we are living on top of each other in that mobile home."

Seth laughed. "Are you sure that you don't want to leave your cat with Sinead? She is going to miss him."

"No, he's my baby. He is part of our family now. You can't deny that you haven't got a soft spot for him. I've seen you talking to him and giving him treats."

"We have an understanding. No, I can't deny it. He has grown on me. He covers my clothes in his white hair and some days we look like brothers."

"He's not that hairy!" she said, laughing.

"So, Jules, my sweet girl. What are we going to sing tonight? It's been a while since we went busking. I might be a bit rusty."

"Just our usual songs. Can we sing Hey Brother to start with? Our voices are just perfect for that one and everyone seems to love it. I was thinking the other night that we should write an Irish folk song. I tried to write a song to the hornpipe, but it was hard going. It didn't happen."

He laughed again. "I don't think it would be possible to make up a song for that one. I think we need to leave the traditional tunes as they are and write our own upbeat love songs. I hate to admit it, but love ballads are really popular. Since making up my proposal song, I have had lots of ideas going on in my head. I've scribbled a few ideas down. So one fine day, I will sing them to you and then you might be able to pick up the tune and chords on your guitar."

Jules smiled, she was starting to feel hot and took off her gloves. "I can't wait to hear you. I loved your first song. I will never forget it. You are really talented."

"I write the words down when I can't sleep. I have a lot of time on my hands at night. You will need to compose the music to go with the words. I know that you will be able to find us some great tunes. I am getting fewer nightmares, but I just can't sleep. My mind is in overdrive as I think up new songs. I am surviving on two or three hours of light sleep a night. I could do with a whole night's deep sleep again. Actually, I was going to ask you if it is ok if we pick up something to help me sleep. Sinead told me where to get it."

"You don't have to ask me. Just be careful; I don't want to find you in a dark alley, with a knife stuck in your back."

The streets of Cork were eerily quiet for a Saturday night. In the icy wind, an empty beer can rolled along the road and rattled as it turned. As they walked along the high street, Seth noticed that there were homeless people sleeping in doorways. Although they were covered over in blankets, he knew that they were probably frozen to the core. He tutted. "It's a crying shame. This is not a night to be sleeping rough. What do you say we buy them a hot coffee and a sandwich? I've spotted six sleeping along here already. There's a coffee shop up the road that is open late. Do you mind if we spend a little money on these poor souls?"

"No, Seth, that's fine. It's hard to walk past them and not worry for them." *He has the kindest heart.*

When they had distributed the coffees and the free cakes the cafe had donated to them; they decided to visit The Elbow. It was too cold to busk and they thought that Mick might have a gig slot available for them. The Elbow, the pub, was jam packed with people. Sonar Cell were on stage, and their following had doubled. The pub was warm and welcomed them in, promising them sanctuary.

"What would you like to drink?"

"Just a hot chocolate, please. Oh look, there are two seats at the bar. Let's sit there. It's so busy in here tonight."

"Do you want to go somewhere quieter? Really, we should visit all the pubs and bars and check out all the live music to see how we can make our mark," he shouted.

Jules nodded. "If Mick's got nothing for us then we could have one drink here and then go on a tour. We could leave the guitar here and pick it up later."

Mick, seeing them waiting, came over to serve them. Before he got their drinks ready, he asked if he could have a quick word with them in the back room. They left their coats on their seats and Jules brought her guitar with her. Mick let them into the back room which was filled with boxes spilling over with t-shirts and bric-a-brac. Although the room was a mess, it also seemed to be sound proof and quiet. Mick was a large framed man and had some fading tattoos on his arms. He had no hair and his forehead was sweating. Jules noticed tattoos on his fingers. They looked as if they had been drawn by a child.

"Sorry to drag you away from your night out. You haven't been busking have you? It's too cold a night for that. It's really hot in here," Mick said as he wiped his forehead on his arm.

"No, we were going to but like you said it is crazy cold out there. Do you have any gig slots available?" Seth asked.

"I'm afraid I haven't got any room for you tonight. If you are free next Saturday, then I could give you a two-hour slot. It breaks my heart to say no to you. You've been missed. People are asking all the time where S&J are."

"That would be grand. I'm sorry, Mick, we've not been able to make it for a while. The snow was bad at Waterfall and the buses weren't running."

"We're going to get more snow again tonight. My brother lives in Bantry and he's just phoned to say that they are two feet under already. I blame this run of bad weather on climate change. Anyway, I won't keep you. A regular here came in the other night and was asking when you were playing next. I think he works for a big record label, and he asked me about you. He left me his business card and wants you to give him a ring." Mick gave Seth the card.

"Really?" Jules was surprised. "Do you think he wants to sign us up?"

155

Mick laughed. "I don't know about that, but he seemed really interested in contacting you and he did ask if you write any of your own songs. So maybe he is willing to give you a chance. Give him a ring and find out; you've got nothing to lose. He has been talking to Sonar Cell too."

Jules left her guitar in the back room and after they had finished their drinks at the bar, they put on their coats and stepped outside into a blizzard. Fortunately, the most popular pubs were all close by and they gradually worked their way around them, looking for those that had live music. The pubs playing traditional music were crowded, and it was impossible to find a seat. One of the pubs was having a dance off between two men who were river dancing on hardboard. Their reel shoes tapped loudly in time to the music as they each tried to out shine the other. Mesmerised, Jules watched them, marvelling at their agility and talent. They listened and watched them for a while and then moved on to another pub. By the time they reached Sin E, Seth was on his fourth pint. Jules had drunk two half-pints and her head had started to spin. *I'm such a lightweight.*

Seth felt a little merry and he was enjoying his night out with Jules. When he returned with their drinks, she noticed that he was smiling broadly at her and his big brown eyes shone. *He looks so happy tonight.* The pub was not as busy as the others had been and they were lucky enough to be offered some seats by a couple that were just leaving. The seats were in front of the window, and they could see the snow swirling down outside. At the far end of the pub, a traditional folk band was playing. The members of the group appeared to be in their late seventies and they reminded Jules of Seth's parents' band, Windmill. She shuddered as she thought about them. *Push those memories away and live for now, Jules!*

"What are you thinking about?" he asked, taking up her hand.

"Just the past. I try not to think about our time on the farms. It wasn't all bad, though. I like thinking back to when we first met."

"No, it's best not to think about the bad parts. So are you still up for marrying a poor farm boy?"

"Of course. We're not so poor these days, are we? We're doing ok now. If we were to sign a record deal then we could make millions. Would you like to make millions?"

"I don't know what I would do with the money. I like things the way they are. We're in hiding, so we can't really make a name for ourselves. I feel bad, that because of me, I could be holding you back from becoming a star. Isn't that what girls dream of? Becoming popstars?"

"That's not my dream. Yes, I like singing with you and being with you. That is enough for me. Anyway, we can't become celebrities, can we?"

He smiled. "You are the best. You know that, don't you? I adore you. When we've finished our drinks, shall we see if we can get us a room at the Jury's Inn?"

"Are you tired? We should see if we can get you some sleep medication."

Seth shook his head. "I'll have to get Sinead to get some for me. I had a look at the side street I was supposed to go down to get it and I didn't fancy my chances. Anyway, I don't think I will need it tonight. I'm not planning on sleeping much!"

"Why is that? Are you going to sing to me again?" she asked with a naughty twinkle in her eyes.

"I might, but I'd rather show you how much I love you. Every time I lie with you, I close the world off and I breathe when you breathe, my heart echoes your heart beat and I am part of you. I cannot bear to think of you in pain. If you bleed, then I bleed too. Forgive me for loving you too much. Forgive me for letting you down when you needed me most."

Jules stroked his face; his eyes were tearing up.

"Seth, you have never let me down. You must never think that you have. Life throws some ugly curve balls at us sometimes and we have to deal with these things alone. If you wrap me in cotton wool, then I will never learn to fly. I know that something bad happened when Tom drugged me but I will not allow the past to break me. Each day I grow stronger and each day our love grows stronger too. My heart is your heart. We can face our brave new world together. You are the dearest thing. You are going to make me cry if you don't smile."

He smiled at her. "When did you become so strong? I shouldn't have drunk so much; it is making me gush and act the maggot. I can't help it. I am just crazy about you. I need you, Jules, I am aching for you. We should get going and see if we can get a room. The hotels are going to be busy tonight. Look at the blizzard, the wind is howling out there. We'd better try and get to The Elbow and get your guitar. I hope we can make it without perishing."

"I need you too; it's been at least a week since we were alone. We will be fine, we will fight our way through the snow storm together."

They had laughed as they made their way to The Elbow. The snow was ankle deep and the wind was ferocious and hurled hard pellets of snow at them, making it difficult to see where they were going.

It was a relief and a pleasure to step into the warm pub. It was then that they realised that because of the storm, they would be unable to get to the hotel as they had only just made it to The Elbow. Seth sent a message to Sinead to let her know that they were going to stay in Cork for the night. He wasn't sure where they would sleep. There weren't many people left in the pub but those that had stayed were dancing reels and didn't seem to care that the building was rapidly disappearing under a blanket of snow.

Seth watched the dancers whirling around and the music called to him to dance. Jules looked up at him and her bright blue eyes were sparkling.

"You want to dance, don't you?"

He nodded and grinned. "I think we are going to be stuck here until morning, so we might as well make the most of it. Come and dance with me, my gorgeous girl, until the birds sing again."

Chapter Nineteen

Jules woke up and her head ached. She could smell bacon cooking and it was making her stomach churn. Slowly, she opened her eyes and then turned over and groaned. Her body was aching from lying on the pub floor. As the interior of The Elbow came into focus, she could see other people laid out on the floor too. Most were fast asleep with coats and blankets over them. She didn't remember very much about the evening, other than dancing with Seth for hours and then drinking Baileys. *My head really does hurt. How many did I have?*

Seth appeared holding a couple of rolls in napkins in one hand and two cups of tea in the other. "How are you feeling?" he asked as he put the teas and rolls on a table next to them.

"Did I get drunk?" Jules asked. "I've never been drunk before. I didn't make a fool of myself, did I? My head hurts and there is way too much sunlight coming in from the windows."

He laughed. "My poor wee little dote. Here, sit up slowly and drink some tea. I can't believe that two halves and three small Baileys would knock you out. You didn't make a fool of yourself; you just went to sleep in my arms. I was singing you my song, and you went to sleep like a baby."

"Oh, Seth, I feel so mean and reckless. You are going to have to promise to sing your song to me later." She sat up and took the tea, hoping that it would clear her head. "I don't feel too bad really but I don't think I could eat anything yet. You had a bit to drink last night too. You seem to be fine."

"I only had lager, and I drank lots of water last night, so I am ok. I actually slept for four hours, so all in all, it was a good night." He smiled. "I brought you bacon! Mick has been up early cooking breakfast for everyone."

"Oh, dear, I will try to eat in a bit, just let me get this tea down me. Oh my, my hair has gone wild," she said as she tried to pat it down with her free hand.

"You look beautiful, you always do... Jules, it has stopped snowing and it's a beautiful morning. Earlier, I helped clear snow away from the front door. The snow is knee deep and a neighbour said the Lee has frozen over. Can we go and see it before we walk home? I want to take some photos. It's a shame I haven't got the camera with me, but I should get some good shots on the phone."

"Goodness! You have been busy. Yes, of course. Walk home? Oh, my!"

"There are no buses or taxis running and there's more snow predicted." He picked up the phone to check out how long it would take them to walk home. "So, our friend Google Maps says that it will take just under two hours to walk to Waterfall. I would say, because of the deep snow; it will take two and a half, maybe three. Is that ok with you? I don't think Mick wants to take on lodgers. I'm also worried about Sinead too. The stable hands won't be able to get in today and she will need a hand feeding and mucking out all those horses. It's a good job Sinead thought to bring Moss and the other cobs into the barn yesterday, otherwise, we would have had to dig them all out of the snow."

"I'm feeling a lot better, thanks to the tea. I don't mind walking through the snow. It will be fun. What time is it?"

"It's just gone half past seven. It is almost light and the sky is clear, so we should catch sunrise over the Lee. Is it ok if we go when we've had our tea and rolls? Here, please eat, you are going to need some energy. It's going to be hard work walking. I don't mean to make you rush and I know that you are feeling hungover. I think that the fresh air will do you good." He passed to her the bacon roll and she knew that it was going to be difficult to eat it without feeling sick. "What have you got in your roll?"

"Cheese," he said, grinning. "I live for cheese."

They had walked down to the river hand in hand, through knee deep virgin snow. The bridges and river were covered in a white blanket and were picture perfect. She was glad that she was wearing a hat to hide her wild hair. Jules was standing on South Gate Bridge and watched Seth at work. It was so good to see him enjoying himself taking photos. She had no idea where he got his energy from. *He has got his sparkle back.*

The Lee had not frozen over completely and large chunks of ice were floating along the river, shimmering in the morning light. A handful of seagulls swam between the icebergs, looking for food. Seth took several pictures of the river and Jules noticed that he had included a few of her in them. She looked along the road for a place to sit down but did not fancy sitting in snow. She was feeling a little sick. *I shouldn't have drank so much.*

When he returned to her he was beaming. "I think I have got us some great pictures." Then he paused as he saw her face. "You look a bit green."

"I'm fine..." She shook her head. "I'm not. Sorry, Seth; look away." She could feel her stomach churning and then promptly threw up over the edge of the bridge. She stayed there for a moment with her eyes shut until the wave of nausea passed, not willing to see the contents of her stomach on an iceberg. *I shouldn't have had that bacon roll.* All she could remember was the taste of grease on the meat.

"You poor girl, you should have said that you were feeling sick and I would have waited at The Elbow until you felt better. Do you want to go back?"

"I was ok then and it was only in the last few minutes that I felt bad. I actually feel so much better now. I can't eat meat again or drink so much Baileys."

"I feel bad for giving you bacon," he grinned. "If only I had stayed a few moments longer on the river bank, then I could have caught you hurling on camera! That would have been a fine photo for our wall," he said, hugging her.

"Seth!"

"I know, I'm a wicked boyfriend. I have the feeling that you might have a few more moments like this on the way back. I promise you, that by the time we get home, you will be cured. If you need to stop, then I will hold your hair up for you. Come on my gorgeous girl, let's start walking while you are still able to."

It had taken them nearly three hours to get back to Waterfall West. The snow around Waterfall was much deeper than it had been in Cork. Jules had stopped only three times more to be sick and she was in need of a drink of water. As they walked up the drive, May waved to them from an upstairs window and then opened it and leaned out.

"Are you two ok? Sinead said that you got stuck in Cork last night," she called.

"We're fine," he called back. "It's been a bit of a trek home but we survived. I'll clear the path for you later. We're going to help Sinead with the horses first."

"Come and have tea with me this afternoon. I've baked cakes. Lemon drizzle cake! It's your favourite. All the guests were hoping to see you both."

"That sounds grand, we will be over at three."

They continued to wade through the snow and finally made it to the stable yard. It was eerily quiet. The horses seeing them arrive stuck their heads out of their stables and looked at them expectantly. Seth was puzzled. "There are no footprints in the snow. Sinead hasn't been down here yet. It must be gone eleven. I wonder if something has happened to her. Will you check the phone, Jules, and see if she has messaged us?"

Jules put her hand in her pockets. "I haven't got it. You must have it."

"Oh yes, I took those photos. He checked his pockets, found the phone and then looked at it and sighed. "It's dead, we couldn't charge it last night. Let's go and check the mobile; she might have overslept."

The summer field was unrecognizable, and only the tops of the rails and posts of the fencing were exposed. They were surprised to see that the mobile home was almost buried under a snow drift.

Seth shook his head. "The wind must have blown half the snow in Cork this way. The doors and windows are probably frozen shut. At least she will be warm in there. I can see steam coming out of the boiler flu. Sinead is going to be so mad. Brace yourself for a torrent of bad words. I'll go and get some shovels from the yard, and we will dig her out. Are you feeling ok? Do you want to sit in the office for a bit?"

"I'm fine, Seth. Just a bit embarrassed. I actually feel really good now. I'll go and talk to Sinead and tell her that we are here to rescue her. I hope Barney has been good. He doesn't like being shut in. I'm dying to see what he thinks of the snow."

"Ok. See what you can do. I won't be long."

He returned with two shovels and gave one to Jules. "Have you made contact with her yet?"

"Yes, she knows we're here, but I couldn't hear exactly what she was saying. She sounded angry."

He laughed. "That's our Sinead for you!"

Sinead must have heard him and they could hear her sounding off.

After half an hour, they had cleared the snow from the side of the mobile home. Barney appeared from beneath it, stretching his legs and meowing at Jules. He wanted to run to her but after placing a paw on the snowy ground, decided to stay put and meows at her to come and collect him.

"Oh, you poor baby! Did Sinead shut you out?" She went over to him and picked him up to hug him. "There, is that better? Were you sleeping? You are so warm. I'll feed you when we get in."

Seth tried to open the door but it was stuck fast. "Sinead, do you have any deicers in your car?"

"Why the fuck doesn't anyone answer their phones?"

They could hear her clearly now.

"What the fuck is the point of having one, if you don't even look at it? Christ! The temperature in here is nearly a hundred degrees, and still the fucking door won't open!"

Seth looked at Jules and grinned. "She's like a ticking bomb about to explode. Sinead, I'm going to look in your car for some deicer. I won't be a minute."

"Won't you need a key?" Jules asked.

165

"It's not locked, is it Sinead? She's a bit forgetful sometimes."

"You know it's not. Just piss off, Seth!"

While Jules waited for him to return, she thought she would try and calm her down. Still holding Barney, she climbed the step, so she could talk to her without shouting. "Sinead, I'm sorry, we didn't see your messages or calls. The phone ran out of power. We didn't have the charger with us. We had to walk back from Cork and in some places the snow was past our knees. It's really bad in Waterfall and especially bad here."

"I hate fucking Ireland. The weather is ridiculous! I'm going back to England!"

"We'd miss you, Sinead, if you did that. Don't go."

She went quiet for a moment. "I'd miss you both too. Don't listen to me. I am just pissed off and I have cabin fever. Jules, there is so much to do. All the horses need looking after. Is May ok? She didn't even answer my calls!"

"May waved to us when we walked in. I don't think she uses her phone much. Did you try her on the land line? She answers that one."

"No, I didn't think so. Can you see Seth? Are all the cars buried out there?"

"Practically, but you always park in the same place so he will find it. I hope he's quick; I'm bursting for a wee. We will both help you with the chores today."

Seth returned to the mobile home and after soaking the door seals in the fluid, managed to open the door. Sinead was just wearing her shorts and a bra. Her black hair was plastered down around her face. She looked like she had been for a swim.

She smiled at Seth. "I'm sorry I sounded off. I just didn't like being trapped."

"Don't you worry. I'm just glad that you are ok," he said as he gave her a big hug. "You look a fright."

"I so need to go," Jules declared as she squeezed past them with Barney and headed for the bathroom.

Seth shut the door, took off his shoes and coat and put the kettle on. It was really hot, so he turned the thermostat down. "I think we should all stay at the Old Barn tonight. I'll light up the wood burner to warm up the place. Sinead, you can have the sofa bed May gave us and I can build our bed this evening."

Jules came into the lounge.

"What do you say, Jules?" he asked. "Don't you think we should stay in the Old Barn tonight? If there's another snow storm then we could all get trapped in here. I will build the bed, and I am also eager to see if the heat exchanger on the stove heats up the water. What do you think?"

"There's not much furniture and it will feel like we are camping but I think you are right. May won't be able to dig us out here. Yes, that's a great idea. We could stay at the Manor House with May if you prefer."

"No, I'd like to stay in our own home, if that is ok. I know we were planning to move in when we had furnished it properly but it makes sense to stay there tonight at least."

"I'll bring down everything we need, before it starts snowing again and get Barney settled in. When I've done that I'll come and help you with the horses. This will be the first night in our new home. I can't wait."

Chapter Twenty

"It looks ok," Jules declared as she pulled out the lasagne from the new oven. "I think I've got the hang of this cooker already. We will have to eat on our laps, though; until we buy a table." George Ezra was singing Shotgun on the radio and her spirits were high.

Sinead was walking around the old barn, admiring some of the photos on the wall. "Seth took these, didn't he? He's taken some great photos. This is going to be a great place to live. I like the space in here and the kitchen being part of the living area. Open plan living they call it, don't they? It's hot in here. Your wood burner is really warming the place up. It was ridiculously hot in the mobile. We've been so busy today. Thanks for all your help. When I do up the piggery, I am going to do something similar to this. You two will help me, won't you? I haven't got a clue."

"Of course we will. We're nearly done in here. The barn will look so much better when we furnish it properly. Seth is turning into a flat pack king." Barney jumped up on the work surface to be stroked and Jules tutted. "Barney has made himself at home already. You naughty thing! You can't come up here. You'll get fur in the dinner," she said as she picked him up. After hugging him, she put him on the floor.

"I don't want you two to go, but you need your own space. You should stay here from now on. I can still come down for dinner," she said with a cheeky grin.

Seth came out of the bedroom and walked into the kitchen. He was holding the instructions to make up the bed and looked puzzled. "The bed is done," he said. "The thing is, I have some screws left over. Maybe I should have read the instructions first. I've tested the mattress and made up the bed, so we don't have to worry about it later. We're going to be snug as a bug in there. Dinner smells good," he said, inspecting the lasagne. "Is it ready? I'm starving? Where are the plates?"

"I think they are in a box somewhere... I know, they are under the sink," she said, opening the cupboard door. She pulled out the box and put it on the work surface for him to open. "Sinead will you sit on the sofa, and I'll bring some dinner over to you. I have found the trays. I've done garlic bread too."

"Thanks, Jules. You too, Seth. I'm quite happy to sit on the floor," she offered.

"No, I couldn't let you do that," he said.

"I don't mind," Jules said, taking a plate from Seth.

"Are you sure?" he asked. "I'll find you something to sit on. If I sit on the floor, then I don't think I'd get up again. Your old man's body is aching today. I've got flat pack back!"

"It doesn't bother me. I'll sit on a cushion, and I can lean against the arm of the sofa. Oh, look it's snowing again," she said, looking towards the bi fold doors leading to their courtyard garden. Large white flakes floated down. Jules had a vague memory of seeing snowflakes like these covered in a rosebud pattern. *What on earth! You are one crazy woman!*

"I don't think we are going to get much snow tonight. I said that yesterday and look what happened. It's going to warm up soon, but it will take a few days for the roads to be cleared. Is it me or is it boiling in here?" he asked.

"It's perfect, it feels like the tropics," Jules said as she passed them their plates of food.

"Did you bring your shorts, Sinead?" Seth asked with a mischievous grin. "You should be warm enough tonight. I'll put a couple of logs in the burner before we go to bed."

"About that," Sinead said. "I am going to stay with May tonight. Although the Manor House has guests, May stays in the annex all by herself and she could do with a bit of company. It's also Sunday and you two didn't have your usual lie in, did you?" She was smiling. "I know what you two get up to when I am up at the yard on a Sunday morning!"

"I have no idea what you're talking about," he said.

"Oh yes, you do. As well as feeling hot in here the air is also thick with pheromones. The sexual tension between you two is almost tangible tonight. I know that the moment I step outside, you'll be ripping each other's clothes off!"

He was surprised and a little embarrassed. "You really don't have to do that. We might have a cuddle but nothing more than that. I am shocked that you think that there is anything more going on!"

Jules laughed. "Is it that obvious?"

When Sinead left them, she had winked and blown them a kiss. Jules turned the lights down low and stood by the courtyard doors watching the snow fall. "It's so pretty when it snows nicely, don't you think?"

Seth came and joined her. He had taken off his top and had turned off the radio. In a reflection in the door, she could see them side by side watching the snow together. His muscular arms and chest in the half-light put her snow watching on pause as she remembered running her hands over his body. Her heartbeat was starting to pick up as she secretly gazed at his reflection, too captivated to look away.

"I like the snow. My song is about the snow, and it's about when we first met," he said quietly.

"Will you sing it to me?"

"I will, but you've got to promise to stay awake this time. I need to hold you and slow dance with you," he said as he drew her to him.

She could feel his smooth strong chest against her hand. He smelled good, a heavenly mix of citrus and his own unique odour. *Pheromones!* She could feel his heart beating hard. "Don't be nervous, Seth."

"I'm not nervous. I'm just having trouble controlling myself. You don't know what you do to me." *Come on, Seth, sing to the girl.*

As they danced, he sang to her. She could feel his hot breath in her ear.

I watch you from afar
Not knowing who you are
Across golden fields I see you
Do you even know me?
Tell me that you do
I want you to free me
Tell me that you see me.
Tell me that you see me.
See me.

I watched your light go out
What is love about?

I hope you feel the same
Tell me that you do
I want you to free me
Tell me that you see me.
Tell me that you see me.
See me.

I fought for your heart
And after a shaky start
From a hill high above
Now I think you know me
We found a secret love
Tell me that you love me
Tell me that you love me
Love me

We will walk hand in hand
Now we understand
You are my Juliet
And you know you own me
My heart is in your net.
Tell me that you love me
Tell me that you love me
Love me.

I really need to know
Am I waiting for it to snow?
After our first kiss
Did I hear you say you love me?
Those words I didn't miss.

Now you'll always love me
Now you'll always love me
Love me
Now you'll always love me
Now you'll always love me.
Always love me
Will always love me

"Did you like that?" he asked, kissing her neck. "It might need another verse."

"I loved your song. It was about us. We so have to record it. We don't need a record deal. We can still record our own music."

"I thought we could sing that one together."

"Tomorrow, we will..." She could barely get the words out, her whole body was throbbing with desire.

"Jules, I love you," he said as he led her into the bedroom. His heart was beating hard in his chest, and he needed her so much that he was in pain.

For a moment they just stared at each other and then with urgency, they tore each other's clothes off, and discarding them came together. Hungry for each other, they kissed passionately and then tumbled onto the bed, desperate to feel skin against skin. Their hot bodies entwined as they found each other. In a frantic rhythmical dance they became one, each eager to pleasure each other. With their hearts pounding and nerve endings exploding, they could hold back no more and they cried out into the night as their bodies shook with orgasmic pleasure and exhilaration. Lost in each other's being. Out of breath, they smiled at each other, kissed and then holding hands, they lay side by side to recover - spellbound.

It was early when Seth woke and it was still dark outside. He reached for the phone on the floor and disconnected the charging cord. The bedroom was chilly and he shivered. *Oh, it's only four forty, too early to get up. But I should. I need to put some more logs in the burner to warm the house up.*

Jules lay on her side; her bare shoulder was sticking out of the covers and her tattoo was partially exposed. He turned on the torch so he could see the Dara Knot better. Moving her hair to the side, he could see that Sinead had drawn individual leaves on the oak tree and the S and the J had been delicately scribed in a heart. "Beautiful, like you," he whispered as he traced his finger around the heart. She stirred, and Seth ran his hand over her cold shoulder and pulled the duvet over it to keep her warm. He loved the feel of her skin and the shape of her body. *Will you wake and let me make love to you again? No, let her rest. Behave yourself!*

"Can we sleep a bit longer?" she mumbled.

"Sure, we've got a couple of hours yet." He lay back down and stared at the dark sky through the window in the roof, willing sleep to claim him. He sighed. *I can't sleep.* Pleasant memories of their crazy lovemaking flooded his mind. As he thought about it, he realised that they hadn't used protection. *It was just the once. No, actually twice! Our first time as well. Why did I forget to use a condom? Oh dear, that's risky. I don't think she has had a period since we've been together. God! That's more than six months. Could she be pregnant? We need to talk. I'll go and work out and keep my mind occupied until she wakes up.*

Seth got out of bed and looked in a bag of clothes for his gym kit but realised that most of his clothing was still in the mobile home. *We will bring everything else down later.* He put on his boxer shorts and wandered out into the kitchen and lounge area. *This barn is perfect for us.* It reminded him of an art gallery.

Barney was asleep on the sofa. Hearing Seth getting himself some water, he meows at him and then stood up, stretched and jumped off the sofa, ready for his breakfast. "You'll get nothing from me, until your Mam wakes up." Seth put two logs in the burner and then got on the floor ready to do some chin ups. Barney walked over to him and started rubbing himself along his side. Seth laughed "That tickles, no, don't. Christ! Ok, I'll feed you then." Seth was sitting cross-legged on the floor and stroked Barney's fur. He meowed, enjoying being loved. "You're welcome."

Jules came out of the bedroom, bleary eyed and was looking for the bathroom. She was wearing his t-shirt and was looking hot. "Morning, beautiful, are you looking for me?"

"Oh Seth, I forgot where I was for a moment. I was looking for the bathroom. I know where it is now," she said as she turned around and walked off towards it.

Seth got up from the floor and found the bag of cat biscuits. Holding his breath, he tipped the chicken biscuits into the cat bowl and went back into the bedroom to wait for Jules. *I need to ask her if she is pregnant. I don't think she is. I would know, surely?*

The living area was quiet when Jules came out of the bathroom. Barney was sitting on the sofa washing himself. As she walked into the bedroom, she saw Seth sat on the side of the bed. He smiled at her, but she could tell that there was something on his mind.

"Come and sit next to me. I want to ask you something."

175

Jules sat next to him but she was starting to get worried. "Is everything ok?"

"Oh dear, do I look that serious? Everything is grand."

"What's the matter then?"

"I just wanted to know. This is hard to say, and I don't know why I haven't asked before. We've had unprotected sex twice now and I've been thinking. You don't seem to have had a period since we've been together." *Ok, just let her answer. Let's not jump to any conclusions. She's colouring up. Is she going to cry? Oh God, she's crying. What did I say?*

Jules took in a deep breath and tried not to cry but she couldn't help herself. *What is wrong with me? Why am I crying?* She had to explain to him why this was but he might not like what he was about to hear.

"Don't cry, please don't cry. If you think that you are pregnant then that is fine."

"No, Seth. It's unlikely I am pregnant. I don't... I don't eat enough to have periods. The doctor said..." Memories of doctors asking her personal things, questioning her about her eating habits and lack of calories overwhelmed her. She had been angry with them. Angry that they were accusing her of being anorexic. Angry with herself for choosing not to hear them. "Look, Seth, I haven't been hiding this from you. From myself yes, but not from you. You know what I'm like. I have been trying to eat better. In fact, I have never felt better about eating and I am actually enjoying being a vegetarian. I do have trouble dealing with putting weight on, but you make things feel so much better when you say you like the way I look. I don't know if I've made myself infertile by being underweight but if I have then I am sorry. I want to have children with you but because I'm so stupid it might not happen. I'd understand if you wanted to end it. No, I wouldn't. Please don't do that," she sobbed.

"Christ, no! Don't be daft. I'd never dump you. It doesn't matter if we don't have children. As long as I have you in my life, then that is all that matters. Please don't cry."

Chapter Twenty-one

The wintery weather had lasted until the end of February, making running a riding school and getting supplies in difficult. It was March, and spring was edging its way in. The last of the ice, in defeat, had seeped into the thawing earth and was eagerly embraced by thirsty roots. New life began to breathe in the hedgerows, in the fields and in the darkest of places.

Jules was busy at the Manor House changing beds. She had six more bedrooms to clean before midday, before a coach load of American guests arrived, keen to explore Cork. She made the bed and with her hand, she ran it over the white duvet until she was satisfied that every crinkle had gone. Pleased with her work, she picked up her drinks bottle and drank the cool water. The sun was shining into the room and she was feeling hot.

Jules looked out of the window to check on the sheets that she had hung out to dry earlier that morning. *There's nothing better than the smell of air dried linen.* The sheets billowed gently in a breeze. *I'll have to bring those in before the guests get here.* She could see the stable yard in the distance. *I wonder how Seth is getting on? It's another busy day for him. At least we have Sunday off together. Just two more days to go.*

The Manor House and the riding school had been very busy since the snow had gone and the horses were eager to work after their winter rest. Sinead and Seth had asked her if she wanted to teach at the school, but she had declined. She would have to go on a training course, and she didn't think she could be as confident as Seth and Sinead were when they taught. Jules was also really enjoying working for May, and she liked having the afternoons off to do as she pleased. After work, she spent the time cleaning their lovely new home, reading, listening to music and finding and learning new songs for them to sing at The Elbow. They had managed to get into Cork for two gigs since the snow had gone. They had sung Seth's new song together and had got a round of applause. She had seen Seth beam with pride and her heart had melted at seeing him so happy.

May, apart from being a great boss, was also turning out to be a good friend. Since Tom had gone, May had been concerned about her and constantly apologised for his wicked ways. Jules had told her not to worry and that she had moved on. Over time, her tale of why she and Seth had fled to Ireland had leaked out. She hoped that Seth wouldn't mind her telling May everything. She had made her promise not to say anything to him. May had listened to her and given her support and practical advice. For her, talking to her new friend about their troubled past had helped heal her soul. *I have no regrets in confiding in her. I didn't realise how much I needed to talk.*

With the bedrooms done, Jules walked out of the laundry room and into the back garden to collect the sheets from the lines. They looked white and crisp and as she ran her fingers over them she thought about the white wedding dress she had bought in Cork. She had spotted it in a charity shop and had immediately fallen in love with it. The dress was simple and had a low neckline with small puff sleeves. It had fitted her perfectly. The dress reminded her of the garments that Elizabeth had worn in Pride and Prejudice. She wasn't sure what she was supposed to wear to a handfasting and hoped it wasn't too much. She had told Seth about the dress, and he had kissed her and said that she could wear whatever she wanted but she might have to wear thermal underwear as April could be cold. This was not quite the ethereal look she had in mind. She had asked him what he would wear and he had laughed and said that his white shirt, black jeans and his snow jacket should be suitable for a hilltop.

Not knowing exactly what a handfasting ceremony was, she had Googled the word 'handfasting' and had discovered that it was a simple ceremony where country folk bound their wrists together with a braided cord and literally tied the knot to commit themselves to each other. Unable to find a hill with a view that meant anything to them, they had decided to hold the ceremony in the summer field with Moss and the other cobs. Seth's brown eyes had lit up when she had suggested it. *He is such a dear thing.*

Sinead was going to carry out this ritual for them. The only drawback of handfasting was that to make it legal, they would have to be married by a registrar after or before the ceremony. Seth was happy with just being handfasted. Jules thought differently, but hadn't said anything and had decided to see if she could find a registrar that didn't require them to show identification documents. *I would like it all to be legal.*

After Jules had put sheets through the press, she folded them and then left them in a neat pile in the linen cupboard. It was nearly lunchtime when she finished work and she was starving. All she could think about was eating cheese and pickle sandwiches, and she put this down to Seth's obsession with cheese. *He is happy when he sees me eat. I have to get over always wanting to be thin. But I fear that we are fast becoming two cheese eating monsters!* She sighed and knew that Seth and Sinead had been working through their lunch breaks to cover all their bookings. *I'll check the book in the office and see. You never know, Seth might have half an hour free.*

May was in the office and she was taking a call. She sounded angry and slammed the phone down. "That's the third time!"

"Is everything ok?"

May jumped when she realised Jules was stood by her. "Oh, my! I didn't see you there. That was one of those 'you've been in a car accident' calls again. It's not like you can tell them you don't want them to call anymore as you have to talk to a blooming robot!"

Jules laughed. "We get those too, but we don't answer them and let them go to answer phone. We only have your and Sinead's number in our phone. They do make us nervous though as each time we think it could be the police. May, everything is ready for the guests this afternoon. Do you need me to do anything else?"

"No, pet. You keep on top of things so well that I barely have anything left to do myself. I don't know what I'd do without you. I was going to put something by you. Before I got ill, I had been in the process of getting the Manor House licensed so people could be married in the orangery. I sent off the application yesterday and if you wanted to make your marriage legal, then I could get a friend of mine, who is a registrar, to marry you in the orangery before you are handfasted. I will vouch for you both. I'm sure the police don't check the registers to see if their escapees have got married. What do you think?"

Jules grinned. "I was just thinking about looking for a registrar. I love that idea. I hope Seth does too. I just came to see if he was free for lunch. If he is going to have a break soon, then I will ask him."

May looked at the day's riding schedule and shook her head. "He has lessons all day. Sinead too. That's no good. They will burn themselves out if they carry on like this. I can take both one o'clock lessons. They are easy ones, and I am sure Mrs. Clarke and Jack won't mind letting me teach them together. It will be good to help out and teach again. I have missed it."

"If you're sure. You know Seth will protest."

"He will, but he will do as he is told. He's got to rest." She flicked through the book, looking at the lessons. "Goodness! The riding school is booked up for weeks. They really need to take on another instructor."

Jules felt a bit guilty for not wanting to learn to become one. *I'll have a look at the course again.*

"I'll have a chat with them this evening about hiring someone," May said as the phone rang. "Let's hope it's not one of those nuisance calls again. You go and make them some lunch, and I'll send them down to you."

Seth kicked off his riding boots and left them on the doorstep outside of the barn. Sinead did the same. They were both laughing as they walked into the kitchen. Sinead's hair was now a bright red and it glistened in the sunlight.

Jules was sitting at the table and was watching a film. She had made them a huge pile of cheese and pickle sandwiches and alongside the plate was an even larger pile of crisps. She pressed pause and smiled. "You look like two naughty school kids. Did May tell you off then for working too hard?"

"She certainly did. I guess we should think about hiring someone else. It's not good to do long shifts without a break," Seth said as he kissed her hello. "How's my wife-to-be? I've missed you."

"She's missing you too. I've had a good day. I've decided that I will train to be an instructor but it might take me a while before I am ready. In the meantime, you should hire someone to give you both more time off."

"You sweet girl. I knew you'd come around to the idea eventually," he said, hugging her.

Sinead washed her hands in the kitchen sink. "I can't believe that you two are still like love sick puppies. Perhaps when you are wed then you will calm down. I've never been to a handfasting, let alone marry someone. What do I have to say?"

"I'll think of a little speech. It will only be a few words. Jules and I will write something tonight for you to practice. Don't panic, though."

"I'll try not to but I might need to read from a piece of paper as I know I will forget what to say. I can barely remember what happened five minutes ago. Do you have to have someone to give you away?"

"No, only if you want to. There are no rules. Jules, do you want someone to walk you to me?"

She hadn't thought about it. Her Dad's face popped into her mind but then she imagined him crying as he walked by her.

"Jules?"

"May can walk with me. I'll probably have to hold her up. The summer field is lumpy, and she isn't that good on her feet. Yes, I'd like May to walk me to you. Oh, I was going to tell you. May has a registrar friend that will marry us legally in the orangery first. She will ask no questions. I'd like to do that if it's ok with you. Do the police get notified if a fugitive gets married?"

"I'm not sure. But thinking about it, making it legal does make sense. I'll talk to May about it later."

"How about you, Seth?" Sinead asked. "Do you need a best man?"

"No, I can make it there myself." He then thought about Charlene. "I would love my sister Charlene to be at the handfasting. I'd be stoked if she could make it. But it is what it is."

"I guess I'd like my brother to be there too," Jules said. "Somehow, I don't think my Dad would want to come. I wish we could tell them, at least. Tell them that we are ok and perhaps give them the chance to come over if they wanted to."

Seth sighed. "There is a way we could contact them."

"How? If we call them, then that might put us at risk."

"It's been nearly six months since you came over here and they haven't caught up with you yet," Sinead said. "The police probably have bigger fish to fry now. You are not Bonnie and Clyde."

"You say that, but if my Dad's body is found, then it will make them look even harder for me. They will think it very fishy that I absconded on the day that he went missing," Seth said.

"You don't think that, do you?" Jules asked. "Your family wouldn't report him missing to the police. Your mother, Margaret, was happy that he drowned."

"I'd be lying if it hadn't crossed my mind."

"It would be good if we could talk to Charlene and find out what happened after we left. I feel bad that we left her with so much to deal with," Jules said as she picked up a sandwich.

"I know, I do too. I was thinking that we could go and see my aunt and granny in Dingle. My aunt has all my family's contact numbers. I know she has Charlene's number. If anything happens to Granny, then she will ring Charlene rather than Margaret. Aunt Bridie and Margaret don't speak to each other anymore. You wouldn't think that they were sisters. Some of my brothers and sisters say that something bad happened in Dingle, and that was the reason that my warped parents came to live in Sussex."

"Now there's a surprise," Jules said as she nibbled on her sandwich. "How far away from us is Dingle?"

"Have a look on Google Maps," he said as he looked at his dirty hands. "I better wash these before I eat. I'm just going to use the bathroom too. I won't be a minute."

Jules looked up Dingle on Maps. "Heavens! Dingle is a remote village on the west coast. The village is surrounded on three sides by the Atlantic. The land looks like an island," she said, showing Sinead the screen. "Dingle has got an aquarium, though," she said, laughing. She clicked on 'Directions' and typed in Waterfall to Dingle.

Seth returned to the table, sat down and picked up a sandwich and a couple of crisps. "So, how long will it take us to get there from here?"

"Three hours and thirty-six minutes if we start at Bishopstown. We will need two buses, including the number forty, the bus we took, when we first got here. Could we do that trip in a day?"

"I think we should go up there on Saturday evening after work, stay in a bed and breakfast and then visit them on Sunday when they come back from church. We haven't got a gig at The Elbow this weekend. Sinead, you wouldn't mind feeding Barney, would you?"

"Of course not. I'll drop you two off at Bishopstown as well."

"Thanks. I'm kind of looking forward to seeing my granny again. She's got a soft spot for me."

Jules typed in 'hotel' and Maps showed her two hostels. "There are a couple of hostels in Dingle. We could stay there. Do you think they will be open this time of year?"

"They are sure to be. I would have suggested that we stay with my aunt, but she is a strict Catholic woman and we would have to sleep separately. They live in a tiny fishing cottage so there really is no room for us. Although my granny managed to bring up eight children in that house. I don't know how she did it."

"I'd prefer to stay in a hostel. I am starting to feel worried about seeing your aunt. She sounds a bit scary. I hope she likes me."

"She is sound and my granny is hilarious. There is one thing that is bothering me. It will be interesting to see if the police have been round there. If they have, then it is going to be hard to explain to Aunt Bridie why the police are after me."

"Seth, just tell her the truth," Sinead said.

"Maybe I will. We will see. I need to bring her some good strong Irish cheese and then her cold heart will soften."

Not cheese again! Jules thought as she helped herself to another cheese sandwich.

***

I will not rest until I lie with you again. I am sorry for the pain I have caused you. Please forgive me. I love you

Chapter Twenty-two

Heavily pregnant ewes with thick winter coats spilled out onto the lane and stopped the bus from reaching Casement Station on time. Jules and Seth had waited for over ten minutes as a farmer herded the nervous animals into the next field. The bus driver had tutted and had called out to him to get a move on. The farmer had cursed. *So not all the Irish are friendly.* Jules thought as she briefly came round from her snooze.

They ran for the 275 bus at Casement Station, and out of breath, they had climbed aboard ready for the second part of their journey to Dingle. The bus was busy and had standing room only. Jules couldn't find anywhere to hold onto, so she clung to Seth who had grabbed a rail above his head. Smiling, he put his other arm around her to keep her from falling over. The bus sped along and the people in the bus chatted happily to each other. *The Irish people are so talkative.*

Jules noticed a young teenage girl staring at them. *She's checking Seth out!* He was daydreaming and was unaware of the attention he was getting. Horrified, Jules held onto him a little tighter and hoped that the girl would find someone else to stare at.

At the next stop, a handful of people, including the teenage girl, left the bus. Jules and Seth managed to find a seat together. They had just under an hour's journey to Dingle and both were feeling tired.

Seth slid down in his seat, folded his arms and was ready to shut his eyes. As well as teaching all day, he had been showing Luke, a stable hand, how to take a lesson. Luke had his own horse at the stables and was interested in becoming a part-time instructor. *It's going to be good to have a third person taking the classes. Sinead and I are on our knees.*

Jules and Seth had slept part of the way on the first bus, but he still felt tired. He checked that Jules was ok and could see that she was listening to music. *She still looks tired too. She will be asleep again soon.* He didn't want them to miss their stop. "I need to shut my eyes again. Would you set an alarm to wake me up in fifty minutes? I'm sorry, I'm not much company tonight."

Jules pulled an earphone out of her ear, and she smiled sympathetically at him. "You poor lamb, of course I will." She set the timer and then snuggled into him and he put his arm around her and drew her close. As she settled, she plugged the loose earphone into his ear. "Now we can both listen to chill out music while we sleep."

"That's perfect," he said sleepily. He could smell her sweet hair and feel her warm body next to his. "I love you," he whispered as he drifted off into a deep sleep.

It was after nine when they got to Dingle and the streets were dark and quiet. Seth breathed in the cool Dingle air to see if he remembered what it smelled like. *I can smell the sea. Dingle smells like Dingle.* As he walked, he put on his back a small backpack which held their overnight things. Also in the bag were two beers, a storage box with some cold pizza inside and another with a large wedge of Cork Coolea Cheese for his aunt and granny. They planned to heat the pizza up in a microwave when they got to the hostel. *It was a good call to bring food with us as all the shops we have walked past are closed.*

"I hope the hostel staff haven't all gone to bed," Jules said. "I feel bad coming here so late. It's weird but I don't feel like we've been travelling for three and a half hours. I don't know where the evening has gone to. Did we time travel?"

"Maybe," he said. "I think we might have been asleep the whole way here. That makes the time fly by. The hostel will have night staff on. Hostels don't really close, although I wouldn't like to check in after eleven. This is Dykegate Street. The reviews say that the Grapevine hostel will give you a lovely welcome. Let's see if they do."

"I don't think I can sleep now," Jules said as she zipped up her jacket. "After we have had our pizza, shall we watch a movie? I remember the password for Dad's Netflix account. We haven't watched a film together for ages. We could always watch Paul."

Seth laughed. "I remember what happened the last time we tried to watch that film. Is Paul the code word for you want me?" he asked.

"Maybe," Jules replied. Then she smiled. "Definitely!"

***

Jules and Seth were standing hand in hand, on a very windy Inch Beach. They were alone apart from the odd bird that ran along the edge of the sea looking for food. The wind blew fine sand along the shore and spread sand grains over their shoes. The sun was out but the wild wind had a cold bite to it, making them shiver. With her free hand, Jules tried to control her hair and then gave up, allowing the wind to do its worst.

Seth watched a small white boat navigating its way around the spit head. The water was choppy, and the boat was struggling to get out to sea. "We should go on a boat one day, but not today. It is too rough. There's lots of islands to visit around here. When the weather is better, perhaps in the summer, we could take a boat to Inishtooskert and watch whales."

"I'd like to do that."

"We could spend some of the day here and swim. I remember coming to this beach when I was small."

"Did you make sandcastles?" she asked as she turned to face the wind so he could see her face.

"Yes, I did. I must have been three or four. I remember swimming in the sea and playing football on the beach with my brothers and sisters. I also remember Charlene crying because a seagull had eaten her sandwich. It was a hot day. A really hot day and the sand was too hot to walk on without shoes. I remember waiting for the bus home. I was burnt to a crisp, and my shoes were full of sand. Those were happy days. Apart from that, I can only remember playing in the fields around our farm north of Dingle. When I look around Dingle today, it is all new to me. The only street I know is the one that my granny and my aunt live on. Slea Head Drive is not far from here. They should be back from church by now. Are you ready to meet them, my sweet girl? I am feeling nervous and excited at the same time. I don't know why."

"It's been a few years, hasn't it? You will be fine once you start talking to them."

The houses that lined the streets of Dingle were all brightly painted. The small houses, painted blue, red or green, with the odd white house between, reminded Jules of Brighton. She thought Dingle was a pretty seaside village and she liked the way it smelled. Brighton and the beach at Worthing were just a vague memory now.

Seth took a deep breath and knocked on the door. Silently, they waited for Aunt Bridie to open the door. Jules squeezed his hand to reassure him. The door opened slowly and a tiny grey-haired woman, wearing smart clothes, peeped out. She gasped when she saw Seth and her eyes widened with alarm.

"Oh, for the love of God! You've just missed her. Only five minutes ago, I prayed that I would see you alive again, Seth Hearn. Come in quickly, before she sees you. You too, dear. Oh, my days! Thank goodness you are safe. Thank the Lord you are both alive!"

"We are sound, Aunt Bridie. What's happened?"

Bridie led them into a tiny reception room, and cautiously, she lifted the net curtains and looked out into the street. She shook her head and sighed and then turned around to face them. "It's been thirty years since I last spoke to my sister Margaret and today of all days, she turns up on my doorstep. You missed her by five minutes. I don't know what to do, Seth. I can't let her hurt you. Who is Ann? Are you Ann?" she asked Jules.

"No, I'm Julia. Jules actually. Did you say Margaret? Do you mean Margaret Hearn? Oh, my God! She knows that we are alive!"

Bridie nodded, her face was twitching with anxiety. "Seth, what did you do to Ann and Jethro?"

Seth was confused. He looked up at the picture of Jesus over the mantelpiece. He remembered looking up at the picture as a child and wondering why he looked so sad.

"What is going on?"

"Bridie, this is going to take some time to explain. I have done nothing to Ann or Jethro. Ann died nearly twenty years ago. Jethro drowned last year. So you say Margaret was here?"

"Why do you call her by her name now? Oh, Seth, I saw her turn into a monster before my eyes. She is not the sister I once knew. She scared me. You look white, Seth. Sit down, and I'll make us a cup of tea. You too, dear. Jules, you say. I'm sorry that you find us not at our best."

"Bridie, Jules is my fiancée. We are going to be married on the nineteenth of April. We are living in Waterfall now. Do you remember I used to live there a few years ago?"

"Oh dear, yes I do. I told her that you might be in Cork. She seemed desperate to find you. At first she was charming and then when I told her to go... She turned on me. I could smell alcohol on her breath and she came in a car! On God's day! This is all too awful. I hope I haven't caused you any problems."

Seth sighed. "It's not your fault. She is one evil woman. I think you need to sit down. I'll tell you what happened in a moment. We will make the tea. Where's Granny?"

"She's in the kitchen getting the vegetables ready for lunch. You must both stay for lunch. Please don't tell her any of this. Her blood pressure is sky high at the moment, and she won't take her tablets."

"Granny?" Seth called out as they walked into the small kitchen at the back of the house. A tiny grey-haired old lady with no teeth was sitting on a stool at the end of a kitchen table, peeling sprouts. She looked up and smiled.

"So the wandering traveller boy returns. Come and give your granny a hug. It's been too long." She gave Jules a quick look up and down. "So when is the wedding?"

Seth hugged her and smiled. "This is Jules, my fiancée. You should know when the wedding is. It's soon. It is next month on the nineteenth. There will be a full pink moon on that day. I want both you and Bridie to come if you can."

"So you have been listening to your old granny then. Your marriage will last until you both pass and you will have plenty of strong children. You must make sure the light of the moon shines on your arse when you fuck on your wedding night."

"Granny! You are too much and are making me blush."

Jules smiled. *She really is something else! She's a bit crude, though.* A moment of laughter had been replaced by a gnawing pain inside her stomach as the reality of the situation sank in. *Mad Margaret Hearn is looking for us. Looking for Ann!*

Seth made a pot of tea, put it on a tray with cups and saucers and covered the teapot with a hand knitted cosy. He asked Granny if she wanted tea and she shook her head and pointed to a large glass of sherry on the table. "Keeps me oiled," she said, laughing. "I'll do a little extra if you too are staying."

"Yes, please, but no meat for me. I have some lovely Cork cheese for you both in my bag."

"You eat like a peasant. Your sperm won't be able to swim if you don't eat meat."

"You're being embarrassing again. My poor wee dote is going pink listening to you."

"Take no notice of her," Seth said as he walked up the stairs. "She is really quite nice most of the time. Jules, I'm going to tell Bridie everything but not about going to prison. Is that ok?" he whispered.

"You don't need to tell her that, it's not relevant."

Jules was sitting in an armchair that had lace arm covers and a lace antimacassar over the back of it. She looked at the needle work and wondered if the two women spent their evenings making lace. The room smelt of furniture polish. The dark wooden furniture in the small room had been polished until it glistened. She looked at Bridie and could see that she was nervous as she was wringing her hands.

"Seth, there is something I should have told you a long time ago," Bridie announced. "Now that Jethro is dead, I am not afraid to tell you a little about what went on here. First, I need to know why Margaret is looking for you. Who is Ann? Margaret is eager to find her," she asked as she poured the tea with a shaking hand.

Seth looked around the room, hoping that someone would come forward and tell the story for him. He didn't really want to talk about their past life as he had managed to put all the anguish and pain in a box in the far corner of his mind. "This is hard for me to talk about, Bridie. Ann is Jules's aunt. She had an affair with Dad eighteen years ago and they produced a son, Jake. Margaret couldn't handle her best friend having an affair with Dad and killed her. They left her body in a deep pool in woodland on Farm End. Margaret decided to bring up Jake herself as Jules's uncle wanted nothing to do with him."

"Did Margaret tell you this?"

"She told both of us. Jules looks very much like her Aunt Ann and for some reason, Margaret and my Dad thought that Jules is really Ann and that she has risen from the dead to haunt them both."

"That woman is unhinged!" Bridie said angrily.

"On Patrick's fortieth birthday, my Dad tricked Jules and got her to meet him in the woods by the pond. Still thinking Jules was Ann, he nearly raped her. I came along just in time and knocked him into the pond. We fought and he drowned. I just survived." He looked up at the picture of Jesus and hoped that he understood. "Margaret..."

"You poor dear. Go on, Seth."

"Margaret came down to the pond and pushed Jules into it, still believing her to be Ann and wanted rid of her. The pond has steep sides, and we couldn't get out of it. She left us both to die. Before she went, she told us that she had murdered Ann and also said that she was sick of having to look after Jethro's illegitimate children. She was glad that Jethro was dead. She also said that she was not my mother."

Seth took a sip of tea and shook his head. "We managed to tread water until morning and then Jake and Jules's brother Peter pulled us out. I can't call her Mam anymore. She left us there to die. We both feared for our lives and fled here to Ireland. I hoped that she thought we had drowned, but she obviously knows that we are alive."

"You reap what you sow," Granny announced. She was standing in the doorway and had her fists on her hips. "I should have drowned Margaret at birth! She came out feet first and I knew she would be trouble."

"Mam, she wasn't all bad. When I gave Seth to her when he was born, she took him on willingly. She had eight of her own by then and another one didn't make much of a difference. Seth, I couldn't keep you. Single mothers and illegitimate children were frowned upon in those days."

He was shocked and was lost for words for a moment. He looked at Jules with wide eyes and then looked back at Bridie. "So you are my mother?"

"I am, Seth, dear."

"Is Jethro my Dad?"

"Yes, I am afraid he is," she said in a quiet voice.

"So the bastard is dead!" Granny declared. "Thank the good Lord for that! There never was a man that I hated more.

195

Margaret, or you Bridie for that matter, should never have taken up with him. He must have slept with every fertile woman in Dingle. One night the men of the village joined up and ran him out of town. They should have cut it off there and then! Margaret sold the farm and they moved to England. I stayed at Crow Farm for a while and helped Margaret with the kids and then when I saw that she was coping, I came back to Ireland. I couldn't look Jethro in the eye, but I certainly told him what I thought of him. It sounds like he carried on much the same there. Good riddance to bad rubbish, I say!"

"Mam!"

"Don't Mam me. So Seth, are you feeling any better for knowing the truth?"

"Not really. I don't know what to think. I can't believe Bridie is my Mam. I should be angry with you both but I'm not. This is all so surreal."

Jules sipped her sweet tea, hoping it would soothe her. She was worried about Seth and as shocked as he was. She studied Bridie's face to see if she could see any resemblance. She had pale blue eyes, a delicate nose and gaunt sunken cheeks. *No, I'd never have guessed that she is his mother. He looks like Jethro.* "So what do you think we should do about Margaret?" Jules asked them. "Why has she come after us? It's nearly been six months since we left Sussex. We have kept her dirty secrets and not gone to the police. I'm scared for us."

"She is not in her right mind," Bridie said as she walked to the window and lifted the net curtain to make sure she wasn't outside. "I don't think you could reason with her. I would tread carefully from now on."

"Don't worry, Jules, if she bothers us in Waterfall then we will deal with her," Seth said, taking her hand. "She needs psychological help. Bridie, can I get Charlene's number off you and give her a call from here. I'll leave some money on the side. When I left Crow Farm, I forgot my phone so I haven't got any numbers with me."

"My poor wee boy. Of course you can and you don't have to give us money for the call. It's the least we can do," Bridie said as she walked over to a side table. Out of a drawer, she produced an address book and passed it to him. "Charlene is under H."

"Thanks, Bridie. I wonder if Charlene knows what is going on."

Granny tutted. "It's a crying shame that it has turned out this way. Now I know why the tarot cards have been out of sorts. You two must keep your babies safe. Don't let her take them."

***

I will find you and you will hear me!

Chapter Twenty-three

Charlene's phone rang and then went through to her messaging service. Seth left a message to call him on Bridie and granny's number and was just about to sit down when his sister returned his call. He ran back into the hall and picked up the phone. "Charlene?"

"Yes, it's me. Oh, it's so good to hear your voice, Sweetie."

"Yours too. Jules and I are at Aunt Bridie and Granny's and I have put you on the speaker phone. I've told them what happened to us."

Their phone was old and had large buttons and a chord. Granny mumbled something about missing a phone you could dial on. Bridie and Granny were, however, amazed that they were all able to talk to Charlene without speaking through the handset.

"Oh thank goodness, you two are ok. I have been so worried. Seth, Mam has gone. She's packed her clothes and took a taxi somewhere. Patrick says she has gone on business, but I know he is worried about her. He's been a complete donkey's arse since you left. I think Mam has gone to Dingle looking for you two. She doesn't stop talking about you and Ann. Jake or I didn't say anything, I promise. It was her that followed us down to Southampton on the day you left. It was a shock to see her in the car park. I didn't know she could drive. She saw you speed off in her car." Charlene was about to cry.

"It's ok, don't cry. She doesn't know we are at Granny's. She was here earlier and is on her way to Cork to find us. She doesn't know we are staying at Waterfall West."

"Mam said that she wanted to drive us home in my car but she lied and followed you all the way to Fishbourne. I couldn't stop her. I asked her where Dad was, and she said that she didn't know. She's told everyone that he has left her."

"Charlene, it's Jules."

"Oh my! I'm sorry, Sweetie. It's been a hard few months. Mam has not been herself. I think she is sorry for what she did to you both. Are you ok, Jules? I've missed you two so much."

"Charlene, we really are ok. Thank you for everything you've done. I can't imagine what life at Crow Farm has been like for you. We feel bad for leaving you with so many problems. We wanted to speak to you before now, but we didn't have your number. Please will you tell Peter and Dad that we are ok?"

"Of course I will, Sweetie."

"Is Dad out of hospital yet?"

"Yes, Peter says he is having counselling sessions. Your Dad is working in the new farm shop. We get all our cheese and butter from them. They both miss you too. Your Dad thinks you are backpacking around the world. Jake is doing a grand job with Connor, but he still gets drunk now and then. Peter has to look after the horses sometimes. I think that Jake and Peter both have a broken heart. They miss Ivy and have become good friends. How bizarre is that?"

"You sound tired, Charlene. Are you ok?" Seth asked.

"I am fine, Sweetie. Just a little tired but that's because Joe and I are having a baby. We are having another boy soon. The baby is due on the twenty-second of April."

"That's wonderful news. We were hoping you might be able to come to our wedding on the nineteenth of April," Seth said. "I guess you will want to be at home if the baby is due."

"I usually go past my due date. We will be in Killarney the weekend before that. Joe's parents are having their fiftieth wedding anniversary. We could stay on and then come to your wedding. Where is it going to be held?"

"At Waterfall West. In the Manor House's orangery and then outside, by Moss's field for a hand-fastening ceremony."

Charlene laughed. "I might have guessed. I would love to come, but it will be cutting it fine. As long as Finn doesn't come early, then we will be there. Maureen is going to look after the kids for me while we are away. I am sure she won't mind looking after them for a few more days. Little Bryony might have something to say about that. She is quite a drama queen these days!"

"I'll keep my fingers crossed," Seth said. "I'll text you our phone number, so we can keep in touch. You and Joe can stay with us. We have our own place now."

"I'd like that. Jules, do you want me to tell your Dad and brother about the wedding?"

"It's ok. I don't think they will be able to leave the farm. I don't want Dad to know that I am not travelling. Tell Peter please, and I will let him decide if Dad can handle me marrying Seth. I hope you and Joe can make it. I've been longing to see you again."

"Charlene, we're going to be at the wedding too," Bridie announced.

"Oh Aunt Bridie, I forgot you were there. How are you and Granny?"

"We're fine, dear. Today has not been the best of days but we are bearing up," replied Bridie.

"I love you, Granny."

Granny smiled. "You're a good apple. I'll see you at the wedding. I'm going now, I've got to check on the roast. Kiss all my grandchildren for me. How many do I have now?"

"More than twenty, I think."

"You are all breeding like rabbits! There must be something in the water."

"Bye, Granny."

"Charlene, I will ring again soon. There are a few things I want to ask you and there is lots to tell. Take care," Seth said, smiling.

"Seth, be careful. Mam is ill and could be dangerous."

"Don't worry. Now we know she is looking for us, then we can be prepared if she turns up. Bye, Charlene. Love you lots."

***

Jules and Seth, waited for the bus to Cork at a very dreary Casement bus station. It had started to rain. Seth was deep in thought. The first bus had been too busy to discuss the morning's events. Seth needed a hug, and he pulled Jules to him. There was nobody around, so no one was going to stare. "I need a hug, please. It's been quite a day."

Jules hugged and kissed him, and he held her, not willing to let her go. She didn't mind and was happy to be in his arms. "How are you feeling?"

"The same; still numb inside. I can't get over how matter of fact Bridie was when she told me that she was my mother. She didn't seem to regret what she did or show any emotion when she told me."

"Bridie had no choice. That was how it was back then. I guess if your aunt is a devout Catholic, then she would have brought shame on the family. You have kept in touch with her, so she got to see you and knew that you were doing well. I know it's sad."

"You're probably right. I could never call her Mam, though."

"You don't have to. She doesn't expect you to. At least Bridie is a normal mother and not an unhinged, crazy woman like Margaret. Do you think she will be waiting for us when we get back to Waterfall?"

"No, she doesn't know we are there as she would have gone to Waterfall instead of coming to Dingle to look for us. She knows I have a horse, but I don't think I told her where I kept him. She will probably stay in Cork for a few days and ask around. This might sound strange but I want to talk to her. I need to make her understand that you are not Ann. She has to leave you alone. Why does she want to see Ann, when she left her to die in that pool? She is not sorry."

"Who knows, she has become obsessed with Ann. She sounds psychotic. I am glad that nobody reported your Dad as being missing. That is one less headache to deal with. Where do you think she will stay?"

"I don't know; a hotel perhaps? I can't actually remember her leaving the farm, except when she went shopping and Dad always drove her to Asda. It is really odd that she has travelled this far. I had no idea she could drive, either. I really don't recognise her anymore."

"If she drove over here in your Dad's old black car, then we could check all the hotel car parks to see if it is there. It's raining, so I doubt that she will be out visiting Cork's tourist attractions. We could have a look when we get to Cork and see if we can find out where she is staying. We could pay her a visit. Why don't we?"

He laughed. "You so should have been a detective. I would never have thought to do that. I don't think we need to hunt her down. I don't want to be dragging my lovely fiancée through the wet streets of Cork looking for a nutter. Why don't we get a Chinese takeaway instead? I already told Sinead that we will get a taxi back tonight. She said she would collect us, but I feel bad that I keep asking her to ferry us around. If only we could get a car."

"May said that she would teach me to drive. Sinead did too but she has been so busy. I wouldn't be able to take a test here without giving out my personal details but it would still be good to learn. We've got two hours on this bus before we get to Cork. I hope it comes soon. I'm starving. I've never had a Chinese takeaway before. An Indian but not a Chinese."

"You're kidding me! In that case, I will select only the finest dishes for my sweet girl. Sweet and sour chicken, perhaps?"

"Hold the chicken, Seth, just tofu, vegetables and rice will do. Do they do that? I'll have what you're having. Your aunt was disappointed that I didn't eat any lamb. I couldn't face it."

"You do know that all the healthy eating you are doing is making you look fantastic. I know you don't like to hear that but it's true."

"Thank you, Seth. I am a lot happier with myself these days." *If only it were completely true.*

***

I saw the bastard force you into that taxi and I feel for you, Ann. Do you see my headlights?

Chapter Twenty-four

Jules hadn't slept well. It had been a week since they had been to Dingle and the thought of seeing Margaret Hearn again was causing her sleepless nights and making her stomach ache. The steering wheel of Sinead's car felt unfamiliar and cold. She took a deep breath and tried her best to absorb all of May's instructions. *This is my first driving lesson. I must stay calm and stop thinking about crashing Sinead's car.*

"Jules? Did you hear me?" May asked.

"No, sorry. I'm feeling nervous. I don't want to damage Sinead's shiny new Mini."

"You won't. You know where the brake is and the stable yard car park is empty. We are just going to drive around here for a bit and then head down to the Manor House. If you think you have lost control, then just slam your foot down on the brake and even if we stall then no harm will have been done."

"Ok, I'm ready now."

"We are going to go very slow. Now, I've told you what to do to make the car move and stop. It will take a few goes to get used to raising the clutch. So first of all, we must make sure the car is in neutral, and the hand brake is up."

Jules did this and ran through the list of things to do in her head to make the car move. *Right, Jules, turn the key. Riding a horse is so much easier.* She started the car, and May talked her through the process. Feeling surprised, Jules saw the car had started to move forward. *This isn't so bad.* As she picked up speed, May asked her to change into second gear. She felt like she was doing everything in slow motion, and didn't put the clutch down in time when she changed gear. The car stalled. "Oh, nuts!" *Perhaps I am going to be as bad at driving as Peter is.*

May laughed. "Don't look so sad; your first couple of yards was excellent. You are young and you will learn quickly. Have another go."

After stalling for the sixth time, Jules managed to drive around the car park twice. She was starting to enjoy herself.

"You are doing really well. So when you're ready, I want you to drive around the car park one more time and then head down the drive to the Manor House. When we get to the car park, I want you to drive into the entrance and look for a parking space. When you find one, look in the rear view mirror to make sure you are not being followed by another car, slow right down and then drive into that space. There are cars there, so you will have to drive slowly and take your time."

"Ok, I'll do my best." Her heart was pounding in her chest, and her palms were sweating. Jules started to move forward and she stalled again.

May patted her hand. "You can do this. I'll be with you all the way, and I will talk you through."

She took another deep breath and focused on her mission. With her foot on the clutch, she put the car back into neutral and pulled up the hand brake. Again she started up the car and knew what to do without May telling her. "Mirror, mirror, action. May, I think I can remember what to do."

Jules drove them around the car park and then headed down to the Manor House along the driveway. The gravel crunched as she drove over it.

"Jules, look in the rear view mirror and then indicate left and brake gently."

"Ok, where's the indicator?" May pointed to it and Jules moved the lever down. As she turned into the car park, she noticed a black Honda Accord parked in the middle space. Her heart lurched in her chest with fear. For a moment, she forgot she was driving.

"Jules, are you with me?" She nodded. "Good, drive slowly into the space next to that black car. Gently apply the brake and when your wing mirrors are level then press the brake harder and the clutch down until you stop."

Shaking, Jules managed to do as she was asked but pressed the brake down too sharply and the car shuddered as it stopped.

"Well done. We made it!"

"Only just. At least I didn't stall again. May, do you know who that black car belongs to? It looks familiar. We borrowed Seth's Dad's car to get us from Southampton to Wales. It could be the same car."

"I think it belongs to Mr Jennings. He is checking out today. How does it feel to drive to work?"

Relieved, Jules smiled. "That was fun, but a bit surreal and nerve-wracking."

"We will do this every day and then when you are done at twelve you can drive us back to the stables and then you will get the hang of driving in no time."

From the sand school, Seth could see part of the car park and he had seen Jules stall the Mini a few times. He was trying to teach Mr Jennings some more advanced riding techniques but Soldier was not responding well. Seth couldn't help himself from stealing a glance over to the car park to see how the driving lesson was going. *I can't wait to tell her how proud I am of her. If only Margaret wasn't trying to hunt her down. It's been a week since she came to Cork and we haven't seen or heard from her. I guess she has gone home. I hope so.*

Thanks to Luke taking the nine o'clock lesson, Seth had an hour to himself to catch up on paperwork and run some Facebook ads advertising the riding school. He had taken some decent photos of the facilities there. At midday, when Jules had finished at the Manor House, she was going to come out on a hack with him and eight others. Luke was going to take a beginners lesson at one which meant that Seth could have lunch with her. He treasured that hour with her. Luke really liked teaching and this meant that he and Sinead were getting a break now and again. *I'll pop down to see Jules after this lesson and see what she thinks about driving a car. I miss driving.*

His attention returned to his student who was trotting around the sand school. "Mr Jennings, you are doing a grand job. In the second corner, I want you to sit back and put your inside leg in the forward position on the girth. Put your outside leg behind the girth. When Soldier breaks into a canter, I want you to keep sitting back."

It was another good drying day, so Jules decided that she would hang out the sheets and duvet covers. She put the basket of laundry on the grass and then started to peg a white sheet to the line, making sure it didn't touch the floor. Despite stalling so many times, Jules was really happy with her driving lesson. It was exciting trying something new.

She shivered and looked over her shoulder, and for a moment she was sure that she saw someone standing by the garden gate. When Jules looked again there was nobody there. *It might have been May.* She then remembered that May was helping Mr Jennings check out. After that she was going to meet someone from the council, to see if the orangery was a suitable building to carry out wedding ceremonies. Jules could feel butterflies in her stomach and didn't know why. *Perhaps I am just looking forward to being married to Seth.* She held up her left hand and looked at her ring shining in the morning light. *I can't wait to become Mrs Hearn.*

"I'm sorry, Ann, I came as fast as I could."

Jules gasped and spun around. "Margaret!" Margaret Hearn was behind her; only a meter away. She was grinning at her. Jules tried to make the apparition go away and shut her eyes for a moment. *No! Please no!* She was still there. *What on earth are you wearing?* She was dressed in a beige rain mac and beneath this was a floral dress which was low cut and exposed her ample breasts. Her grey hair was swept up into a French pleat and her face was made up. Jules could not believe how different she looked. It was probably the black high-heels that shocked her most. *Why are you dressed like this?*

"I came for you, Ann. I know you have forgiven me for trying to hurt you. We were lovers once. We can be lovers again." She put her arms out, inviting Jules to come to her.

She was shocked and she struggled to reply. "I don't want to. I'm not Ann." Desperately, she looked for an escape route out of the garden and then saw Seth by the gate. "Oh Seth, thank God!" He looked cross and stormed over to Margaret.

"You need to leave now and never come back. This nonsense has got to stop. This is Julia, not Ann. Do you hear me?"

"Oh, it's you! Typical! Crawl back under your rock and die with the rest of Jethro's runts – so, so many babies for me to deal with. I should have buried you with the rest of them at the farm."

"You're out of your mind! I am not going to ask you a second time. Leave us alone now!"

"YOU CAN'T HAVE ANN! SHE IS MINE AND ALWAYS WILL BE," she screamed.

Jules could see the fury in Seth's eyes. "I am going to call the police if you don't go now."

Margaret sneered at him. "Really? We both know that is not going to happen. They came looking for you at Crow Farm. All it would take is just one phone call."

Seth's eyes narrowed. "You are not going to call them either. We know quite a lot about your evil doings. You say there are more runts buried at the farm. I'm sure the police will be interested to hear more about that."

Margaret looked confused for a moment. She frowned. "You think you are so clever, but Ann knows her place is with me and we are going back to Crow Farm, even if I have to drag her. She will thank me one day."

"Mrs Hearn? I'm not Ann. I don't want to live with you. I love Seth, and we are going to be married soon. Please go home. I'm sorry, but I can't come back with you," she said firmly.

"You are only a child. You don't know what you want." She walked over to Jules and grabbed her wrist. "You always were disobedient, but we liked it that way, didn't we?"

210

"Please, Mrs Hearn, you're hurting me."

Seth could take this no more and took hold of Margaret's arm and pulled her off Jules.

"NO, SHE HAS TO COME WITH ME," she screamed.

Trying to control his temper, Seth dragged her out of the garden and down the drive towards the road. "YOU NEED TO GO!"

"Get off of me. Ann needs me. I need her."

"Look, you crazy woman, it is not Ann. Seriously, I will hurt you if you ever show your face here again." He saw her car and dragged her towards it. She staggered along, resisting him.

Margaret started to cry. "You can't treat your Mam like this."

"You were never my mother. Bridie is my mother now. You mean nothing to me. Get in the car and drive out of here. If I see your face again in Cork then I swear I will drown you in the river Lee! Just fuck off and leave us all alone."

Still crying, Margaret started the car and reversed out of the space, scraping the side of Sinead's car as she went. She then sped off down the drive and didn't stop.

Seth sighed. "That is one weird freak!"

Seth found Jules sitting on the back step with her head in her hands. She was crying. He sat down next to her and pulled up her head and wiped her tears away with his thumbs. "She's gone now. I don't think she will be back."

"I am just getting so tired of people trying to hurt me. Seth, that woman is a maniac. She has openly admitted to killing babies. The only reason she kept Jake and you alive is because you belonged to people she loved. She needs locking up. We could leave an anonymous tip with the police. I could get

Charlene to contact Inspector Simon Black with everything we know."

"We might have to. It seems wrong that she is walking free and getting away with so many crimes. What would you do if you discovered that your Dad had killed Ivy? Would you tell on him? I need to sleep on it and speak to Charlene. I told that lunatic that you were Jules and not Ann. I said that I would drown her in the river Lee if she came back here. I've never seen her cry and I have never seen her wear clothes like that. It is like she has become a completely different person."

"Seth, she is sick and she will come back here at some point; I know she will. She is so unbalanced that she may well try and kill me again if she is angry. If we tell the police, then she will tell them that you are on the run and then they will come for you. I couldn't bear that."

Seth drew her to him and hugged her. "I promise I won't let her hurt you."

"Your granny knows that she disposes of unwanted babies. I just know she does. That's why she said what she did when we left their house in Dingle. Do you remember what she said? *You two must keep your babies safe. Don't let her take them.*"

"Granny is a sandwich short of a picnic. Don't listen to her. I think you are in shock. Let me help you hang these sheets out and then come back to the yard with me and stay with me in the office. I can't bear to see you cry."

"I can't, Seth, I've got lots to do here. I will be ok," she said, drying her eyes on her sleeve. "That witch won't come back here for a while. Don't worry about me. Margaret is just a sad old woman and we can handle her. I am so looking forward to going on a hack with you at lunchtime and I still want to go busking and perform at The Elbow later. I just love singing with you. I've been working on various harmonies for your new songs. We are going to blow them away tonight."

Seth laughed. "You're amazing. You really are."

Chapter Twenty-five

Jules was standing in the space where Jethro's old car had been. *I wonder how many times this week Margaret has come here to watch me. How did she find out we live here?*

"Jules, you don't need to drive again today. Is everything ok?" May asked. "You haven't been yourself this morning."

"Oh, May, I haven't had the chance to tell you. Seth's mother turned up here and she tried to force me to go back to Crow Farm with her. She still thinks that I am Ann. My aunt and Seth's Mum, Margaret, were in a relationship at one point. This is so creepy and frustrating because we can't seem to get it through to her that she is being crazy. It was lucky Seth came up to the house and heard everything. He managed to get her to leave, but I know she will be back. He said he would drown her in the river Lee if she returned. She scares me so much. How can we stop her from coming up here without involving the police?"

"Oh, you poor dear. She sounds like she is very ill. Normally, you would apply to the courts for an asbo. Then, if she comes near you the police will arrest her."

"She didn't threaten us, but she does have a temper. She killed Ann all those years ago and pushed me into the pond to die when she was angry. If she thinks Ann is alive and I keep rejecting her then I fear that she may try and kill her, me, again. May, I think my life is at risk and I should run."

"No, you mustn't do that. I am sure Seth will be able to get rid of her if she bothers you again. Although I wouldn't recommend drowning her in the river Lee. These things have a way of sorting themselves out. When she is out and about in Cork, she will probably pick a fight with someone and end up getting arrested anyway. Look, I'll drive you up to the stables. Are you going for a ride? You've changed into your riding things."

"Yes, I'm going out with Seth on the twelve o'clock ride. It must be nearly twelve now. I think that you'd better drive as I don't think I can concentrate on it now. Is that ok? I will definitely drive in the morning."

"Quick then, jump in. A ride out will do you good. Let's see if I can still drive."

"Oh, May, I didn't think. I'll run up to the stables if you like."

"No, I think that I will be ok. I've been doing yoga again, so I am almost as flexible as I was."

**

From Moss's back, Seth watched the drive for the Mini and then sighed with relief when he saw the little car zoom up the hill and into the car park. It was twelve o'clock and the ride was about to leave. He watched Jules run around to the back of the car, open the boot and pull out her hat and crop. As she ran to them, she put on her hat and adjusted the chin strap.

"I'm sorry, thank you for waiting for me."

"It's only just twelve. You are not late," Seth said.

Luke was waiting at the mounting block with a large pony named Beth. She was black with a white blaze. Jules hadn't ridden her before and was a little nervous. She hopped up onto the mounting block and got into the saddle. Beth was eager to join the group and immediately started to walk towards them all. Luke pulled her to a stop and let Jules adjust the stirrups to the right length.

"Thanks, Luke. I'm ready now."

"Jules, come and ride next to me. Ok, everyone, follow Jules and I. We are going to go on the road first and then turn off onto the bridle path into the woods. Look out for cars when we cross the road and keep a good space between each other. Let's go. Let's have some fun."

Beth was quite a lively pony and was happy to be at the head of the ride. As they all walked down the drive, Jules noticed that Moss was shedding a lot of fur. She could see patches of his glossy summer coat below.

"Seth, Moss is going to look so good again when he loses his old coat. You are leaving a fur trail behind you."

"I know, I got the edge of the rasp over his coat this morning and was up to my knees in hair. I can't believe how much is coming off him. It was a cold winter, and I'm sure that all the horses grew extra thick coats this year. But, for some reason, Moss seems to be extra hairy." He looked behind him to make sure everyone was following and were looking confident. Satisfied that all his students were ok, he looked down at Jules and grinned. "I'm sorry you couldn't have your usual horse but Jane is a bit too big for Beth. You actually fit Beth perfectly. She's a New Forest pony, but I would say the size of a small horse. How do you find her?"

"She's quite sweet. I'm not used to riding anything so bouncy. I have a feeling that she will take off when we reach the gallop fields. You might not see me again."

"Don't say that. I have to keep you in my sight from now on. How are you doing?"

"I'm doing ok."

They reached the road and a car pulled up and let them walk across the road. The ride continued on its way, up the lane towards the bridle path.

It was a pretty walk through the woods and the group trotted through them on the soft wood chip path. When they reached a gate, Seth opened it and allowed everyone to file through to the first of the gallop fields. She waited with him. Moss, eager to canter, was fidgeting and was making it difficult for Seth to hold the gate open.

"Jules, please, can you take the gate, he won't keep still. Moss didn't go out yesterday. He is like a tightly wound spring. I will have to go ahead. Catch us up as soon as you can." She held the gate until the last of the riders had gone into the field and then closed it behind her. Beth complied but was eager to join the others. As she reached the bottom of the field, she could see Seth battling with Moss and he was trying to stop him from charging up the side of the hill. As Beth trotted, Jules could feel her getting excited too. She and Beth waited with Seth as each horse and rider took their turn to canter up the hillside. Seth had managed to calm Moss a little by turning him around so he couldn't see the other horses. "You go next. He can't wait any longer. I will follow you."

Seth laughed. "Here he goes. I'll see you at the top." Moss didn't need any encouragement and spun around, setting off in a fast canter, eager to catch up with the others. Jules kicked Beth on, and she did a quick trot and broke into a smooth canter. *She is such a nice pony to ride.* In the distance she could see Seth and Moss charging up the hill, the strong horse pounding the ground and throwing up mud as he flew.

When they returned to the stables, Seth jumped off of Moss's back and patted him. "You did good, my boy. You worked hard." A stable hand came over to take Moss from him. "Do you want me to put him back in the barn for you?"

"Thanks, Gemma that would be grand. You couldn't quickly run the curry comb over him and get some of this fur off him, could you?"

"No problem. All the other horses are the same."

Seth looked around for Jules and saw her talking to one of the riders. When he got closer, he realised that it was the lead singer from Sonar Cell. He had his riding hat under his arm. *I didn't recognise him with a riding hat on.* Seth took off his hat too and ran his hand through his thick hair and then walked over to them.

"Seth, this is Shawn, he's the lead singer in Sonar Cell. They are playing before us at The Elbow this evening. They've got a record deal," Jules announced.

"Nice to meet you. Congratulations! You deserve it."

"Thanks, Seth. It's a bit of a dream come true. We're making our first album and we are going on tour in the summer. That was a brilliant ride out, by the way. My girlfriend Jane is crazy about horses, and I don't like to admit it but I do enjoy riding too. You know, you two should get a deal too. Roger, our manager, has been trying to contact you. He's been really impressed with all those new songs you've been singing. I could give you his number."

"That's kind of you. We have been really busy lately. All that snow cut us off and stopped us going into Cork as much as we wanted to. We're also getting married Friday week and there's been lots to do."

"Congratulations to you too," he said, hugging them both. "Don't tell Jane."

Jane came over to join them. "Tell me what?"

"Seth and Jules are getting married soon. I was saying that it would give you ideas."

She laughed. "I'll get you to marry me one day, Shawn Smith."

"Look, if you like, we could back you tonight for a couple of songs. Some of the guys in the band really like your song Waterfall Way and would be up for a collaboration. Roger will be at The Elbow tonight, and you never know. I bet when he hears us, then he will be offering you millions to sign up. Seriously, you should think about it. You both have so much talent, and you deserve a break too."

"We could try, Jules. What do you think?"

"Even if he's not interested then it doesn't matter. It will be just amazing playing with you all. I'm so excited."

Chapter Twenty-six

It was just starting to get dark when Seth and Jules found their favourite spot outside the Echo office on Princes Street. The evening was mild, and the streets were busy with shoppers, tourists and those seeking evening entertainment.

Seth was perturbed and had secretly searched the area for Margaret. He would protect Jules from her, no matter what. Hiding behind Cork's twinkling façade lurked vice and corruption. On their way through the city, Seth had spotted a few unsavoury characters lingering in doorways and in dark corners. Some were too high on drugs or too drunk to notice predators watching and waiting for them to stray their way. He squeezed Jules's hand to reassure her and to let her know he would protect her from all evil. She had looked up at him, her bright blue eyes questioning his unease. An image of his ex-mother filled his mind. *Why did she dress herself up like a bit of mutton? What the fuck! I mustn't let that lunatic get near her.*

"Seth, you are away with the fairies. Are you ready or shall I get you a coffee?" Jules asked as she put her guitar strap over her head.

"I'm grand," he said as he rubbed his hands together. "Just a few nerves. I'll be fine when I get going."

"Shall we do our usual routine or do you want to do one of your songs first?"

"I think that it's better to do popular songs on the street. Let's do Pink's 'Walk Me Home' first. Everyone loves that one. What do you think?"

"I guess the folk songs only make money during the tourist season." She started to strum her guitar and she smiled at Seth, longing to hear his voice again. *He is not himself tonight.*

As they sang, people stopped to listen to them. Their voices harmonised so well at times that it sent little chills down her spine. A small crowd assembled around them and it was such a good feeling, knowing that people were enjoying listening to them. It was a little overwhelming.

When their fourth song finished and the applause faded, Seth took a sip of water and watched the crowd move on. His spirits were high again. *I just love watching everyone's faces. We really should see if we can make a go of this.*

Jules bent down and collected the money from the guitar case and then tucked it into a side pocket.

"Someone has left us a five euro note. We've made over thirty pounds so far!"

"We're on fire today, Jules. Let's sing a couple more and then get something to eat. We can dine in style tonight. What shall we..." Seth stopped talking.

She looked over to him and he was looking worried. "What's wrong?"

"Look up Princes Street and tell me that I'm not seeing things. Is that Margaret walking, or should I say staggering our way. Is she drunk?"

Jules scanned the busy street ahead and could see her weaving her way towards them. "Yes it is! Let's go! Before she sees us," she said as she threw the guitar in its case.

"There's no time." He pulled her to him, and turning his back on the passers-by, kissed her and hid her the best he could, from Margaret's eyes. Somebody shouted at them to get a room but Seth didn't care and carried on kissing her until he was sure that she had gone by. He chanced a quick look over his shoulder and then relaxed.

"Don't stop, Seth. It's kind of hot kissing you in the street."

He smiled, gave her a quick kiss and pulled away. "I'd rather save myself for later. Did you see the state she was in?"

"It was probably a good thing she was drunk. She was just focusing on walking straight and not what was going on around her. I hope she doesn't come back. Let's get out of here. Is it ok if we go and eat now? My stomach is churning and is crying out for food."

"Yes, of course. I'm starving too. Where do you want to go?"

"Let's go to that vegan restaurant we went to with Sinead. Oh, I was going to tell you. She is going clubbing tonight. I said that we could get a taxi home together but she said if she got lucky, then she might not be back until tomorrow. Sinead said to ring her when we are heading home, just to check."

Seth zipped up the guitar case and put it on his shoulder. "She will end up wrecked. She always does," he said, laughing. "Come on, let's get something to eat and then we can go and see who's playing at The Elbow."

The Elbow was packed and the atmosphere was electric. Both young and old were all enjoying a mixed programme of music. The pub had become known as the place to be to discover new bands and to experience Irish music culture at its best. As usual, there were very few tables free, so they left the guitar and their coats in the back room and joined the crowds around the stage. A rock band they hadn't heard before were playing, and their lead singer was strutting up and down the stage singing and clapping his hands above his head, encouraging the audience to clap too. Jules wasn't so sure about them. The musicians were looking nervous and didn't seem to have the same confidence as their lead singer.

"Oh dear, they're not that good, are they?" whispered Jules into Seth's ear, but he couldn't hear her. She tugged his arm. "Let's get a drink." He nodded, and they made their way to the bar. When they got there Shawn and Jane were ordering drinks.

"I'll get these," Seth announced and then looked at the barmaid to confirm this. She nodded.

"Thanks, mate," Shawn said, surprised to see them. "We've got a table under the dolphin. Come and join us."

Seth looked across the room and saw a plastic dolphin attached to the wall. "How have I not seen that dolphin before?"

Jane laughed. "You can't miss it. I can't believe you haven't noticed it before. See you in a minute," she said, carrying a tray of drinks away with her.

"Ok, we won't be long. What would you like, my sweet girl?"

"Just a small lager. I don't want my head to spin."

"A pint and a half of lager as well, please."

Shawn introduced Jules and Seth to four other band members and their girlfriends. Jules sipped her lager and enjoyed how cool it felt as it went down. She was feeling really full after eating her favourite vegan burger and fries. Seth was enjoying chatting to everyone and was making them laugh. She admired his ability to make friends with everyone instantly. He didn't forget her and made sure she joined in. She was grateful as Guy, the guitarist, was loud and gregarious and she was struggling to make herself heard.

When the band went off to get ready to play, only Jane remained sat with Jules and Seth. They chatted for a while. As Sonar Cell walked on to the stage, cheers and applause from their fans echoed around the pub.

"They are going to be a hard act to follow," Seth said.

"Nonsense, you two are great," Jane said. "Is it alright if I leave you two and I get a bit closer to them? I am going to record them tonight. They sound better close up."

"No, that's fine. You go, we're going to have another drink," Jules replied.

Jane disappeared into the crowds.

"What can I get you?"

"Just a coke with ice, please. Seth, I'm feeling kind of weird."

He looked concerned. "You look a bit pale. It's quite hot in here. Do you want to go outside for some air?"

"No, I guess I am just a bit tired and my dinner is taking a while to go down. It has been a crazy day. If I sit here and rest with a cold coke, then I will soon rally." She smiled. "I do love you."

"I love you too. I won't be long, the bar isn't too busy at the moment."

Seth returned with their drinks and they watched Sonar Cell, enjoying their music and both were itching to get on stage. When it was quarter to ten Seth finished his pint and looked at Jules to see if she was ready to perform. She had only drunk half of her coke. She smiled back at him, but she didn't look well.

"Let's go and get ready. Do you want to bring your drink with you? You still look pale."

"I am still feeling weird. I probably ate too much. Your fiancée is turning into a fat bloated whale."

"Are you in pain? Do you want to go home?"

"Oh no, I'll be ok. I wouldn't miss singing with you for the world."

Chapter Twenty-seven

Jules and Seth were standing by the stage waiting for Shawn to invite them up. Jules was feeling a whole lot better as she had visited the toilets and had thrown up. She hadn't told Seth as she didn't want him to worry. He was super excited about them performing together. *He's got stars in his eyes and he wants a record deal, I just know it. Do I want that too? Maybe. It would be a shame not to try.*

Shawn introduced S&J as being his close friends and as being brilliant musicians with a great song. As they walked up onto the stage ready to sing Waterfall Way, the crowds around clapped, whistled and cheered, surprising them both. They couldn't help grinning at each other and their audience, thanking them for their support.

As discussed earlier, Sonar Cell played a melodic introduction piece, before Seth and Jules sang. Jules loved the intro and the backing music and she hoped the audience would like Seth's new song as much as she did. Her heart was beating hard with nerves as she waited for Seth to begin. *I am so proud of you.* He started to sing, and she watched the audience's reaction as she waited to join in during the chorus and for the next part of the song. *They like it!* Jules strummed on her guitar waiting for her moment.

JULIA'S BABY

Nearly lost our lives when the sun went down
To a crazy man and a withered clown
We fled golden fields for County Cork
Too poor to eat, so we found work
We declared our love with a Claddagh ring
Now all we do is dance and sing
You laughed and stole a kiss
I kissed you back and made my wish

If you are going Waterfall way,
then please stay. I want you to stay.
I can't wait another day
Marry me and be my wife
I've waited for you all my life
I am asking you to stay
If you're going Waterfall way,
then stay, please stay.
I can't wait another day
Hey, hey, hey, please stay
I want you to stay.

Don't dance with that bad ass guy
You know he will make you cry
Be with me instead cos he's in another girl's bed
You know what I'm saying is true
All I want is to dance with you

If you are going Waterfall way,
then please stay. I want you to stay.
I can't wait another day
Marry me and be my wife

I've waited for you all my life
I am asking you to stay
If you're going Waterfall way,
then stay, please stay.
I can't wait another day
Hey, hey, hey, please stay
I want you to stay.

Together we can climb our tree
Seal our love, just you and me
We don't need to think, just let our bodies' link
I'm crazy, you're always in my head.
Can't wait until I get you into bed
So I'll steal a kiss and make my wish

If you are going Waterfall way,
then please stay. I want you to stay.
I can't wait another day
Marry me and be my wife
I've waited for you all my life
I am asking you to stay
If you're going Waterfall way,
then stay, please stay.
I can't wait another day
Hey, hey, hey, please stay
I want you to stay.

The audience erupted into applause and whistled as they closed the song. Feeling overwhelmed, Seth scanned the crowd and saw all their approving faces. There was no better feeling than this. The buzz was out of this world. He looked over at

Jules and could feel nothing but pride for what they had achieved. He took a deep breath in and grinned. *That was amazing!*

After an hour of singing and watching everyone enjoying themselves, they had left the stage and hugged each other, jubilant and were on an all-time high. As they made their way to the back room to get their coats, Mick waved them over to him.

"Congratulations!" he called out. "Roger is waiting for you in the back room. You just have to talk to him."

Roger was sitting in a chair and was on the phone. He was a large man, dressed in a black suit and his fingers were adorned with gold rings. When he saw them, he waved them in and they waited while he finished his call. When the call ended, he shook his head, put his phone in his pocket and then looked up at them, revealing his yellow teeth. "Look, you two, you must know that you have a career in the music industry. You will need a manager. I've seen you grow and flourish. We can all make some serious money from your music. Have you spoken to anyone else about signing up?"

"No," Seth said. "Not yet."

"Good! Come by my office on the nineteen of April at two pm and we will have a chat. Here's my card." He pulled a card out of his top pocket and handed it to Seth.

"Could you make it another day?" Jules asked. "We're getting married on the nineteenth." He hadn't yet made eye contact with her.

"It's ok, Jules, we can get married in the morning and then see you in the afternoon."

"That's good news. Have a good evening," Roger said as he got up. He walked towards the door and before he left he grinned at them. "We have a great future together."

Seth watched the door close and then he turned to Jules and he could see by the look on her face that she wasn't impressed.

"He's a bit slimy. I don't think he will make a good manager," she said. "He is just out to make money. He doesn't like women. He didn't make eye contact with me."

"No, I didn't like him at all. He didn't care that we were getting married. If he was decent, then he would have given us another time to see him. You're not going to be mad with me if we don't go?" Seth asked.

"No, not at all. We are doing just fine as we are. Wasn't it amazing tonight?"

"It was the best. Come here and give me a hug. You are looking so much better."

Jules ran to him, and he lifted her off her feet as he embraced her. She laughed as he put her down and then kissed her passionately, pulling her to him. The phone began to ring, and Jules not wanting him to stop, tried to ignore the sound.

Seth stopped kissing her. "It's probably Sinead. We'd better answer the call. She'll go mad otherwise."
Seth took the phone out of his coat pocket and having missed the call rang her back. He put it on loud speaker so they could both hear her. He was bursting to tell her about how their gig had gone. "Hi Sinead, are you ready to go back to Waterfall? No luck tonight, then?"

"Seth, I've got a problem. I think I am with your mother. She is smashed and keeps talking about losing Ann to a shithead called Seth. I don't know what to do."

"Fuck! Just leave her there. She can call a taxi to take her to her hotel."

"I was going to do that but she isn't able to tell me where she is staying. She keeps crying and I think she's pissed herself. Margaret wants to go to Waterfall."

"No way is she coming back home with us. Fuck! That woman is the bane of my life."

"I'm sorry, Seth, I know what she has done to you both but I can't leave her. We're in a very dodgy bar and she will get mugged or worse. I was thinking that I could take her back to the mobile and then in the morning when she has sobered up, call her a taxi to take her back to the hotel. That's all I can think of. I'll need your help to get her into a cab."

Seth was starting to feel cross and he knew he would have to contain his anger. He wasn't angry with Sinead, just angry at the world for dealing him with so much shit. He looked over at Jules and could see she was in shock. Seth sighed. "Ok, I'll get a taxi and we will meet you at the bar. Really, I should leave her to rot. Jules you will have to go in the front of the taxi. I don't want her anywhere near you. Sinead, where are you?"

"We're in the Cloven Hoof night club on Oliver Plunkett Street. I wouldn't come in. She can still walk, so I am sure I can get her into the street but I will need you to be there as she is sure to fall over when the fresh air hits her."

"If she is too much, then just leave her. I will find you." Seth ended the call. "I did the right thing, didn't I?"

She nodded and then shivered. "What a nightmare!"

Seth got out of the cab in Oliver Plunkett Street and he could see Sinead and his ex-mother at her feet. A crowd had started to form around them. He asked the taxi driver to wait and walked over to them.

"I'm sorry, Seth. Margaret fell over when she was being sick and now I can't get her up."

"It's ok, Sinead." In disgust, he looked down at the woman he had once called his mother. She was lying in her own sick, unable to get up and her forehead was bleeding. Margaret focused on him for a moment and he could see that she had recognised him. She put out her hand for him to help her up.

He ignored her and looked back at the taxi driver to see if he would have a drunk in his car and he shook his head before he had even asked him. "She can't get into the taxi like that. I am going to call an ambulance and say she hit her head. Thanks for staying with her. I can deal with it now. Are you going back to the club or are you going to come back with us?"

"I'll come back with you. I'm knackered. It was hard work trying to stop her getting herself arrested. She was bothering everyone and yelling at them. Aren't you going to go to the hospital with her?"

"Are you joking? Would you tell the taxi driver that I won't be a minute?"

"I could go with her if you like."

"You've done more than enough. She will be fine. The emergency services can deal with her. She is not my responsibility."

"Ok, if you are sure. I'll tell him."

Seth got out the phone and noticed that a man in the crowd was talking to the emergency services. He put away his phone and took one last look at her pathetic face pleading with him for help and he hoped that he would never see her face again.

As he walked over to the taxi, someone in the crowd shouted out that he was a bastard. Seth spun around with his eyes blazing and his fists clenched. Whoever had shouted was not willing to face him. He waited for a moment in case that person wanted to add anything more. Nobody spoke, and all eyes were now fixed on Margaret who was throwing up again. Seth relaxed and shook his head. *Just walk away.*

Chapter Twenty-eight

Seth opened his eyes and he could hear purring. The purring intensified and his eyes focused on the source of the noise. A tip of a fluffy white tale moved along the side of the bed and then on reaching the corner of the bed returned. They had forgotten to close the bedroom door when they had gone to bed. He didn't want to move, but he knew that at any moment, Barney would jump onto the bed demanding food. Jules was fast to sleep and lay in his arms, she was the perfect spoon, her warm bare skin next to his. Still purring, Barney jumped up on the bed, meowed at him and started to walk towards Jules.

"Ok," he whispered. "Don't wake your Mam up."

Every Sunday, it was the same. Barney demanded his food at six every morning even if it was their day off and they were having a lie in. Reluctantly, Seth got out of bed, and naked, he walked into the kitchen. Barney followed him and rubbed his body against his legs as he got his bag of food out of the cupboard. It was almost light outside and it was raining hard. The wedding was just a day away, and he hoped the weather would improve.

He visited the bathroom and then after closing the bedroom door climbed into bed, keen to snuggle up with Jules. In her sleep, she acknowledged his cool body next to hers. Seth knew that it was too early to wake her, but he was aroused and he was finding it difficult to stop himself. Gently he kissed her neck and shoulder. He rubbed his hands over her full breasts until her nipples hardened. She was starting to wake up. He smiled. Gently, he ran his hand over her hips and onto her stomach, moving himself closer so she could feel him. He was going to nibble on her neck when all of a sudden, he felt something move in her stomach. Surprised, he ran his hand over her tummy to see if he could feel that strange rippling movement. Again, he could feel something shift inside her. He inhaled sharply. "Christ!" Slowly, that precious moment in time hit him. *I am feeling my baby move for the first time!* There was no doubt in his mind that Jules was pregnant. *How has she not noticed?*

Stunned and unable to move, a dark thought crossed his mind. *Is it Tom's? No, it can't be? He used a condom, and the baby is too big to be his. So how far gone is she? My God! I got her pregnant the first time we did it, back in August.* He felt the baby move. *Was that a kick?* He was starting to feel tearful. *She must be about seven months pregnant. My poor wee dote has no idea.* He just wanted to hold her and let her know he was there for her. He wrapped his arms around her and held her tight. *I can't wait to tell her. She must know, surely?*

Jules woke up and checked the phone for the time. It had just gone nine. She needed the toilet desperately and pulled back the bed covers and looked over to Seth's side of the bed. He wasn't there; just his nightshirt lay on the bed. Jules slipped it on and remembered being in his arms that morning and being aware that he wanted her. She walked into the kitchen and saw him by the cooker making breakfast. He was wearing shorts and a t-shirt and looked like he was ready to workout. He smiled when he saw her.

"Morning, beautiful. Are you up for a little scrambled eggs on toast?"

"I thought you would be lying in. You are so sweet. I'll have a little," she said. "It's a bit early for me but I'll try. I'm sorry if I didn't wake up for you this morning. I wanted to, but I couldn't open my eyes. We didn't get to sleep until late. Are you disappointed in your wife-to-be?"

"Goodness, no! I don't know how you put up with me. We will have to be good tonight, though, as Charlene and Joe will be staying over with us. Can you believe that we are going to be married tomorrow?"

"No, it's all a bit of a dream. I've got to wee, Seth. I won't be a minute."

He watched her go, and he was bursting to tell her about their baby. He had never felt so happy. He hadn't realised how much he had wanted children.

After relieving herself, Jules went back into the bedroom and put on her joggers. The waist band was feeling tight. *I know I shouldn't eat too much today but I am so hungry. I don't want to be a fat bride.*

She joined Seth at the table, sat down and looked at her scrambled eggs. *He has cooked this perfectly but I am not really up to eating so early.* She had a sip of tea and then saw that Seth was staring straight at her with an unusual look on his face. "You've done a great job. Your cooking is really coming along." *He's grinning now.* "Are you ok?"

"I'm grand, Jules. I'm the happiest man alive." *I must let her eat before I say anything.*

"That's good," she said as she started to eat. "Are you looking forward to seeing Charlene?"

"I can't wait. It has been just over seven months since we last saw her. Thirty-three weeks and five days."

"That's very precise? Are you sure you are ok?"

"Yes, I'm fine. I am not sure what to tell Charlene about her Mam. I told her that she still thinks you are Ann and that she wanted you to be her lover again. Charlene didn't take that very well. I know she believed me but it is a difficult pill to swallow when you find out that your mother, your own flesh and blood, is a bisexual psychopath."

"I don't think we should tell Charlene about leaving the emergency services to take care of her when she fell over drunk. It was the only thing you could have done," she said as she cut into her breakfast.

"I am going to tell her about that. They were close once. I don't know if they have been in touch. Charlene might know about that already."

"We will have to play it by ear. We haven't seen Margaret for a good few weeks. With a bit of luck, she might have gone home or been admitted into the loony bin."

"I guess so. Jules, I've got something really good to share with you."

"I knew there was..."

The phone began to ring. Seth picked it up. "It's Charlene. I'll put it on speaker phone, so you can hear her too." He swiped the green phone icon to take the call. "Hi Charlene, are you ok?"

"Morning, Sweetie. I am grand. We are just a bit tired. We were on our feet all day yesterday and my ankles have swollen up. I swear that I am going to give birth to a monster. Seth, we are in Waterfall already. Is it ok if we come over early?

I couldn't stay at Joe's parents any longer. They were fussing over me and driving me mad."

"That's fine, your room is all made up for you. I can't wait to see you both."

"I think that we have just gone past your turning. I saw a drive and a big Manor House. Joe, turn around, please. Where do we go after that?"

"Drive up past the Manor House to the stable yard. There is a car park there but if you keep going through the yard, if it is clear of horses, then drive through and you will see a track leading downward on the right. It's a bit rough, so take it slow. I don't want you giving birth in the car. You will see the Old Barn on your left. I'll be waiting at the door for you."

"Ok, Sweetie. See you in a minute."

Jules looked down at her breakfast; she just had time to finish it but would have no time to dress. "Seth, I'm not dressed. What will they think?"

"You look fine. They won't mind. You are glowing. You never looked so good."

"Seth? What were you going to tell me?"

"Ok, I can't hold out much longer. Let's just see Charlene and Joe first."

"You are driving me mad now." *What does he want to tell me?*

Seth smiled at her and finished his breakfast. "I can hear their car." He opened the door to wait for them.

As the car drew up, Jules finished her last mouthful and joined him at the door. "It's a shame it's raining," she whispered. "The barn looks so pretty in the sunshine."

They welcomed them in and they hugged each other. Joe got their cases out of the boot and joined them. Jules was amazed to see how large Charlene's bump was. It was good to see her big brown eyes and her dark hair was shining. *She looks amazing!* Joe came in, hugged Jules and then shook Seth's hand. "Good to see you both alive and well. We've been so worried about you both."

"We're doing just fine," Jules said. "We've had a few problems with Margaret, but I think that's over with now." Jules hadn't expected Joe to be so tall; he had thick ginger hair and a beard. He had strong arms and looked like he worked hard at Crow Farm. *He's got kind eyes.*

"I love your new home. It's so bright and airy," Charlene announced as she turned around to look at the barn. Her eyes focused on Jules.

"We love it here. It's perfect for us."

"Jules, you are looking wonderful. Sweetie, are you pregnant? You look like you are. I've seen enough pregnant women in our family to know."

She was taken aback. *I really must have gotten fat.* "I..."

"She's seven months pregnant," Seth announced.

In disbelief, Jules glared at him. She was getting cross and could feel her cheeks going red with embarrassment and anger. "I'm not pregnant. I'm just fat, ok! Seth, we talked about this!"

He hadn't expected her to react this way. *I've got to save this.* "Jules, while you were sleeping this morning, I had my hand on your belly and felt him or her move. Not once, but several times. I felt our baby move, Jules! That is what I was trying to tell you. You are just starting to show. You are pregnant. I am not joking. That's why you have been saying you have been feeling bloated and weird. There have also been all those urgent trips to the toilet. You must see that I am right?"

She looked at everyone and could feel all eyes on her. She was embarrassed, but memories of being sick and feeling a strange fluttering feeling in her stomach and thinking it was gas were all starting to add up. Her temper was cooling as the reality of what he had said began to sink in. "Do you really think so? You said earlier that you are the happiest man alive. Is that why?"

"Yes, my gorgeous girl! We are going to have a baby!"

"Charlene, could I be seven months pregnant and not know it?" she asked as her hand went to her stomach to protect the little being inside her. *It's true. I know it. Oh, my God!*

"It's possible. Our sister Claire had a baby and didn't know she was pregnant. It happens. It's only after six or seven months that a baby really starts to grow."

"I feel really stupid now." Jules smiled at Seth as she imagined holding a baby with dark hair and big brown eyes. "Do you think I need to do a test?"

He shook his head. "There's no need; you can see that you are pregnant. Are you happy about this, Jules?" he asked as he held her hands and gazed lovingly into her eyes.

"I am a bit shocked, but yes, I am happy. More than anything." Seth gave her a hug and then grinned at her.

Charlene laughed. "I bet that you are really glad I turned up. I'm becoming more and more like Granny with her third eye, every day. I'm surprised she didn't see it too. Talking of which, Joe is going to pick up Bridie and Granny later." She looked at Joe and he rolled his eyes.

"That's going to be an interesting journey. They never stop talking. Are they going to stay in the barn with us as well?" he asked.

"I hadn't thought about where to put Bridie and Granny. Hopefully, May has a room free at the Manor House," Seth replied.

"There's a couple of rooms on the ground floor that are available. I'll give May a call," Jules said. "I'll tell her about the baby too. She is going to be so surprised."

"Is it ok if I sit down, Seth?" Charlene asked.

"Oh dear, I am a bad brother. Come and sit down on the sofa and put your feet up. I'll put the kettle on."

Charlene waddled towards the sofa. Joe followed.

"You really have done this place up so well. We need a bigger place," Joe said. "The cottage is all very nice, but it only has three bedrooms and we won't be able to move when this one comes along. I'll have a chat with Patrick," Joe said as he helped Charlene sit on the sofa.

Jules was sitting on a chair and shut her eyes for a moment and tried to concentrate on the little being inside her. She had spent quite a few months doing her best to ignore her expanding girth, hoping that it was just a temporary glitch and her stomach would return to normal if she ignored it; didn't look or touch it. It was a relief, not to worry about her weight anymore. *I can actually stop thinking about getting fat and enjoy being pregnant for the last two months. Goodness, just two months to go!*

After lunch, Charlene had gone to rest in the guest room, and Joe had headed off to Dingle to get Bridie and Granny. Entwined, Jules and Seth lay on the sofa watching a film. Seth felt a little guilty that he wasn't driving to Dingle as it was he that had invited his aunt and his granny to their wedding. It was going to take Joe four hours to get there and back.

Seth was enjoying watching The Greatest Showman and Jules was engrossed in the film too. He kissed her cheek. He was feeling euphoric that they were having a baby and thankful that Jules was happy about it. He had his hand on her mini bump, eager to feel their baby move again. When he eventually felt her tummy shift, he placed her hand there too and she exhaled with surprise. "Is this the first time you've felt him? Surely not?"

She laughed. "It is actually. I told you that I felt a fluttering feeling early on but just thought that was down to all the vegetables I was eating. So, do you think it's a boy?"

"I do, I don't know why. I don't mind either way. Back home, some of my sisters suffered from morning sickness and they all thought that the baby was more likely to be a girl because of that. You haven't felt sick really, have you?"

"No, I suppose not. Seth, when the baby is born, I want to keep working. I like working at the Manor House in the mornings. I don't think that I will have time to learn how to become a riding instructor. I could bring the baby to work with me. Is that ok? I don't think that May will mind. You don't want me to be a stay at home mum, like the other Hearn wives, do you?"

"Of course not. I want you to do whatever makes you happy. I will of course expect my dinner on the table when I return from a hard day's graft and expect you to tend to my every need," he said, laughing. "No, you don't have to do that, really. Darragh is probably going to dictate how we operate from now on. Babies tend to do that. Our lives will never be the same. If the baby is a boy can we call him Darragh? It means strong like an oak tree."

"I hadn't thought about a name. I like it. Yes, I love it," she said, thinking about their tattoos. "I love you, Seth. Shall I rewind the film? We've missed quite a bit. I was thinking of doing a soya mince Bolognese for everyone. Do you think they will eat it or do you think...?"

Charlene emerged from the bedroom and it was evident that she had been crying. She was holding her phone and had just ended a call. Shocked to see her like this, they both sat up.

"What's wrong, Charlene?" Jules asked.

She shook her head again and holding her back lowered herself into the armchair.

"The baby's not coming, is it?" Seth asked, his eyes wide with concern.

"No, not yet. It's Claire. She just rang me. Jules, Claire is our youngest sister. Oh, Seth, she is in a terrible way. She has just given birth again and thinks that Mam or the social services are going to take her baby away. She's not been well recently and is at the mental health hospital in Worthing. I can't believe what she told me. Claire is saying that Dad is the baby's father. Oh Seth, you don't think he is, do you? That would be too awful. She must be delusional."

Seth felt sick hearing this bad news, but knew that Claire was telling the truth. "Charlene, we have to face the fact that our parents have turned out to be two sick evil bastards. I think I know what happened to Claire's last baby. That had to be Dad's too. When Mam was last here, she told us that she has had to get rid of his illegitimate children, me included. Over the years Mam has murdered Dad's unwanted babies and buried them on the farm. God knows how many she has buried and how many of our sisters he has got to."

Charlene started to cry. Jules got up and found a tissue for her. "Charlene, I know this is hard for you," she said, rubbing her shoulder. She hesitated before she spoke again. "He didn't touch you, did he?"

She shook her head. "No, Sweetie, he spared me. I hope he didn't abuse anyone else. It is all too awful! I think I know where these poor babies have been hidden. I am sure that they have all been buried around the silent pool. I remember playing down there once and seeing Dad digging a hole. He said he was digging it for a dead lamb. I remember thinking that it was a sweet thing to do. Farmers don't bury dead lambs, do they? Oh, Seth... we need to get the police involved. This has gone on for long enough." Charlene dried her eyes and then smiled weakly at them. "Everyone back at home is going to be so shocked. I hope they don't hate me."

"I should have rung the police a long time ago," Seth said bitterly. "I don't like to see you so upset."

"You can't get involved with the police. You said that Mam came here. Do you think that she is still in Cork?"

"We saw her in town a few weeks ago; she was drunk. She fell over and a member of the public called out an ambulance for her. I couldn't go with her. I couldn't bring myself to. I'm sorry."

"I understand, Sweetie. I wouldn't have gone with her either. Not now." Charlene shook her head. "I am going to call the police. It has to be done."

Chapter Twenty-nine

You are beautiful, you are my life,
Meet me at eleven and be my wife.

Jules found the post-it note on Seth's pillow and smiled as she read the words. She wished she could see him, hold him and tell him how much she loved him. *It won't be long until we are wed. Eleven o'clock is just two hours away.* She longed to see him dressed smartly and to see his smiling face when he saw her walk into the orangery.

Jules had managed to find Seth some smart black trousers and a white dress shirt in her favourite charity shop. She knew that he really wanted to wear jeans, but she didn't want to look over dressed in a long white gown. He hadn't minded too much and said that he would wear the clothes if it made her happy. *I hope my dress still fits me.*

Please don't rain when we are handfasting. Seth looked up at the sky to make sure there were no angry clouds threatening rain. Sunshine streamed out from behind a cloud. *Perfect.* Satisfied that it was going to be dry, he waited for Annie to join him in the sand school. She had asked to change horses as she found Beth too difficult to ride. Annie was one of his more nervous students. He had two more classes to teach before eleven and he would then have an hour to get himself ready. He had shaved but Sinead thought that he needed a quick haircut. He ran his fingers through his long hair and wished he had gone into Cork to have it done. Sinead had cut his hair before and had taken too much off. *Just two more classes before I make my gorgeous girl my wife. I wonder if she has found my note yet.*

Today is the first day of another chapter in my life. At lunch time I will be Mrs Hearn. Jules was curious to see how the orangery had been decorated. May hadn't allowed her in to see it and she had spent a lot of time in her new wedding venue, redecorating the derelict building. Jules had noticed a lorry arriving from an architectural plants company and had dragged herself from the window so she couldn't see what was being unloaded.

May hadn't allowed them to pay for anything. Seth had wanted her to let them pay for the registrar at least but she wouldn't let him and said that it was her wedding gift to them. He had made her promise not to spend too much as he really only wanted a simple ceremony before they handfasted. By accident, Jules had come across the catering invoice left on the side in the kitchen. Her jaw had dropped when she had seen how much May had spent.

Jules pulled the covers back and sat on the side of the bed. Her stomach was aching. She felt it to see if she could feel Darragh move but all was quiet. *I need to give you some food? What do you fancy? A cheese omelette? Why do I think that you are going to be a big fan of cheese? We'd better see if Charlene and Joe had a good night.*

She gathered together some clothes, ready to shower and wandered out into the kitchen to see if anyone was up. She was particularly concerned about Charlene. She had cried a lot after dinner, and everyone had assured her that she had done the right thing by calling the police. Granny had been the most supportive and said that Margaret was the Devil incarnate. Her bluntness was always shocking.

The soya Bolognese had been warmly welcomed and nobody had complained about the mince being plant based. Granny had, however, moaned about the pasta being a little too foreign for her. Nonetheless, she had eaten it all. Sinead had whispered to Jules that Granny reminded her of a miniature Mrs Brown. They had laughed quietly together.

Barney came over to greet her and meowed for food. She looked in his bowl and saw that he had left a couple of biscuits. "Seth fed you. You can't want more!"

"Oh, I fed him too. I'm sorry; he was desperate," Joe said with an apologetic look on his face.

Joe and Charlene were sitting at the table. *Charlene is looking a lot brighter this morning.* "That's ok, he will be sorry when he is the size of a basketball and can't jump on the sofa. Did you two sleep ok? You're the first to sleep on the new bed."

"We did, thank you. I was going to say. Peter said he can't make it. He doesn't want to leave your Dad just yet. He hasn't told him that you are marrying Seth. He sends his love and will try and make it over during the dry season. Does he mean the summer?"

Jules laughed. "No, he means over the winter when the cows are dry. There is less to do on the farm then."

"Oh, I see. Jules, I have been worrying about something. I've just had your Inspector Simon Black on the phone. He's going to send a team down to the silent pool to check for human remains. If they find anything, then they will issue a warrant for Mam's arrest. I told them that Mam had told me she had buried babies there. I said that Mam was in Cork. I don't know what she is going to say to the police when they arrest her, but there is a chance that she will say you are staying here. I feel bad now that your hideaway has been unearthed. What if the police come for Seth?" She was tearing up again.

"You mustn't worry about us. There is a chance she will say something, but that woman needs locking up. She can't be allowed to get away with it. Too many people have died or nearly died because of her. The police will be more interested in all those dead babies and won't worry about Seth." *I hope that is true.* Jules suddenly felt a sharp pain in her stomach and cried out. The pain passed quickly. "That hurt!"

"Ouch, I felt that. It could be your muscles stretching. The baby is growing quickly now. That can be painful," Charlene suggested.

"I hope so. I'm ok now. It's probably trapped gas. Have you both got everything you need? I'm just going to have a shower and then do battle with my hair."

"We're fine, Sweetie. I'll do your hair for the wedding. Only if you would like me to. We will go and have a look in the lane for some tiny flowers to weave into it. It's a beautiful morning for a wedding."

"I'd love you to do my hair, although you may regret offering. This mop of curls can be quite a challenge."

"You have beautiful hair. I will do my best."

Jules turned on the shower and waited for the water to warm up. As she stepped into the cubicle, water gushed out of her and ran down her legs. She looked down as the clear fluid mixed into the water and watched it wash away. Her stomach ached for a moment. *Did I just wet myself? Does pregnancy make you incontinent? I'll ask Charlene. At least that happened in here, and there's nothing to clean up. How weird.*

Jules found Charlene and Joe outside collecting spring flowers. Charlene was pointing out the ones she wanted, and Joe was picking them for her and held a delicate spray of flowers in his large fist. Barney was rubbing himself on Joe's leg and was making a nuisance of himself. Jules laughed. "He's not helping, is he?" She went over to him and picked Barney up. Her stomach started to spasm again. She breathed in sharply and gasped. She looked at Charlene and could see that she was concerned. "These pains are contractions, aren't they? I thought I had wet myself in the shower, but now I think my waters have broken."

Charlene looked concerned. "Shall I get Seth? You really need to go to hospital."

"Oh dear, no. I want to get married first. I feel fine between the cramps. There is just an hour before the ceremony. It could be anxiety. I get cramps when I am anxious. The contractions need to be close together before the baby is born, don't they? I think that I have been having one every twenty minutes."

"If your waters have broken, then you are in labour. The thing is, Sweetie, the baby is premature and will need assistance when it is born. It's best not to take any chances."

"I know, but I really don't think he is coming yet. We really are ok. Please, don't say anything to Seth until after we are married. I promise that we will go straight to the hospital. I'll put my dress on and put the radio on to relax us. Will you still do my hair for me?"

"Of course I will. I am here for you."

Jules put the silky white dress on and pulled the puff sleeves onto her shoulders. The zip at the back of the dress only just did up. She looked at herself in the mirror and was pleased with how her body filled the dress out. *Being pregnant certainly has some advantages.* She looked down to see if she could see her tiny bump. It was hidden under folds of material. *If Darragh is born today, then it will feel like I've only been pregnant for one day. How strange is that?*

As Charlene did the last touches to her hair, Jules put on a little makeup, trying to make herself look as natural as possible. She inspected herself in the mirror and was pleased with what she saw. *I look like an elven princess.* They had decided to leave her hair down and Charlene had twisted back and fastened strands from each side. She had woven tiny flowers into these strands.

It was ten minutes to eleven, and Jules had managed to hide four contractions from Charlene and Joe. She was determined to be married before giving birth. Sinead pulled up outside the door in her Mini. The Mini was decorated with ribbons and balloons. This was a surprise as Jules thought that she was going to walk down to the Manor House. *Thank goodness you are here.*

Jules stepped out of the barn and Sinead's mouth opened wide when she saw her. "You look amazing! Everyone is waiting for you in the orangery. Seth is sweating a bit. I've never seen him so nervous. I'm going to apologise now. I might have cut a bit too much off his hair but I think I did a good job. He looks really hot. Are you ok, Jules? You suddenly look very pale. I didn't scalp him or anything."

Jules shook her head as she felt another contraction. "Just give me a second."

"She's gone into labour," Joe said. "This is going to be one very quick wedding."

Sinead looked shocked. "Seth told me the news this morning. Oh my, Jules! Shouldn't you be going to hospital?"

"It's early yet. It could be hours before Darragh arrives. Please, Sinead. I've got time to marry Seth."

"Ok then, but if it all gets too much then just say and I'll be ready to rush you in. The hospital is about ten minutes away."

The ride up to the Manor House was a bumpy one. When they reached the car park she felt her stomach contract. Jules got out of the Mini and then held onto the roof until she got her breath back. As she recovered, she looked at everyone and smiled. "That was a strong one. I'm ok now, really."

They walked along the front path through the garden and then took the path to the right by the side of the house that led to the back garden. Jules stopped for a moment and looked at the white building at the foot of the garden. The panelled windows were filled with fairy lights. May was standing in the doorway surrounded by white lights and she could see her waving and smiling at her. *It must be eleven.* "I can do this but not the handfasting after," she announced. Another contraction took hold, and she clenched her fists tight, determined not to let it show.

"They are coming faster now, Jules. You haven't got much time," Charlene warned.

As they reached May, she saw her switch on a CD player and music began to play. Jules gasped with surprise. She could hear Seth singing Waterfall Way. She was amazed. "Who recorded us?" she asked May.

"A very nice girl, called Jane, dropped a CD by this morning. She said she had caught your whole performance at The Elbow the last time you were there. I listened to the CD this morning while I was getting this place ready. You should both be on the radio. You look beautiful by the way. Are you ready to get married?" May asked.

"I can't wait."

"Come on then. Seth is going crazy waiting for you."

Charlene, Joe and Sinead slipped by them to take their seats. Jules took May's arm, and they walked into the sunny orangery filled with tropical plants which were all covered in white lights. A walkway with chairs dressed in large white ribbons either side led up to a small table covered in a white cloth. Behind the table was standing a smartly dressed lady, with curly blonde hair and a kind round face. *She must be the registrar.* "It looks so beautiful in here, May, thank you," she whispered as they walked towards her. *Where is my lovely Seth?* He was standing to the right of the table with his back to her. As she approached, he turned around and gave her a huge smile. She breathed in sharply when she saw his handsome face and his newly shorn hair. *He looks so smart and hot.* His big brown eyes met hers, and she could see the love in them. She grinned back at him, eager to be by his side.

My beautiful girl is here at last. I have waited all my life for this moment. Seth could feel his heart almost bursting with joy. He scanned the room quickly and noticed that everyone was watching her. *I am just so proud of her.*

As Jules passed the row of chairs, she heard Bridie and Granny whispering with Charlene. *Did I hear the word police?* As she reached Seth, she could feel her stomach muscles contracting and contorting. She gritted her teeth together. *Be strong, Jules, you can do this.* May patted her on the back and then sat down next to Sinead.

Seth took Jules's hand and then noticed her tremble a little and he could see a look of alarm in her eyes. *There's something wrong. I can sense it.* He took a quick look at Sinead and immediately knew that his fears were correct. *Why isn't*

Sinead smiling? He looked back at Jules and could see she was in pain. Her beautiful face was pale. "What's wrong?" He whispered. She looked surprised that he had noticed her pain. "You do still want to marry me, don't you?"

"Of course I do, you daft thing. Seth, we need to be quick, the baby is on its way. Please can we be married? I want that more than anything and then we have to go to the hospital. Darragh is coming too early. He is going to need some help when he is born."

"Oh my God! My poor wee dote. Are you sure? You are being serious. How long do we have?"

"I don't know. The contractions are about five minutes apart. I have just had one as I walked up the aisle."

He turned towards the registrar who was looking horrified. "Are you able to carry out an express ceremony?"

She nodded and smiled. "This is going to be a first for me. Here goes. Now, I am going to ask each of you in turn to declare that you know of no lawful reason why you should not be married to each other. Ok?"

"That's fine."

"Sebastian Hearn, please say the following words after me. 'I do solemnly declare that I know not of any lawful impediment why I, Sebastian Hearn, may not be joined in matrimony to Julia Bridgewater.'"

Seth repeated her words.

Jules mirrored his declaration and then took a quick look over her shoulder to see if anyone objected. Their song Waterfall Way had ended and the room was quiet. She felt relieved that her Dad hadn't burst in through the door ready to drag her home.

"Now the moment has come for Julia Bridgewater and Sebastian Hearn to contract their marriage before you, their witnesses, family and friends. Do you have the rings?"

"Yes, we do," Jules said as she slid the Claddagh ring off of her finger. She gave her ring to Seth. He took his ring off too and gave it to her. He was looking serious, and she hoped that he wasn't annoyed with her for wanting to be married in such a rush.

"Sebastian, please say the following words after me," the registrar asked. "I give you this ring as a sign of our marriage and I call upon these persons here present to witness that I, Sebastian Hearn, do take thee to be my lawful wedded wife." Seth repeated the words and slipped the ring on to Jules's ring finger with the heart pointing towards her own. She breathed in with relief as the ring was replaced.

After being prompted by the registrar, Jules said the same. "I give you this ring as a sign of our marriage and I call upon these persons here present to witness that I, Julia Bridgewater, do take thee to be my lawful wedded husband." She smiled and slipped the ring on his finger with the heart pointing to his heart. The hearts on the ring were now set to send their never-ending love to each other for eternity.

"Sebastian and Julia, you have both made the declarations prescribed by law and have made a solemn and binding contract in the presence of your witnesses here today. It therefore gives me great pleasure to declare that you are now legally married. I need you both to sign the register and then Sebastian, you may kiss your bride."

The registrar pushed a registry book across the table to them and offered Jules a pen. Elated, Jules signed the blank square with her name printed next to it and gave the pen to Seth.

He signed the book too. She looked up at him and could see that he was smiling broadly. His eyes met hers and she could see the happiness in them. "Mrs Hearn, you have made me the happiest man alive," he whispered and then took her into his arms and kissed her.

She could taste his sweet breath and she could feel his heart beating in his chest. Jules wished she could stay like this for ever, safe and warm in his aurora. He pulled away and held her face "Are you doing ok, Mrs Hearn?"

She nodded and placed her hand on his cheek. "I love you with all my heart." Her stomach was contracting again and she held onto him, waiting for the pain to pass. "Seth, we need to go to the hospital now. The contractions are only a couple of minutes apart and are really starting to hurt."

"You disgust me, Ann! How can you do this to me?" Margaret yelled. She was pointing a shotgun at them.

Everyone gasped and turned in their seats to see who had spoken.

"IT SHOULD HAVE BEEN ME! NOT HIM!"

Granny stood up and marched over to Margaret. "This has got to stop, this instant. You are making a fool of yourself! Put that gun down before you do something stupid."

"Mam, what are you doing here?" Charlene called. Margaret looked around the room. "Charlene too! You are all in this together. I should have known! Don't you see? That bastard has stolen Ann from me. You should be helping me." She pointed the gun in Seth's direction and her finger quivered over the trigger. Seth pulled Jules behind him to protect her and glared at his ex-mother.

Granny tried to take the gun from her but she pushed her away. "Give me the gun, Margaret. You need to listen to your mother for once. You stupid headstrong girl; you've got to get a grip. Seth has just married Jules. That girl is not your precious Ann. Whoever the fuck she was," Granny said, with her hands on her hips. "What would your dear father say if he saw you carrying on this way?"

"Mam, please, put the gun down. We need to get Jules to hospital. She's going to have a baby. Can't you see that she is in pain?" Seth shouted out.

Margaret's eyes narrowed. "I thought as much. Another of Jethro's stinking runts for me to deal with. Ann, what is wrong with you? How could you lie with him again when you promised yourself to me?"

Instinctively, Jules knew that at any moment Margaret was going to shoot Seth. There was no reasoning with her. *I can't let her kill him. I have to do something.* She pushed Seth's arm away and stood next to him to face her. The shotgun was still pointed at Seth. She tried to stay focussed. "Margaret, please forgive your little Ann. I am sorry that I have hurt you. Please put the gun down. If you love me... If you love me, then you will do as I ask." She was feeling faint and then bent over as pain surged through her stomach muscles. She gasped and cried out. "Margaret, please give me the gun. How can I be with you if you shoot Seth?" She could see that Margaret was beginning to soften.

Seth pulled her back. "No, Seth. Please, she will give me the gun."

"No, I can't let you. I don't trust her."

Margaret sneered at Seth. "You make me sick. Look what you have done to Ann. Why can't the Hearn men keep their dicks in their trousers?"

Horrified, Jules saw Margaret take aim and her finger touch the trigger. "NO!" she screamed and then she saw Joe leap up from his chair and launch himself at Margaret. The gun went off. A bullet exploded from the barrel and drowned out the music. The sound was deafening. Margaret and Joe went flying across the room, entangled. They hit the ground together and her head smashed against the tiled floor. The shotgun slid across that floor and stopped short of Jules's feet. Jules thought that her heart might explode.

Margaret lay motionless on the floor. Joe got to his feet and was cursing his mother-in-law. He then looked towards Jules and Seth with a look of horror on his face. Jules followed his gaze. Her ears were still ringing. The wall behind her was splattered with blood. Slowly, she looked down and realised that there was a body lying across the table with blood dripping from their head onto the registry book. Their signatures were now beginning to distort with the oozing fluid. *Oh no, she's dead! The registrar is dead!*

"Seth, look," she said, barely able to take in what she was seeing. He was no longer standing next to her. She looked down and screamed. Seth was lying on his back with his eyes closed. She dropped down to the floor, and she scanned his body looking for a bullet wound. *There was just one bullet, wasn't there?* His white shirt was pristine, and his beautiful face unmarked. She held his cheeks in her hands and kissed his face all over, willing him to open his eyes. His eyes opened and he looked shocked.

"Jules, I'm ok, I just fell when the gun went off. I thought that was it. She always was crap at shooting. Was I unconscious? Where is the witch?" he asked, sitting up and he rubbing the back of his head.

"Oh Seth, the registrar is dead. She shot her. I thought you were dead too."

"No, I'm fine. It's not my time."

She flung her arms around him. "I'm so glad you're alive." He hugged her back, and he looked around the room. Everyone was standing up not knowing what to do. He got to his feet and helped Jules up. "I'm sorry everyone. Joe, you saved my life. Are you all ok?"

Joe came over and hugged him. "I couldn't let her kill you. That woman has been the bane of my life. I'll not rest until she is behind bars. With a bit of luck she'll be out cold until the police get here. That poor woman over there. Just look at her," he said, pointing to the registrar.

Seth went over to May; she was crying, and Sinead was trying to comfort her. "May, I'm sorry about all this. I never imagined that she would turn up with a gun. I'm going to have to leave you to sort all of this out. Jules needs to go to the hospital. I'll pay for any damage, and I am sorry about your friend. Does she have a husband?"

"I don't care about the damage. All that matters is that you and Jules are both safe. My poor friend, she lives alone, so at least I won't have to face telling a partner. It is such a shame as she was a wonderful person. Seth, I can't imagine what you have been through living with that monster as a child. You are all a mother could wish for. You have been like a son to me. You two have the rest of your lives to live now and I am glad for you."

"Oh God, Seth! Another contraction. I've got the urge to push now. I won't, not yet," Jules said, holding her stomach.

Sinead was by her side. "Can you walk to the car?"

"Yes, I can, but not for a few minutes. It should pass but this hurts so much. The pain is making me feel sick," she said, hanging onto Seth's arm.

"It's ok, just breathe through it. I'm here for you. Don't argue with me. I am going to carry you to the car when the pain stops," Seth said. He looked over at Charlene and wanted to speak to her before they left. Charlene was on the phone, and he knew that she was talking to the police. "Joe, will you tell Charlene that I will give her a ring when I am at the hospital? The barn is open, so make yourself at home. Would you mind feeding the cat? I don't know when I will be back tonight."

"Look, don't worry; just get Jules to the hospital."

"I will. Thank you again for saving my life," he said, looking over towards Granny and Bridie. Granny was telling his aunt off and Bridie was crying. *I can't face talking to them yet.*

"Come on, Seth; we have got to get going," Sinead said, getting her keys out of her pocket. "Jules is going a funny colour."

Seth smiled at Jules and then scooped her off the floor into his arms. "Darragh needs us now. Put your arms around my neck and hug me tight if you get another contraction. You are my beautiful wife, and I will always be there for you."

Chapter Thirty

Jules lay on the back of Sinead's Mini with her head on Seth's lap and her knees bent. She gripped his hand tightly as she battled with the pain and the urge to push. She could hear him telling her to breathe through the pain, but she couldn't relax enough to do this. The contractions were now so close together that she barely had time to recover before the next contraction started.

"We are nearly at the hospital. It's going to be ok," he said, trying to soothe her. He felt her hand relax and knew she would have a few seconds to recover. He squeezed her hand to reassure her. "I love you," he whispered. "You are doing just fine."

"For fuck's sake!" Sinead yelled as the traffic lights turned red. She tapped the steering wheel while she waited for them to change. "Just one more junction to go before we are at the hospital. I'm sorry I swore. How are you doing back there?"

"Hanging in there," Seth replied. "You're doing a grand job, Sinead. Stay calm; we are going to make it to the hospital in time."

The lights turned green and Seth prayed that there wouldn't be any more delays.

"We're through the lights. Yes!" Sinead exclaimed. "I can see the hospital."

Jules groaned through gritted teeth and her body contorted with pain. "I can't hold him back. I don't want to push but... I can't stop him. Oh please, no! Seth, please help me!"

"We're nearly in the car park. Sinead, find a place to pull over; she can't hold on any longer."

Sinead, seeing the emergency ambulance bay, ignored the no admittance signs and sped into a space next to an ambulance.

"Don't move, Jules, I'm going to go around to your passenger door to help you," he said as he leapt out of the car and ran to the other side. He could hear her yelling at him to hurry. He flung open the door and found her with her dress pulled up around her waist. She was struggling to remove her underwear. He helped her take her white lacy briefs off, and he could see Darragh's tiny head crowning. Seth got onto his knees and held out his hands, ready to catch their baby. "It's ok, Jules. I'm ready for him. You can let him go. It's ok."

"God it hurts! I am having another contraction. I really have to push." She gritted her teeth together as she strained to push him out.

Seth's eyes widened as he watched the tiny baby slip out of her and into his hands. *I was only just in time. That was so quick!* Seth was in awe. Seeing his son for the first time was something that he would never forget. "He is perfect. He has fine dark hair, and he is quite small but just perfect."

The baby began to cry with such a loud shrill, ear piercing sound that it took him by surprise. "Jules, we have a boy like we thought. Darragh is fine, just a few smears of blood and some white stuff on him. You are bleeding a bit. My gorgeous girl, he is strong like you. No more pain. You are a Mam now. Christ, I'm a Dad too. I can't believe it. What shall I do with him? He needs his cord cutting."

"Seth, I want to hold him. Is he breathing ok?" she asked as she sat up and pulled her dress down to cover herself up. "Oh, look at him; he is so tiny." She stroked his cheek with her finger to try to stop him crying. "He has hair just like yours. We need something to wrap him in."

"I can't believe that you gave birth, Jules. You look so normal," Sinead said. "I'll go and ask those ambulance men for help. No, it's ok, someone is coming over to us."

A paramedic dressed in green appeared next to Seth, and crouching down, he looked into the car and smiled. "You nearly made it in time." He looked sympathetically at her. "You are not the first to give birth in the car park. Your wee boy has got quite a pair of lungs on him. He is small, is he a preterm?"

"Yes, he is early. He is thirty-three weeks and five days old." Seth replied. "Why is he still crying?"

"That's a good sign; it means his lungs are well formed, and he is breathing well. I am going to cut the cord." He stood up and opened a box he had brought with him. "I am going to put some towel under your hands and then you can lay him on it." With the towel in place, Seth gently placed Darragh on the paper, not wanting to let him go. He was still crying and his arms and legs kicked out as he cried. Seth stood up, allowing the paramedic to attend to the baby.

The driver of the ambulance came over to them with a thermal blanket. Quickly, she wrapped their baby up, and feeling secure, Darragh stopped crying. "He thinks he is back in the womb now," she said. "We need to keep him warm. When they are this small like this, they get cold easily," she said as she put a woolly hat on the baby's head. "He is such a wee, diddy little thing. I love babies," she exclaimed.

"Are you able to get out of the car by yourself?" the paramedic asked Jules. "I am going to take you up to the maternity wing in a minute. Your baby will have to go into an incubator unit to keep him warm. He will be monitored for a while, and he needs to be able to feed properly before he can go home."

"I can walk. I'm ok but I am bleeding." Slowly, Jules put her feet in the foot well and stood up. She was feeling sore and there was blood and afterbirth on her dress. Feeling a little embarrassed, she looked at the mess on Sinead's back seat. Trying her best to avoid this, she climbed out of the car. "Sinead, I'm really sorry about your car seat. I will clean it up when I get home later."

"Don't worry. I'll do it. I've seen a horse do a lot worse. I am just so happy that you are ok. Both of you." She was tearing up and hugged Jules and then hugged Seth.

He hugged her back. "We are ok, it has been one hell of a day! Thank you for being there for us."

Sinead wiped her eyes with her sleeve. "Look, I am going to head back and see how May is. Do you want me to bring you some clothes later?"

"I'm ok, but Jules will need something and probably a wash bag and overnight things. I'll go out to the shops later if we need anything else."

"I hate to ask you, Sinead, but I would really appreciate something to change into. This dress is ruined, and I am going to get some odd looks wearing this in the hospital." Her stomach contracted again and she squealed and held onto Seth. The placenta slid out of her and slopped onto the tarmac.

"We will have to bring that with us and make sure it's all there. Hold on, I'll just get you a chair and some towel for you to sit on," the paramedic said as he walked back to the ambulance. Jules looked at the friendly driver who was holding Darragh. "I'm sorry, I have made a terrible mess."

"Don't you worry, you are doing fine. We will take care of you."

She sat down in the chair and looked up at her baby. "Is it ok to hold him?" she asked.

"Of course, he is sleeping now." Jules was given her baby and she cradled him in her arms. She looked lovingly at his tiny face and saw him move his mouth. "He is the most beautiful little thing I have ever seen."

"He's gorgeous. I couldn't help noticing but are you wearing a wedding dress? It wasn't a shotgun wedding, was it? Sorry, that was in bad taste," she asked.

Seth laughed. "Jules and I have only been married for half an hour. A relative tried to kill me but my brother-in-law pulled the gun away just in time. She never liked me. She ended up shooting the registrar through the head instead. This hasn't been the best of days!"

"No! Really? We just heard about that shooting on our radio. She must be the elderly lady that is being blue lighted here with a suspected bleed to the brain. The registrar is going to the morgue. You've had one hell of a wedding, haven't you?"

"I hope the police are with her. She is a lunatic."

"Yes, she is in police custody. What a nightmare. At least you weren't hurt. We'd better get you all to the maternity unit and get your little one checked in. We will drive you over in the ambulance. Your little Darragh is one tough little cookie," said the paramedic as he started to push Jules and Darragh towards the ambulance.

"He's just like his Mam," Seth said, following them.

Jules and Seth were sitting side by side staring into Darragh's incubation tank. All he was wearing was a tiny nappy and his skin looked pink and warm. He lay in a small white nest pillow and was attached to wires that were monitoring his heart and oxygen levels. His eyes were closed as he slept. He had a surprising amount of dark hair for someone so small.

Jules looked at all the tanks containing preterm babies. Other parents were sitting by them and they were looking a little shell shocked. One woman was breastfeeding her baby quite openly. Her large breasts were on display for all to see. For some reason it reminded Jules of a cow in the milking shed. "I'm glad Sinead is going to get me some clothes. These hospital gowns are not very nice to wear and the paper pants feel strange too! I had to throw my beautiful wedding dress away. Oh, dear, I left my wedding pants in Sinead's car. I feel bad that she is going to have to clean up my mess. I hope she will speak to me again. At least I am clean. It was such a relief to have a shower. I'm still bleeding, but they said that was normal. Do you think I will have to stay in overnight?"

"Yes, I think you will. Just to make sure you are ok. From what I've been reading, Darragh will have to stay in here until he can feed properly and he is strong enough to sleep outside his incubator. It might be a couple of weeks at least before he is ready to come home. We are going to have to come in everyday to see him. I have next week off but after that you will have to come in on the bus by yourself and I will come over after work. I feel bad about that."

"That is a long time. It is going to be hard to leave him each day. "I'm sure he will start feeding by himself soon as he is so strong. I will be fine on the bus alone. Don't feel bad."

Seth smiled and held her hand. "I am so happy. I can't keep my eyes off him. I can't believe he is here. I also can't believe that you are sitting here next to me and are not in bed recovering," he said, squeezing her hand. "You are like superwoman."

Jules laughed. "I am tired, but apart from that, I feel like I am in a dream. A good dream. I just want to feel his skin and hold him. When he wakes up I will ask if we can both have a cuddle."

"Do you remember, when I first met you, you told me that you had to hold your friend's baby and that you didn't like doing that? I promised you, that you didn't have to hold a baby at my party."

"I do. That was the first time I saw you and that is when you weaved your magic spell over me. I love you, Seth. I love being married to you."

A nurse came over to them and checked Darragh's monitor and charts. She turned to them. "He is doing fine. It's Julia Hearn, isn't it? I can't help thinking that I've seen you both before... Oh, it's just hit me. You sing together at The Elbow. S&J! Oh my! I am one of your biggest fans. I heard that you two were married today. Congratulations! I bet you didn't imagine you'd have a baby on the same day!"

"No, we didn't," Jules said. "We are just glad that he is here, and he seems to be doing ok. Although we are not prepared. You will have to tell us what we need to do or get him."

"I'll give you a list. He won't need much. Just a few clothes and a lot of love. He is still growing, so he will sleep a lot. To help him grow, I need you to hand express a little colostrum for him. As much as you can. Even if it is just a teaspoon full. I will give you what you need and show you where you can express. For the next few weeks, you are going to have to express milk for him, every two hours and once at night. I'll show you what to do."

"Goodness! I didn't realise. Yes, of course. I've worked with dairy cows, so I should be able to express milk without training. It's a bit weird though, doing it on yourself."

She laughed. "I'll go and get you what you need." The nurse walked across the room to a cupboard.

"She was sweet. I don't think she knows what else happened at the wedding. I hope May is coping. I didn't like to see her cry," Seth said as he ran his fingers through his hair. "God! Sinead cut this short."

"I like it like that, you still have the length on top but your shorn sides make you look so hot."

"If you like me this way, then I am happy. Hot, you say?" he said, smiling. "When you've finished pumping, shall we get some lunch? It's nearly three and I bet you haven't had anything to eat yet. I'm not nagging you, but I don't want my lovely wife to keel over."

"You're right. I need something. I am really hungry. I need to keep strong for Darragh, if I am going into mass milk production!"

Chapter Thirty-one

Margaret ripped the collar off her neck and sat up. The police officer guarding her was talking to a nurse. *I know his kind. He has a dick for brains*! She felt the back of her head. It was sore but no more than that. *A bleed to the brain, my arse!* She got to her feet and the room spun for a moment, but her dizziness soon passed. *I'm out of here.*

The accident and emergency unit was busy, and she knew that she would be able to get away easily. Her eyes narrowed as she planned her next move. She found her heels under the bed and slipped them on. Jethro had never allowed her to wear heels, but Ann liked them on her and she liked to look her best for her.

Margaret smiled as she thought about her lover. She had looked so beautiful in her wedding gown. Her golden curls, laced with meadow flowers, had melted her heart. She longed to kiss the nape of her neck again and breathe in her sweet perfume. *Why did that bastard marry her? If only I had been there in time to stop that. He is dead now. I have saved Ann. We have a new baby to look after.* She picked up her handbag and slipped out of the bay unnoticed. From what she remembered, the hospital's maternity unit was only a five minute walk away. *Poor Ann needs me more than ever now. Jethro or Seth can't hurt you anymore.* She looked back at the police officer lapping up the attention he was getting from the nurse. *What a dickhead!*

JULIA'S BABY

***

Jules and Seth had met Sinead outside of the hospital's café. Sinead handed her a holdall and Jules took the bag to the nearest wash room and selected something to wear. Sinead had brought her jogging bottoms to wear and a selection of t-shirts. *Loose fitting clothes, thank goodness!* There was a packet of sanitary towels in the bag too. *Thank you, Sinead, for thinking of that. I've never bled like this before.*

She changed in a toilet cubicle and now stood in front of the washroom mirror to make sure she looked ok. Her breasts looked huge and were spilling out of her bra. *I look like a dairy cow. I hope I was able to produce enough colostrum for Darragh. I can't believe that I am a mother now.* She still had a few wilting flowers caught in her curls, so she pulled them out and then inspected herself again. *Not too bad, but I look a bit tired.*

When Jules got back to the cafeteria, she found Seth and Sinead were sitting by a window. Seth had bought her a cheese sandwich and a cup of tea. Carefully she sat down on the chair, still feeling a little sore. "Sinead, thanks for bringing me everything I needed. You even remembered to bring sanitary towels. You have thought of everything. Seth, you are going to have to buy me a couple of feeding bras."

"Christ!" he said and his eyes widened. "Where do I get those?"

"Mark's maybe. I will look on the internet in a minute and tell you what size I want. I am so happy to be wearing my own clothes, Sinead. You are a lifesaver."

Sinead was staring out of the window deep in thought. When she turned her head to reply, Jules could see that she was sad. "That's all right. I knew what you needed. I remembered packing a bag like yours, when I had my baby."

"I didn't know you had a child," Seth said. He was surprised.

"I don't have one anymore. I was fifteen when Augusta was born. She was only twenty-four weeks old when she arrived. Augusta had a heart defect. She didn't survive."

"I'm sorry, Sinead; this must be bringing it all back to you," Jules said. She was sad for her.

"It's ok. The baby wasn't wanted, but I do miss her now and again. It was a long time ago. Anyway, I am glad that little Darragh is doing ok. You two look a bit tired, though. Are you going to come back with me or are you going to stay here tonight?"

"We will stay until this evening and then get a taxi home. It will be hard to leave the little dote. He is going to be in the NNU for a couple of weeks at least," Seth said. "How is May doing?"

"She's ok. I was worried that the stress might bring on another stroke, but she seems to be coping with everything. May was doing some yoga when I left her. I doubt she will be able to hold any more weddings in the orangery. Your mother is one sick woman. You do know that they brought her to this hospital, don't you? I hope that woman bleeds to death."

"The ambulance man told us she was here," replied Jules. "I don't like to think about her being in the same hospital. It gives me the creeps. At least she is in police custody."

"Is that so?" Sinead said, staring out of the window again. "Is that her walking through the gardens towards the main entrance?"

Seth couldn't believe his eyes. "For fuck's sake!" he yelled, his eyes flashing with anger for a moment. People started to stare at him.

"Seth, Margaret is after me again! How does she know we are here?" Jules asked. She was feeling scared, and her heart was beating hard.

"Calm down, you two. I am sure the police will be close on her heels. She must have escaped from A&E. She will be looking for you in a maternity ward. She won't think to look for you in the NNU. I am going to call the police and then we can just wait here until they catch her."

Seth got up. "I am going to get her and hold her until the police get here. She is a dangerous woman. She shouldn't be near babies. Jules, stay here, please. I don't want her to see you."

"I'm frightened for you, Seth. She might have a gun."

"No, she won't. That nutter has just been in A&E with the police. She won't be armed. You really need to stay safe here, with Sinead. I've got this."

Sinead started to talk to the police and Jules looked up at Seth and sighed. "I'll stay here, but promise me that you won't do anything stupid. Promise me."

"I promise. I am only going to hold her until the police come to take her away."

Jules watched him leave the cafeteria. He was fired up and she hoped that he would keep his word. *I have to let him handle this.*

When Sinead finished her call to the police she looked towards the door. "He was so angry, wasn't he? The police are on their way. She has escaped from the emergency department. They will be here in minutes. The police officer that was guarding her is going to get a roasting."

"I am worried about Seth. Do you think he will lose control?" she asked.

"I know he hates her but he won't hit her, he wouldn't hit a woman," Sinead said. "I know you want to protect him, but this time, you must let him sort this out. He needs closure."

With his arms folded, Seth waited by the main doors for Margaret to appear in the reception area. He took in slow steady breaths, attempting to calm his breathing. *There mustn't be a scene here. Outside yes, but not in here.* The phone in his pocket was recording everything, ready to pick up her words. *She's taking her time. Have I missed her?*

He looked over his shoulder and scanned the room to check all the corridor entrances, to make sure she wasn't creeping off into the hospital. He checked the main doors again and then sighed. He could see her approaching. *At last!* As soon as she entered the hospital, he grabbed her elbow, spun her around and then he escorted her out.

Margaret gasped, shocked by his appearance and rough handling.

"NO! But you are dead! I shot you. You should be dead. Take your filthy hands off me! You are hurting me. I need to see Ann. She needs me. Her baby needs me!"

"You are one sick woman," he said through gritted teeth as he frogmarched her back into the hospital gardens. He let go of her in view of the cafeteria window and quickly looked up to see if Sinead and Jules were watching. They were. *Good.*

"Sinead, I can see Seth and Margaret outside. He's brought her out here, so we can see them. Why?"

"He wants you to see him dealing with her sensibly. I am going to ring the police back and tell them where she is."

"Just tell me one thing," Seth asked. "Did you ever care about me?"

"NO, NEVER!" she snapped back. "I had to tolerate you for my sister and Jethro's sake. You were never special to me; not like Jake. You know Ann wants me and not you. I need her. I will take care of her and her baby. I know it is another of Jethro's runts, but I will love the baby, like I love Jake. In time Ann will learn to love me again."

"You sick bitch! Jules is not Ann. You killed Ann twenty years ago."

"I did it out of temper. Jethro had so many women and so many babies to dispose of. This time it will be different. I regret killing Ann. God has forgiven me now and given me a second chance. He has given Ann back to me. You cannot have her. She is mine."

"What about Claire's baby? What happened to her baby? She's had another, you know. Was that Dad's too?"

Margaret looked wounded for a moment. Her eyes narrowed and then she looked disgusted. "Not again! How could Claire open her legs for her Dad like that? What was she thinking of? One day, she called me to the barn and there it was, another one of his bastards, lying there covered in blood and hay. I wrapped him in a blanket and left him by the silent pool to die. So many new-borns have had to die. I've had to smother so many of Jethro's stinking runts. How could he do that to me? How could he leave me with so many babies to take care of? Did Ann have a girl or a boy? Tell me!" she yelled.

"She didn't have another child. Ann is gone and will never forgive you. She hopes you rot in Hell! You are wasting your time here," Seth said calmly. He could see a police car with flashing lights at the edge of the gardens. Two police officers jumped out of the car and started to walk towards them. Seth took out his phone and showed it to her. "I've got everything you said on this phone. You are going to get life. I hope you die there; alone and afraid."

Margaret looked behind her and her mouth opened. "You bastard. You have set me up. You will go to Hell too for what you have done and I will take you with me!" She started to run, but her high heels slowed her down and a police officer caught her up and he grabbed hold of her. She struggled, but she could not break free. The policeman read out her rights. She was being arrested for the suspected murder of Ann Bridgewater, the murder of Eileen Goldberg, the registrar and fifteen counts of infant murder.

Fifteen counts of infant murder! A strange sense of calm and sadness came over Seth as he watched her being dragged towards the police car. *We can live in peace now.* He sighed and looked sadly up at the café window. *Now, I just need to say goodbye to my beautiful wife.* He could see Jules looking out of the window; her face was pressed against it, and her eyes were wide with fear. He held up the phone and smiled at her. He was sure that she would know what he had done.

"Oh, my! Margaret's being put in the police car. Seth's holding the phone up to me. Does he want you to call him, Sinead?"

"No, I don't think so."

"I know what he's done," Jules said. "He's recorded their conversation. Clever Seth; he's got Margaret to confess. He's got it on tape. Why isn't he coming back?"

A police officer came over to him. "He's talking to the police. I think that they want him to get in the car too."

"Why does he have to go with her?"

"Perhaps they need to take a statement from him and let him play the recording to them."

"This feels wrong. Oh, Sinead, he can't get involved. No, it's ok, he is walking away. He's not going with them. He's coming back to us."

Jules waited patiently to see Seth appear and as soon as she saw his face, she knew that something was wrong. He sat next to her and held her hand.

"I'm sorry," he said. "I've got to go with them. They need me to make a statement, and I need to sign our phone over to them. That recording will put her away for life. When I am at the police station, they will realise that I am on the run. It was only a matter of time before they caught up with me. I need you and Darragh to be strong and I will be back with you in no time. Ten months is not that long. The time will go by quickly. I will ring you every day, and you can email me pictures of..." He was starting to cry.

"NO, PLEASE! You can't go. I am lost without you. You have to tell them about Jake. You are innocent. He should be in prison, not you," she sobbed. Tears were streaming down her cheeks.

"You know I can't. I love you so much. We can get through this. Ten months away is nothing compared to what we have been through. When I come back, then I will be a free man."

"You will look after them both for me, won't you, Sinead."

"I can't bear this." Sinead was crying too. "Of course I will."

He drew Jules to him and kissed her. He held her face in both his hands, and gazed into her blue eyes. "Kiss Darragh goodbye for me." He was crying. "I am going to miss you both so much. We can live in peace now." Seth pulled her to him and hugged her one last time. He took a deep breath in, stood up and then walked away. His heart was almost breaking. *Just ten months, and then we will be together again.*

Chapter Thirty-two

It was February and ten months since Jules had said goodbye to Seth. Ten months since her and Seth had been married and ten months since Darragh had been born. The grass was thick with frost and dark clouds in the sky threatened snow. Jules was standing outside Ford Prison gently rocking Darragh in his pram, trying to get him to go to sleep. Her heart was beating hard in her chest with excitement as she waited for Seth to appear. She had waited ten long months for Seth to be released from prison, and today was the day that they would be reunited. She would be able to hold him, smell his sweet body and be one with him again.

Jules looked at the high green fencing around the prison caging in hundreds of petty villains and her poor innocent husband too. She imagined all the prisoners saying goodbye to Seth and then shaking his hand and wishing him all the best.

Darragh was still awake and was babbling at a toy that was hanging from the hood of his pram. She smiled and stroked his warm cheek. His big brown eyes stared back at her and he smiled. "Are you looking forward to seeing your Daddy?" she asked, tucking his blanket in around him to keep out the cold. "You are getting so big now. Wait until your Daddy sees you. He hasn't seen you for two weeks."

Since Jules had returned to Sussex, she had managed to visit Seth every third week and she had taken Darragh with her when she could. She was sure that each time Seth had seen them, it had given him the strength to cope with prison life, knowing that they were there waiting for him to come home. Somehow, he had kept his spirits up, and he had soldiered on and completed his sentence. The judicial system did not care that he had skipped parole to save his life and had sent him back to prison just as he had predicted.

Seth had kept himself busy in prison and had written lots of new songs for them to sing at The Elbow. Jules had composed music for each one and had sung them to Darragh. Music fed her soul and had helped her to heal her broken heart.

Seth had called her every other day and she always said that they loved him. It was so good to hear his voice. The first time he called her, he had cried. He told her that he was sorry for abandoning them both. Jules had cried too and had assured him that they would be ok and that they were counting the days down until he returned. She had sobbed her heart out when she had put the phone down. It had been such a relief to know that he was ok. That night, Jules had made a chart so that she could tick off the days until they were together again. On the last day, the day of Seth's release, she had drawn a heart with S&J within it. Every day she looked at the heart and watched the ticks racing towards it.

Darragh had spent three weeks in the premature baby unit. It had been an emotional time for her, and she had cried a lot. It had been a shock to have such a tiny life depending on her but over time as she got used to feeding him and holding him, she realised that little Darragh was helping her to get through each day.

One of the most difficult days had been when she had brought Darragh back to the Old Barn. Jules had felt so alone, and she had wished that she could have shared that day with Seth. Some nights, the emptiness she felt inside was almost too hard to endure. Sinead and May had been great and had given her a shoulder to cry on. Sinead had driven her to the hospital every day and had collected her after work. Charlene had been there for her too and had called her every week for a chat.

When Darragh was three months old and he was strong enough to travel, Jules had returned to Farm End with her tiny baby strapped to her. It had been a sunny July day and as she entered the farmhouse kitchen she noticed that the radio was on, just like old times. The dogs had come over to her, and she had ruffled their fur as she waited for Peter and her Dad to appear. It was as if she had never been away.

Jules had called out for them, and they had come out of the study and were surprised to see her. She hadn't told them that she was coming back. Her Dad was looking so much better and she could see a sparkle in his eyes. Peter was looking a little older and had grown a beard. He had run over to her to hug her and the baby. Her Dad had hugged her too. He had stroked the top of Darragh's head with a quizzical look on his face. It had been good to be in the old farmhouse again with them both and she had cried happy tears.

Her attention returned to the entrance of the prison as she waited for Seth. She could feel butterflies in her stomach. Jules was nervous and excited at the same time. She saw men in prison trousers and yellow jackets waiting at the zebra crossing ready to cross the road. *No, none are Seth, just prisoners going to work.* Some of the prisoners had jobs at the prison. Seth had helped in the farm shop 'Serving Thyme' for a couple of weeks and she had gone there, pretending to buy some plants, with the hope of seeing him. He had smiled and when nobody was looking he had pulled her to him and kissed her. He had smelled of citrus and earth, just as she remembered.

Please come out. It must be time.

That weekend, they were going to go back to Waterfall West and they would continue with their lives as if nothing had happened. She couldn't wait. "There he is!" She could see him; he was wearing his jeans and his black hoodie. *He doesn't look like he has been in prison. He looks so strong and proud. My lovely Seth.* "Darragh, your Daddy is over there." *Finally, he has been set free.* "Oh, thank God! SETH!" she called, waving frantically at him.

Seth smiled broadly as the reality of the moment hit him. *I am free. I have waited so long for this moment. There is my beautiful wife and our baby.* The road was quiet, so he ran across it to be with her. "My gorgeous girl!" he said and then picked her up and hugged and kissed her. Tears of happiness flowed down his cheeks. "I've missed you so much. I love you so much." He put her down and looked lovingly at her.

"I love you, Seth. I think that my heart might explode. Just hold me for a moment so that I can feel your beating heart against my ear." He wrapped his arms around her and she could feel the warmth from his body and the steady beat of his heart.

"I can't believe that I am here with you both. And how is my best boy?" he asked as he let her go and went to the pram to see Darragh.

"He looks more and more like you every day. He is just learning to sit up. You have come out at the right time. You have missed the sleepless nights. He is just getting interesting now, and he needs his Daddy. Seth, you must be freezing, you have no coat on!"

"I am too happy to be cold. Is Charlene picking us up?"

Jules smiled. "No, I am going to drive us home in Dad's old Land Rover. I was keeping it as a surprise. I passed my test last week. I've parked it in the car park."

"Really! You are amazing, I knew you could do it."

"Oh, I was going to tell you. You are never going to believe this, but Dad is going to drive us, Connor and Barney over to Ireland tomorrow in the lorry. He offered. Seth, I've missed you so much that I thought I might not make this day." She tried to blink away the tears.

"Don't cry," he said, hugging her again. "We are together now. I will always be by your side. We will never have to be apart again. I promise. Please don't cry."

Jules pulled up in Farm End's courtyard and Seth looked at the farmhouse kitchen window. The light was on and the house looked inviting. "I never thought that I would say this, but it is really good to be at Farm End." He opened the car door and looked down. "The cobbles look icy. Can I get Darragh out of the car?"

"You don't have to ask, silly!"

"You are going to have to show me what to do with him." Seth got out of the car and opened the door behind the driving seat. Julia slipped as she came over to him. He caught her and she laughed. "Steady there! It's like an ice ring out here," he said. "Do you have any grit or rock salt around?"

She nodded. "It's in the bin over there," she said, pointing to a dustbin in the corner of the courtyard. Being careful not to slip, Seth walked over to the bin and then shovelled out the grit and made them a path to the front door. Jules smiled as she watched him work. It was so good to have him back. She was worried that things would be awkward between them. *It's as if he has never been away.*

Seth smiled as he lifted Darragh out the back of the car. He was in a carrier and was sound asleep. "He sleeps like you do. Bombs could go off, and I don't think that he would wake up."

"He's a lot better than he was. He sleeps well in the car seat but not so good in his crib. Charlene gave me the crib. Her baby has outgrown it already. They are all coming over later."

Jules opened the front door and they walked into the hall. She took off her coat and hung it up.

"Where is everyone?" Seth asked. "I am still feeling a little nervous. I didn't get your Dad's permission to marry you, and I am not sure that he likes me."

"He is fine about us being married. Dad has changed. He is not depressed anymore. I barely recognise him. In a good way, though. Dad and Peter are out and about on the farm. They have strict instructions not to come back to the farmhouse until lunchtime."

"Why is that?"

"Well... I thought you, me and Darragh would need some alone time together," she said, smiling. "Do you want a cup of tea?"

"Ok. Where shall I put Darragh?"

"We will take him upstairs to my room. He is used to sleeping in there. I am going to keep him in the carrier. He will wake up if I put him in the crib. Dad has given us his room tonight. I've decorated it for him. You won't recognise it. Come and see."

Seth carried Darragh upstairs and Jules left the carrier facing the window so that when he woke up he would see the sky and the clouds. Seth tucked the blanket around him and then stood up and looked around her old room. It was untidy and clothes were bursting out of the wardrobe. *Just as I remember.* He could see Crow Farm from the window. "Jules, do you see that top window on the side of Crow Farm over there. I used to stand by that window and wait for your light to go out before I went to bed. I couldn't sleep until I knew you were sleeping. I think that I loved you then and didn't know it."

"You are a sweet thing. Come and see Dad's room," she said, taking him by the hand.

They walked into the bedroom and Seth inspected her work. The walls had been white washed and there were photos of the farm and some family portraits on the wall. The old brown furniture had been painted a pale blue. "You've done a grand job. It reminds me of our barn. I am so looking forward to seeing home again."

"I am pleased you like it. Shall I go downstairs and get some tea?"

"How long do we have before Darragh wakes up?"

"About an hour and a bit?"

"That's good, I need to hold you first."

"Just hold?"

"Come here and find out?"

Jules walked over to him and he pulled her into his arms. He embraced her and slowly lowered her onto the bed.

He kissed her on the neck. "You just smell so good. I love you so much. If I am being a bad husband then please stop me and I will understand."

"No, Seth, don't stop. Please don't stop. My body is crying out for yours. I was going to wait until we got home but I can't. I love you so much it hurts."

"My gorgeous girl. My wife. I love you with all my heart. I love you to the pink moon and back."

***

Margaret Hearn's family had disowned her. She stared blankly at the walls of her cell in Bronzefield Prison. She was receiving psychiatric help but it wasn't helping her. *What do they know!* She pushed a plate of food away and watched the tray slip off her bed. She gasped and covered her ears with her hands, surprised by the clatter that the tray and cutlery made as they hit the floor. *I am broken. I will not eat again until my soul lies with your soul at the bottom of the silent pool. Wait for me, Ann, I will be with you soon.*

I hoped you enjoyed Julia's Baby, I wrote this during lockdown.
If you could leave me a small review then I would be most
grateful. Authors are lost without reviews.

You might be interested in reading the final book in the
Waterfall way trilogy 'Waterfall Way.' You can get your copy
by clicking on this link shorturl.at/auSX7

Waterfall Way: a gripping romantic crime thriller series (Book 3) set in West Sussex and Ireland

Seth's song Waterfall Way, has reached No.1 in the charts but his heart is breaking. His family have been taken and he needs your help to find them. Time is running out!

Ireland has welcomed back Julia and Seth Hearn with open arms. S&J are making a name for themselves in the pop world and are staring fame and fortune in the face. Seth, however, is finding the attention they are receiving alarming. There is a price to pay for being famous.

When Covid hits the city of Cork, lives are changed forever. Becoming owners of the Waterfall West Estate proves problematic and all their dreams look like they are about to crumble.

Jules and Seth are horrified when they find another body in a watery grave and things do not look good for Seth. Jules has a guilty secret and dare not share it with him. It is tearing her apart and may be her undoing.

Can Jules and Seth find a way to turn their fortunes around or will destiny seal their fate?

Obsession can be a dangerous thing!

Natasha Murray is an award winning West Sussex author. She is a diverse writer and produces books for all ages. During lockdown, Natasha has written a romantic crime thriller series 58 Farm End, Julia's Baby and Waterfall Way (The Waterfall Way Series). These books are set in Findon, West Sussex and Cork, Ireland. She says, "I enjoy writing and it is both a pleasure and a compulsion. There is nothing better in life than creating parallel universes."

For more information about Natasha and her books, then please visit her website at https://cutt.ly/5fR483w

Or her Facebook page
https://www.facebook.com/NatashaMurray3004 or

Twitter https://twitter.com/UKBookShow_2018

Instagram @natashamurray1426

Goodreads https://www.goodreads.com/book/show/55983155